five reasons why you'll love *this book*

Great for fans of **Percy Jackson!**

What would you ask if an ancient god appeared, offering to answer your prayers?

'Oh, what fun this is!'

The Times

Ali won the **Blue Peter Book Award** for *Frozen in Time*

What are you supposed to do when various half-forgotten deities start hanging out at the bottom of your garden?

'**Kevin Rutley** is so cool,
If you don't read this book you're a fool,
This book is the best,
It beats all the rest,
Abandinus is the hero,
Arimanius is the *ZERO*,
Be careful what you wish for,
Read this book to find out more!'

Amy, Year 6

'**Wishful Thinking** is the sort of book that once you're in it you can't get out of it. It takes me into a magical world of mystery. I love the way the author (**Ali Sparkes**) describes the god, it makes you want to dig deep and find what happens next . . .'

Molly, Year 6

'A brilliant book for anyone, I would say. I was reading late at night and I had to put it away for the night but . . . I could not get my fingers off!'

Ben, Year 6

'I loved this book! It was the kind of book that left you begging for more!'

Rebecca, Year 6

For Nicola Jane

OXFORD
UNIVERSITY PRESS

Great Clarendon Street, Oxford OX2 6DP

Oxford University Press is a department of the University of Oxford.
It furthers the University's objective of excellence in research, scholarship,
and education by publishing worldwide. Oxford is a registered trade mark of
Oxford University Press in the UK and in certain other countries

First published 2010
First published in this edition 2018

British Library Cataloguing in Publication Data
Data available

ISBN: 978-0-19-276961-9

1 3 5 7 9 10 8 6 4 2

Printed in India
Paper used in the production of this book is a natural,
recyclable product made from wood grown in sustainable forests.
The manufacturing process conforms to the environmental
regulations of the country of origin.

WISHFUL THINKING

Ali Sparkes

OXFORD
UNIVERSITY PRESS

Chapter 1

WHAT KEVIN RUTLEY WANTS:

1. Nintendo Wii
2. To be cool
3. Emma Greening to notice me
4. A dog
5. Mum and Dad to get back together
6. Better skin
7. To be good at sports
8. That gooey thing on my toe to go
9. World peace and all that
10. Not to be covered in sick

Kevin handed the list to Nan and she read it through, nodding, smiling, laughing, sighing and then nodding again. She glanced up halfway through, pointed at his bottle of Coke and ordered: 'Drink!' before dropping her eyes back to the list. He slurped at the straw. She was right, he thought, slurping a little more up through the straw. It *was* making him feel better, although the wafts of slightly warm vomit coming up from his jumper didn't help much.

The list had worked quite well too. Written on a paper napkin, it was a way of getting his mind off the car sickness as they'd waited for the Coke, a pot of tea, and two Bakewell tarts to arrive at their table in the little watermill tea room.

'You'll feel better the minute you get some sugary drink down you,' Nan had said. 'And then you'll want the tart. Trust me.'

Pale and droopy, Kevin had just held his head up with his left hand while scrawling his wish list with his right, occasionally sucking on the straw and waiting for the waves of sickness to ease off. He knew she was right. He'd had travel sickness all his life and his nan had dealt with it often enough to know exactly how it worked. As Nan started to read his napkin and the tide of fizzy brown liquid dropped to halfway down the bottle, Kevin found he was able to look at the Bakewell tart without heaving. And a few slurps after that he was able to think about the possibility of eating it.

'Well,' said Nan. 'We can sort out the last bit on your list, can't we? You look well enough to go and sponge yourself off now.' She directed him to the men's toilets as she poured her tea. 'Use hot water and a wodge of loo roll,' she recommended. 'Nice and thoroughly, please. Don't want the car reeking all the way back.'

By the time he got back to the table he smelt a lot better and felt perfectly OK again. He reached for the tart and took a big bite, grinning through it at Nan.

She smiled back, knowing the worst was over now. Kevin only got properly car sick when he hadn't had enough to eat. He would go all floppy and sweaty and end up throwing up what little was inside him if you didn't get parked and get him out in time. After some food he was normally fine. He would make it home without any more trouble.

'Sweetheart—you *do know* that number five isn't really going to happen, don't you?' Nan said, holding the floppy yellow list in her hand and pointing at 5. *Mum and Dad to get back together.*

Kevin shrugged. He knew *better skin* and *Emma Greening* weren't going to happen either. And there was a good chance the gooey thing on his toe would still be there when he was drawing his pension. That was the thing about wish lists. They were about *wishes*. Not about likelihoods. If he'd made a list of likelihoods it would have read very differently.

3

WHAT KEVIN RUTLEY THINKS IS LIKELY:

1. Nintendo Wii for Christmas—maybe—if there's one for the right price on eBay. Or Christmas 2015 when they're old tech and nobody wants one any more
2. I will never be cool
3. Emma Greening will not know I exist unless I smack her in the face with a school dinner tray
4. A dog. Stuffed.
5. Mum and Dad to squabble about who has me for Christmas until they're both in nursing homes
6. Better skin—when I'm 35
7. I'll always be rubbish at sports
8. That gooey thing on my toe will pop during swimming—when Emma Greening is looking
9. World peace? Oh, come on.
10. There will always be sick

'You know—it has been three years since they split up.' Nan was still talking, gently, about his parents. 'If they were going to get back together I think they would have done it by now, Kevin.'

'I *know*,' muttered Kevin. 'It's just a list of wishes! I know they won't come true. My wishes never do.'

Nan tilted her head to one side and regarded him through her spectacles. Her eyes were vivid blue and slightly moist. 'Oh, Kevin. Of *course* some of your wishes will come true! You mustn't think like that.'

Kevin finished the tart and then started squashing the crumbs onto his finger and licking them off, staring out across the River Ouse, which powered the giant waterwheel of the carefully preserved working mill. 'It's OK, Nan. Life's just like that, isn't it? I mean— yeah—if I had my own personal fairy or pixie or *god* who could make my wishes come true, fair enough. But I haven't.' A breeze blew in through the window, scented with water and early summer grass. A small, curled white feather fell on his sleeve. 'My life's all right. I'm not starving in Africa. But I don't get wishes coming true, either.'

'Well—I can make *one* wish come true, anyway,' laughed Nan, getting up. She wandered off into the little gift shop and returned as Kevin was finishing the last of his Coke. With a dog. Stuffed. A soft furry Labrador puppy dog in a paper bag.

'There you go,' she said, plopping it in his hands. 'From your fairy grandmother!'

Kevin grinned and gave her a little hug, looking around to make sure nobody his age was there, watching. 'Thanks, Nan.'

'You want to get something for your mum, while we're here?' she asked, patting his tufty hair.

5

'Yeah—I've got some money,' said Kevin. He mooched into the gift shop and foraged about among the china and jewellery and postcards. There were little packets of flour, ground here at the watermill, and he got one of those, because he felt he should. Also a lavender-scented candle for Mum. And some fudge for them both. He spent most of his money. The girl in the shop put it all in a stout paper bag and Kevin tucked it under one arm as he and Nan headed back outside, holding the toy dog under the other.

They ambled along the river bank towards the car park and the wind blew the napkin of wishes, placed lightly at the top of the paper bag, away towards the river. Nan glanced back and sighed, guiltily. There was no point in chasing it. It was in the water now, drifting along and sinking rapidly.

'Ah well,' said Nan. 'It's probably biodegradable. Hopefully it won't smother a stickleback.' They walked on to the car.

'Pwah!' spluttered Kevin. A flurry of fluff danced around his face. Tiny downy feathers—from some swan's or duck's nest, no doubt. One had gone in his mouth and several of the others settled on his jacket.

'What's up?' said Nan, glancing back, her Peugeot key in her hand.

'Bird feathers in my mouth,' spat Kevin.

'That's good luck, that is!' laughed Nan, making the car chirrup and unlock.

'Good luck?'

'Or—no—that's bird *poo*,' amended Nan, as they got in. 'Bird *poo* is lucky.'

More little feathers blew past him into the car and settled on the back seat as Kevin shut the passenger door. He belted up, and set the paper bag and the dog down by his feet while Nan got the engine going and began to drive out of the watermill car park.

'I've had a really nice time,' Nan said. 'We must do it again soon. It's nice to get you on your own. Even if you do occasionally projectile vomit all over me.'

'I didn't this time,' grinned Kevin. 'I got out of the car first, didn't I?' He'd thrown up in a ditch half a mile from the watermill.

'Anyway. It's nice to have a drive in the country. Just you and me,' said Nan.

Kevin agreed. Just him and his nan in the car *was* nice. He glanced back to see the watermill through the rear window.

And screamed.

Chapter 2

Nan slammed on the brakes but Kevin barely noticed. He was too busy gaping at the man in the back seat.

The man was pale but did not look in any way sickly. His eyes were piercing and directed at Kevin. His white hair was short and curling artistically around his temples, like the sort of hair found on marble statues in museums, and his beard was similarly neat and white, trimmed with perfect symmetry beneath a mouth which looked as if it had been chiselled by a talented sculptor. His nose was long and straight and his cheekbones high and smoothly defined.

He seemed to be wearing a finely woven robe of some kind, which was slung loosely across one shoulder, revealing a smooth well-muscled chest. He held a carved wooden staff in his right hand and what looked like a wet tissue in the left.

Dimly, Kevin could hear Nan shouting at him,

asking what was wrong, but he could not tear his shocked eyes away from the vision in the back seat.

As he stared and stared, his mouth hanging open and his jaw quivering, he noticed other things about the stranger. Little feathers were curled into his hair, stylishly, like a fashion statement. A few clung to his chest too. And there appeared to be fish swimming through his robe. Up and down and around and around, never breaking the surface of the material. As Kevin's eyes bulged, just trying to make sense of what was being presented to them, they also picked up that the pattern of the material on the back seat was visible *through* the man. He wasn't quite solid.

'I can see,' said the man, in a deep, commanding voice, 'that the size and shape of this conveyance makes it difficult to kneel.'

Kevin nodded. He had no idea why.

'Therefore I will accept a bow, as far as it may go,' concluded the man.

Kevin undid his seat belt. He thought it best to go along with the request. He bowed from the waist, awkwardly, given his twisted position.

The man smiled and inclined his head magnanimously, sending a flurry of little feathers through the air.

'I observe you are ill equipped for ceremony at present,' he said. 'We will resume your worship later.'

And then he faded away. He simply dissolved into the back seat until there was nothing left to see but a few little feathers settling onto it.

SLAP!

Kevin spun round, gasping. Nan had just smacked him across the face.

'KEVIN! KEVIN!' she was yelling at him. She looked frantic and now she gripped his face with both hands, peering into his eyes. 'Are you back with me now?'

'Did you see that?' he squawked. 'Did you? Did you see the man?'

Nan put one palm to his forehead. 'You're not well,' she said. 'Maybe it wasn't just car sickness.'

'NAN! Did you see the man on the back seat?' demanded Kevin, swiping her hands away. 'There was a man there! With a curly beard and a robe with fish in it!'

Nan glanced back once and then stared at him and her worried face settled into something like an uneasy smile. She was trying hard to think of the right response, he could tell. 'Kevin,' she said, at length, 'there's nobody on the back seat.'

'I know there isn't *now*!' retorted Kevin. 'He's gone now—but he was there! He was!' He picked up one of the feathers from the seat. 'He had feathers in his hair and on his chest—like these!'

Nan regarded the tiny curl of down in his fingers and nodded. 'O-K,' she said.

'Nan! I'm not making this up! He was right there! He was—he was a bit see through too!' Kevin's heart was hammering in his chest, but he took a deep breath and willed it to slow down.

A car horn sounded. Nan had stopped in the middle of the road and three vehicles were now waiting behind her. She started the engine and pulled away with a jerk. 'I think it must have been a ghost, Kevin,' she said, quite calmly. It was one of the things Kevin loved about her; her calmness in a crisis. Even if she *had* slapped his face.

'Yes,' he breathed, now more excited than shocked. 'A ghost! That's what I saw. Wow!'

'Did he say anything to you?' asked Nan, curiously checking her rear-view mirror, in case the ghost had made a reappearance.

'He wanted me to bow to him,' murmured Kevin, staring at the feather in his palm. 'Said something about worshipping him later.'

'Sounds rather impressed with himself,' said Nan.

'Yes—yes, he was,' grinned Kevin. What an amazing thing to tell Tim! He'd love this!

All the same, as he described the ghost in more

detail to Nan on the way home, he couldn't help a huge tide of goose pimples rising and falling across his skin. It had been a very, very weird experience.

Mum didn't really take it seriously when they told her. She seemed to think it was a joke that he and Nan had cooked up between them on the way home. Kevin didn't mind. He felt elated. Thrilled.

He'd always suspected amazing things like ghosts and superpowers and all that *could* happen for real, but as time went by and he became a teenager, the 'real world' stuff started to take over and it became harder and harder to believe in the spooky stuff. Now, though—he had *seen* it! He had *seen* a ghost. And yes, it had been scary. He knew he had *slightly* screamed. But it had also been amazing.

Did he want to see the ghost again? Well . . . probably not. It felt more comfortable to think that he'd left it safely behind in Houghton. It probably belonged to the watermill. It might be fun to go back one day and see if it showed up again. That would be brilliant. But for now, he'd had enough excitement.

Mum was making macaroni cheese, and Nan stayed to have tea with them.

'Oh, Kevin! Thank you, love,' Mum smiled, digging the fudge and candle and watermilled flour out of the bag. She sniffed the candle and set it down on the side in the kitchen, then, after reading on the packet about how the flour was milled, she put it in the ingredients cupboard. The fudge she put down on the side too. 'We'll have some of that after tea,' she smiled. She looked tired and there was a bit of grated cheese in her dark hair. She suffered the same 'tufty hair' fate as Kevin, so kept it quite short.

'Thanks for taking him out, Mum,' she said to Nan, going back to stirring the cheese sauce. 'I could never have got all my work done if you hadn't.'

'Did you finish it, love?' asked Nan.

'Yes,' sighed Mum. 'But if I have to talk to one more estate agent I'm going to shoot myself.'

Kevin grinned. His mum was a freelance copywriter who worked for PR and advertising agencies. She had to talk to people on the phone and then write interesting stories about them to help get them into the local papers. She quite liked her job, but her current task was to promote estate agents. It wasn't easy. 'Deceptively spacious in the head,' was how she described most of them.

'So,' said Mum, when they had nearly finished eating, 'who came up with the ghost joke?'

'It wasn't a joke!' said Kevin, through his last mouthful of hot cheesy pasta. 'I really *did* see him!'

Mum looked at Nan and Nan shrugged. 'He

13

certainly had a funny turn,' she confirmed. 'I'd rather think it was a ghost than the onset of seizures!'

'It *was* a ghost!' insisted Kevin. 'But he was only there for a few seconds. I'll probably never see anything that freaky again, as long as I live. Can I go upstairs now? I want to phone Tim and tell him.'

'OK,' laughed Mum. 'Get it out of your system!'

Kevin ran up to his room, swiping the 'walk about' phone receiver from its base in the hallway as he went. He dialled Tim's number as he climbed the stairs and it was ringing as he walked into his bedroom.

'Guess what I saw today, Tim?' rattled out Kevin, the second his friend grunted hello at the other end of the line.

'What?' said Tim, who was sitting in his own bedroom, playing a computer game. 'Kev?' he prompted, wondering why a strange gurgling noise was coming out of his phone. 'You there?' The gurgling had stopped, but there seemed to be some heavy breathing going on. 'Any chance you could stop being a weirdo?' said Tim, putting the receiver on his desk so he could seize his control pad and tackle an incoming alien while his best mate got over himself.

Back in Kevin's bedroom there was a small tornado of little curly feathers.

Standing inside it was the ghost from Houghton.

Chapter 3

Kevin opened his mouth to shriek, but no sound came out. His knees gave way and he dropped onto the floor, too shocked to notice the stab of pain from a small blue Lego brick under his shin.

'This is better. This is as it should be,' said the ghost, raising the wooden staff in one hand and waving the wet tissue in the other. The finely woven blue material slung across his chest draped right down to floor level, still carrying its full catch of contentedly swimming fish. It was held firm at the waist with a golden belt which was decorated with two swans' heads at the clasp. The ghost wore sandals, also gold, and there seemed to be webbing between his toes, noted Kevin, as he fell forward onto his hands, gasping with terror. Only a few minutes ago he'd been getting over the whole ghost thing and even kidding himself that he'd quite like to see it again.

Now he felt somewhat different, as his heart hammered inside his ribcage and his head swam with amazement, fear, and confusion.

'Good—good—almost correct,' the ghost was saying now. 'But a full bow to the floor should be better controlled—more stately. You're trying, I can see that. But you still look like a landed trout.'

Kevin looked up, his mouth falling open. Was a ghost *really* criticizing his posture?

'Do not gape, boy!' Now the apparition was screwing up its brow, just like his dad did when he caught Kevin biting his nails. 'Close that aperture! Lift up your countenance and let it be gilded with joy. For indeed, *it is I*. Your prayers have been answered.'

Kevin sat back on his heels, closed his mouth, and narrowed his eyes at the ghost. 'You're a bit impressed with yourself, aren't you?' he said, hardly able to believe he was allowing the words out of his mouth. That staff thing might be able to send out blasts of fire!

'And should I not be?' replied the ghost. 'Am I not your god?'

'My god?' echoed Kevin, astonished.

'Your god!' insisted the ghost. 'I am Abandinus, god of the river and the sky above it, deity to man, bringer of water, protector of avia!'

'You're a *god*?' Kevin shook his head and closed

his eyes. Maybe Mum had cracked after her eighteenth estate agent, gone nuts and put drugs in the macaroni cheese. He was hallucinating.

'Yesss,' came back the so-called god; rather testily, thought Kevin, for an immortal being. 'It is I, Abandinus! Do you not quake? Do you not bow down before me? Do you not whimper for mercy and favour?'

Kevin got up and sat on his bed, flicking away the Lego brick which had embedded itself in his leg. He *was* quaking. He *had* bowed down . . . sort of. 'Should I be whimpering for mercy?' he asked, looking directly into the god's dark eyes. 'Are you going to smite me or something?' He clenched bunches of the duvet in his fists and hoped for the best.

Abandinus regarded him silently for a while and then sighed and sat down beside him, surprisingly making the mattress dip down as if he was a normal being—although a light one. 'You're really not up to speed on all this, are you?' he said, resting his staff down by his feet. 'Kevin, isn't it?' Kevin nodded, staring in wide-eyed wonder at the god on his bed.

'Do you believe in anything, Kevin?' asked Abandinus.

'Um . . . ' said Kevin.

'I thought not,' said Abandinus. 'Go to church?'

Kevin shook his head.

'Mosque?'

'No.'

'Ever chant "Nam-myoho-renge-kyo"?'

'Er . . . no.'

'Stuck pins in any wax effigies?'

'No! Of course not!' Kevin shifted back down the bed. A rather vicious looking pike had just swum past Abandinus's knee and given him a nasty look.

'Well . . . probably just as well,' said Abandinus. 'A clean sheet. Blank canvas. And who am I kidding, anyway? Nobody's believed in *me* for centuries. Not even slightly. Not until this week, anyway.'

Kevin noticed that the god's speech kept going from all 'olde worlde' big stuff to just normal, like he himself talked. He began to feel less afraid. 'Are you *really* a god?' he asked.

Abandinus pointed at his fast flowing robe. 'Have you seen any of these down Top Man?'

Kevin laughed out loud and then clapped his hand over his mouth. How could he be laughing when he was this scared? He noticed that Abandinus looked a bit more . . . substantial . . . than when he'd last seen him, in the back of Nan's car. 'So—so if you're a *real* god, why are you here, talking to me?'

Abandinus looked surprised and slightly taken aback. 'Well, because you prayed to me, of course.'

'Um . . . no—I really don't think I did,' said Kevin.

Abandinus held up the wet tissue and waved it, soggily, under Kevin's nose. 'I beg to differ!' Kevin peered at it with distaste and then realized what it was. There was writing on it—*his* writing. It was his wish list, on the napkin which had blown into the river at the watermill.

'What—where did you get that?'

'In my river. Did you not cast it upon my waters? Men have been casting their prayers upon my waters for millennia! And sometimes, if I am feeling clement towards man, I may choose to answer his prayers. Or . . . ' he seized his staff and stood up in a flurry of little feathers, ' . . . I may not.'

'So . . . ' said Kevin, 'when was the last time you answered man's prayers?'

Abandinus shrugged. 'Time has little meaning to a god.'

'No—go on—when?'

'Um . . . around 1431.'

'Oh—that long ago?' marvelled Kevin.

Abandinus shook his head dismissively. ''Tis but a heartbeat past.'

'And what did you do for him?' asked Kevin. He was getting an excited warmth in the pit of his stomach, overtaking his fear. This was a *wish granting* god!

'I restored the water to his well,' said Abandinus, modestly picking something off the end of his staff.

'Oh. Was that all?' said Kevin.

'All? *All?* I saved the man's crops, his livelihood, his family from starvation! And you say is that *all*?' The fish on his robe began to swim faster with little agitated flicks of their scaly tails. One or two dived up out of it and then splashed back down a moment later.

'Sorry—I didn't mean to say it wasn't *good*,' said Kevin. 'Just—you know—kind of *low key*. I mean—did you ever do any really *big* miracles? You know, like cracking the earth asunder or exploding stuff?'

Abandinus stared at him. 'You are a foolish boy,' he said, at length. 'I can see I have made a mistake. You will not believe in me.' And he began to fade away. Kevin could see the corner of the air-hockey table right through his head.

'No! No, wait!' he called, suddenly desperate not to lose Abandinus. This was the most amazing thing that had ever occurred in his life. He couldn't just let it go. 'I'm sorry! I *do* believe in you! I do! You *are* a god . . . you are . . . ' he threw himself onto the carpet in a face-down bow, 'you are *my* god! *My* god!'

He glanced up and saw that Abandinus had

stopped fading. The god smirked. Just a little bit. 'Very well, boy,' he said, getting less see-through. 'You may worship me. Once a day will suffice.'

'Good! Yes! Thank you!' breathed Kevin, getting up again, his mind buzzing with possibilities. 'And . . . um . . . can I get you anything?'

'Shrine would be nice,' said Abandinus.

'A shrine? Um . . . OK,' nodded Kevin, wondering where the heck he would find a *shrine*. Shrines 'R' Us? 'Anything else?'

'Faith,' said Abandinus. 'Belief, faith, worship, shrine . . . I'd like a hymn too.'

'Oh—OK. I can do hymns,' said Kevin. 'We do lots of those at school.'

'Not just *any* hymn,' said Abandinus, with a slight pout of his perfectly chiselled lips. 'I don't want a second-hand one. Already *used*. Make me a new one.'

'A new one. Um . . . all right—fine.' Kevin started to grin, remembering that Tim played the piano and had a little computer set-up where he could make up music with a keyboard. 'And . . . um . . . what do I get out of it?'

Abandinus began to revolve, slowly at first, but picking up speed. 'You get a god to worship,' he said. 'What man can ask more?'

'But—but you said you were going to answer my

prayers,' spluttered Kevin as the god spun faster and his Top Trump card collection started swirling across the carpet. His wish list was still lying limply on his bed. 'Don't you need that to refer to?' he shouted, pointing at it.

'A shrine,' called Abandinus, although his voice was warped and odd because of the mini tornado going on around him. 'First, a shrine.'

And then there was a whooshing noise, followed by a muffled crack, and Abandinus was gone. Only a few feathers remained, swirling in the air and gradually settling on the carpet.

'Right,' said Kevin sinking back on to the floor. 'A shrine, Kev. That's all. No problem.' He heard a squeaking noise and looked down to see that the phone was lying under his bed.

'Kev? Kev!' Tim's tinny voice was yelling out of it. 'What is going on? What was all that racket?'

Kevin snatched the phone and gasped, 'Tim! You'll never guess what! I've been chosen by a god!'

Chapter 4

Kevin ran all the way to Tim's house and got there inside ten minutes. On the doorstep Tim narrowed his dark brown eyes warily.

'What happened?' he said. 'Did you go off on one of those day camps where everyone sings songs and shares soup and stuff. Did you meet some religious girl you fancy?'

'What are you on about?' Kevin squinted at his best friend in confusion.

'What am *I* on about? You're the one who's suddenly been chosen by God!'

Kevin snorted and then let out a laugh. 'Not *GOD*—*a* god. I've been chosen by *a* god. Abandinus. He followed me home from my day out with Nan.'

'Oh—right!' Tim sounded very relieved. 'You had me going there for a while.' He led Kevin through the house and out into the back garden. His laptop was

23

open on the garden swing seat where he'd been playing on-line games. He moved it onto a nearby table and he and Kevin sat down.

Swinging gently in the warm evening air, Kevin was still shaking with excitement and his sprint to Tim's house.

'So—go on. Who's this god then?' Tim said, pushing hard with his feet so they began to arc back and forth more energetically.

'His name is Abandinus and he's a river god. He was in the River Ouse, he says, and he reckons I cast a prayer on the water and that's why he showed up in the back of Nan's car.' Kevin took a breath, noticing that Tim's dark right eyebrow was arched up and hadn't come back down yet. 'Well . . . I saw him in the back seat and I screamed—I thought he was a ghost. And Nan nearly crashed the car. But she didn't see him. And then after tea, just when I was phoning you, he showed up again in my room. Did you hear him? Did you hear us talking?'

Tim's left eyebrow went up to join his right one and he shrugged and shook his head, grinning. 'No, mate. I did not hear you having a chat with a god. All I heard was a lot of squeaking and blowing and gurgling. I though you'd dropped the phone in the dishwasher!'

'Look—it doesn't matter whether you heard him

or not. He was *there*!' insisted Kevin. 'And he had my list of wishes on a soggy napkin and—look—he's a *super being*! With superpowers! And he can make my wishes come true!' Kevin fixed his dark grey eyes on Tim's. 'Don't you get it? Wishes . . . coming true!'

Tim flopped back on the green cushions of the swing seat. 'Yeah,' he said, with a grin. 'It would be brilliant. It's a good game. We haven't played games like that for a while, have we? We used to play super-powers and stuff all the time in junior school.'

'Not a game! *Real!*'

Tim sat up and stopped grinning. 'Look, Kev—you're a good mate. Kind of weird and a bit out there sometimes, but I quite like that. But you ought to know when to stop taking the—'

'Pick up your laptop—go on line!' cut in Kevin. 'See if there's anything about him. My god, I mean.'

'*Your* god,' said Tim. He gave Kevin a sceptical look, but then sighed and reached over to his small laptop. With a rattle of keys he called up the internet, typed 'Abandeenus' and hit the search button. Kevin peered eagerly over his shoulder. A few seconds later a short list of hits lay across the screen. At the top of the list it said *Did you mean 'Abandinus'?* and it had, in fact, only supplied information on the second spelling.

'Here you go,' said Tim. ' "*Abandinus is a little known god represented in Britain on a single altar stone found in Godmanchester, Cambridge. He is thought to be associated with a natural spring, stream or river in the area. The feather votive inscribed to him suggests he may also have avian links.*" Is that your god?'

Kevin felt all the hairs prickle up across his arms and neck. Yes—he *was* a river god and all those feathers wafting about—and the swans on his golden belt—that was 'avian' wasn't it? Avian meant 'of birds'.

'That's him,' he breathed. 'Any pictures?' Tim rattled the keys a few more times but they didn't find any images of the god. Kevin described Abandinus, including the weird fish-filled robe and the golden belt and sandals. He tried to remember and relate everything the god had said, and when he'd finally finished, with the god's parting demand for a shrine, Tim was looking at him in a funny way.

'What?' said Kevin, after a pause.

'You didn't—like—*take anything*, did you?' said Tim. He looked serious—worried even.

'Take anything? What—you mean drugs?' spluttered Kevin. 'Where would I have got drugs from? My nan?'

'Well . . . she grew up in the sixties,' said Tim, with a weak smile.

'Don't be stupid. Of course I didn't take drugs. What I'm telling you is *true*!'

'All right—so call him up. Let me meet him and then I'll believe you,' said Tim, putting the laptop back on the table and standing up. 'Come on! What are you waiting for?'

Kevin stood up. He pushed his fists into his jeans pockets and sighed. 'He won't come. Not yet. Not until I've made him a shrine.'

'A shrine,' repeated Tim. 'Well, yeah. Of course. What was I thinking of?'

'That's what he asked for, remember? A shrine—and a hymn too. I was hoping you might help me with that.'

'So—where are you going to get a shrine?' Tim folded his arms, looking impatient now. 'Because I think I saw some on special offer down Tesco Extra. Buy one shrine, get one free.'

Kevin sighed. He could see it was hopeless. He was never going to convince Tim. His best friend did not believe him and just thought he was playing an annoying game. He patted Tim on the shoulder. 'Sorry to have wound you up,' he said, and walked back towards the house. Tim made an exasperated noise and followed him, but he didn't say anything as Kevin walked on down the hallway and reached the front door.

27

'I'll see you around,' said Kevin, in a flat voice, not looking back. He stepped outside and headed for home. The sun was setting now and a chill settled on his skin. He could not remember a time in his life when he had left Tim's house and Tim hadn't said goodbye.

'Garden centre,' said Tim, as soon as Kevin opened his front door.

'What?' Kevin screwed up his eyes in the Sunday morning sun.

'That's the place to get your shrine,' said Tim.

Kevin stared at him and then felt a grin spread over his face. He'd been miserable going to sleep last night, knowing he'd walked off in a bad mood—and Tim hadn't stopped him. And waking up hadn't felt much better, either. As far as he knew he hadn't put 'Lose best friend' on his wish list to Abandinus, but that morning he thought he might as well have. Now, though, Tim was back. Offering shrine solutions.

'Does this mean you believe me now?' he said.

'No,' said Tim. 'But I was bored and couldn't think of anything more fun to do on a Sunday than buying a shrine.'

'So—why the garden centre?'

'Well, you know—they have those stone orna-ment thingies, don't they? And they're quite shriney. They'll probably do.'

'How much are they?' Kevin mentally rummaged through his cash stash. He reckoned he might have about fourteen quid saved up.

'I dunno. Never looked at them before,' said Tim. 'But I've got a fiver, if you need it.'

'You'd give me a fiver? For a shrine?' Kevin was quite shocked.

'*Lend* you a fiver—yeah! You can pay me back ten times that when your god shows up and starts granting your wishes.' Tim shook his head and ran his fingers through his short woolly black hair. 'I am so *not* getting why I'm saying this!'

Kevin ran back indoors to collect all the money he could find in his bedroom, and then joined Tim in the front garden, having told his mum they'd be back by lunchtime. He didn't mention where they were going, but she probably thought they were off down the village park as usual. The good thing about liv-ing in a quiet backwater, half an hour's bus ride from town, was that mums and dads didn't freak out if you didn't check in with them every half hour by mobile phone. There wasn't too much heavy traffic to worry about and any strangers were so rare they were spotted

29

instantly and closely scrutinized by all the old ladies on the Neighbourhood Watch scheme. It was a sleepy place and the slightest thing could cause a stir. Some of the old dears still hadn't stopped fizzing about Tim and his parents coming to live there five years ago. They were the only black family in Amberton.

'How far's the garden centre?' asked Kevin. 'Should we wait for the bus?' They paused at the stop, a shelter painted green with a bench inside it. There was graffiti inside, sprayed in yellow and white, helpfully suggesting what Steve Pitt could do with himself. Steve went to their school. If he found out who'd left the message, he would probably spread them across the playground more thinly than their spray paint.

'Nah—it'll only take us half an hour,' said Tim. 'And we might need the bus fare. We don't know how much this shrine's going to cost, do we?' He strode on purposefully.

'So—why are you doing this, then?' asked Kevin, stepping out to keep up with him along the narrow pavement, dodging sprigs of prickly hawthorn which reached out of the high hedgerow. 'If you don't believe me.'

'No idea,' said Tim. 'But you've got some mad scheme going on in that freaky head of yours, so I might as well find out a bit more. So, did your god show up again, when you got home?'

'No,' said Kevin. 'He won't do until we've set up the shrine.'

'Where are you going to put it?' It was a practical question. Kevin frowned with thought.

'I think . . . down the end of the garden—behind the greenhouse and the hedges. There's that wild bit under the old apple trees that Mum doesn't ever get to. You know—where we built the den that time.'

Tim nodded. Then he changed the subject. 'You seen those American kids, yet?'

'What—the students?' asked Kevin. The whole village had been talking about the American students for months. The parish council and their school had agreed to be part of a programme to bring some American students over to study English culture. 'No—are they here?'

'Got in yesterday,' said Tim. 'Haven't seen 'em yet, though. Guess they'll be at school tomorrow.'

'That'll teach 'em,' muttered Kevin. 'When they meet Steve Pitt they'll be put off English culture for life. Oh—but they'll knock themselves out for Mike Mears!' Mike was the Head Boy in waiting in their year. He was top at every kind of sport and fancied himself as a gift to all the girls—especially Emma Greening. He was always trying to chat her up.

31

'Maybe they'll take him back to the States with them,' laughed Tim. 'So he could tell the president how to run things properly.'

'We can always hope,' said Kevin.

The garden centre was busy—full of middle-aged and elderly couples from the town who liked to drive down the country lanes and drift about among the potted herbs, flowers, and garden furniture. Tim was right. There was a whole aisle of stone ornaments and water features. There were plenty of figurines, but Kevin didn't feel comfortable buying a semi nude woman, even if she was made of stone. There were sundials and bird baths too, but he wanted something different. Something simple, which he could stick a candle and stuff on.

'What about this?' called Tim, looking at a terracotta thing up on the wall. It had a face on it, spitting out a steady stream of water into a little trough below.

'No—you need a pump and all that,' said Kevin. 'This'll do.' He pointed to a small stone column with an arched alcove hewn into it. The stone was a pale golden colour and the decoration around it was very simple. Squinting at it more closely, Kevin could see there were feathers carved into it. He felt goose pimples on his skin again. Perfect! How much?

There was no price on it, so they had to ask, and when the man in the garden centre overalls finally came back and told them, it was £5 more than they had. Kevin wailed with disappointment.

'Twenty-two quid?' repeated Tim, looking disgusted. 'For *that*? It's not even half the size of that one over there—and that one's only £27!' The man shrugged. 'And look—it's chipped!' Tim was now crouching down, pointing at the base of the stone column. There *was* a small chip—not very noticeable.

'Look, son, it's £22,' said the man. 'Take it or leave it.'

'Can we talk to the manager?' asked Tim.

'I *am* the manager,' he grunted.

'Well, we'd like to take it, but we can only offer £17,' said Tim, clicking his fingers at Kevin for his money.

'Shame—because it's £22,' said the manager, turning to go.

'We'll have to sing then,' said Tim, with a heavy sigh. 'There's nothing else for it.'

'You what?' The man turned round.

'We'll sing. We'll busk for the extra,' grinned Tim. And then he started. Loudly. A Michael Jackson hit. Not very in tune. Kevin felt his face turn pink with embarrassment, but he took a deep breath and joined in. It was raucous.

'Oi—cut that out!' The manager looked around

him, anxiously, at all the nice customers who were being disturbed.

'Ladies and gentlemen,' called out Tim. 'We are singing for enough money to buy a shrine! Please help if you can. My friend is chosen by a god.' Several people stopped and stared. Tim took a deep breath and opened his mouth to sing again.

'All right! All right!' yelled the manager. 'Seventeen! You can have it for seventeen quid—as long as you shut up and sling your 'ook! Both of you.'

Kevin and Tim staggered out of the garden centre a few minutes later, straining with the weight of the stone, which was in a tough carrier bag held between them. They had just enough money left for bus fare home. Kevin reckoned they'd have ruptured something on the return journey if they'd had to walk.

The bus arrived after five minutes and the driver peered at them suspiciously as they dragged the stone ornament up on to the deck. Kevin set it down on the seat nearest to him while Tim paid and then flopped into the seat across the aisle, looking exhausted.

'What the heck have you got in there? Stonehenge?' came an unfamiliar voice. Kevin and Tim looked round to see a girl sitting two seats behind them, staring in friendly fascination at their purchase. She had wheat coloured hair in two chunky plaits and a turquoise beret on. Her eyes were a similar colour to the beret, and fixed upon the package. Her accent was American.

'Um . . . no . . . just a chunk of Avebury Ring,' grinned Kevin. He'd seen the stones at Avebury once and knew they were much smaller than those at Stonehenge.

'What on earth for?' asked the girl.

'It's a shrine for his god,' said Tim, airily, pointing at Kevin.

The girl stared from Tim to Kevin, quite unabashed.

'I *love* this place,' she laughed, at length. 'You're all *so* out there! Whoa—this is me!' The bus lurched to a stop to let someone off and the girl leapt to her feet. She was wearing jeans and a blue suede waistcoat over her white T-shirt. Her trainers looked different to theirs. More . . . American.

'Nice to meet you!' she called as she prepared to step off the bus and flashed a smile back at them. 'I'm Gracie, by the way. See you around.' And she jumped from the bus and ran off down the road.

'That's one of the students then,' said Kevin. 'She's really . . . '

'American,' said Tim.

'Yeah. Definitely that.'

The short walk between the bus stop and Kevin's house was back breaking. The shrine seemed to get heavier with every step and was beginning to rip through a corner of the bag. By the time they'd reached the side passage, they were drenched in sweat. 'Shhh,' said Kevin. 'We don't want Mum to know about it. She'll ask loads of questions. I was saving that money for a computer game. If she finds out I've got a chunk of rock instead she'll think I've gone nuts.'

'Kev—you *have* gone nuts!' panted Tim.

Mum was inside, singing along to the radio while she clattered around in the kitchen. They ducked down low as they passed the kitchen window and staggered on along the garden. They reached the shady, grassy spot, hidden from view by the greenhouse and some tall conifer hedging, at the far end of the garden. Elderly apple trees stretched above their heads, filled with rhythmically cooing wood pigeons.

'Here,' gasped Kevin, dragging the stone column out of the bag, which was now splitting from the weight of its contents. It slipped in his sweaty palms as he eased it towards a flat slab of flint which lay in the grass—part of an old decorative path which was mostly overgrown here. As he tried to position it, one side of the base toppled the last few centimetres and pounded his left little finger against the slate. Kevin shouted out in pain, whipping it away from under the stone. It throbbed a warning, stinging horribly, and he sucked in his breath as he waited for the first belt of *real* pain. This arrived about five seconds later, leaving him whimpering and cupping the finger which was bleeding merrily by now. 'Oh god, oh, ow, ow, oh *god*!' he wheezed. It was really, *really* painful.

'You all right?' asked Tim, peering over his shoulder.

'Yep,' gulped Kevin. 'Gissaminute.' He rested his uninjured hand on the stone, transferring some smears of red onto it.

'Talk about blood and sweat,' muttered Tim.

'And tears,' said Kevin, wiping his watery eyes. He wasn't *actually* crying, but he would have been just a year or two ago. That was *nasty*.

'Well, I just hope Bandino appreciates this,' huffed Tim.

'It's Abandinus!' groaned Kevin, adjusting the stone column again until it stood upright and firm on the slate.

'Abandinus. Yep. Oi! Abandinus! Where are you? Here's your shrine, mate!' Tim called, grinning and looking up into the trees.

'This one annoys me,' said Abandinus, in Kevin's ear.

Chapter 5

'Bwaaaah!' shouted Kevin, spinning round in shock. Abandinus was *right* in his face, staring at him with those piercing goddy eyes of his. Close to, Kevin could smell him—he smelt like the river at low tide; all earthy and minerally.

'Did I startle you, Kevin?' he smiled.

'YESSS! Don't *do* that!' Kevin backed away from the deity, shivering. He had got caught up in the game of getting the shrine with Tim and had quite forgotten how unnerving it was to see Abandinus in the not-quite-flesh.

'Don't do *what*?' said Tim. He was staring at Kevin, looking a little unnerved himself.

'Thank you for your blood offering,' said Abandinus, pointing to the smear of red on the stone.

'Um—yeah . . . you're welcome,' muttered Kevin.

'I always think a whole pitcher of it is too much,' said Abandinus. 'Trying too hard. Although one could argue that a single smudge is a little miserly.'

'Sorry,' said Kevin. 'I could squeeze my finger if you like.'

'No need,' said the god with a tight smile. 'It's the thought that counts.'

'O-K,' Tim was saying, in a 'playing along' kind of voice. 'Who are you talking to? Has your little god popped up?'

Kevin looked from Abandinus to Tim and back again. 'Can't he see you?' he asked.

The god shook his head. 'Doesn't believe in me, yet. You can't see what you don't believe in.'

Tim shook his head, grinning at Kevin. 'You are *hilarious*.'

'But *I* didn't believe in you yesterday!' argued Kevin. 'And I still saw you!'

'Ah—well, that was only because *I* believed you believed in me,' explained Abandinus, patiently.

Kevin screwed up his face and shook his head. 'What made *you* believe in *me*?'

'You cast your prayer upon my waters, remember.'

'But I told you . . . that wasn't a prayer, it was a . . . ' Kevin shut himself up. What was he saying?

Here was his god. His *own* god. Telling him he wasn't even casting a prayer to begin with was not a good idea if he wanted this superbeing to hang around and grant him some wishes. 'Whatever,' he finished, lamely. 'I believe in you now, so that's OK.'

'Please stop him doing that,' said Abandinus. Tim had walked across to the space which Kevin seemed to be talking at and was waving his hands about to distract him—right in Abandinus's chest. His hands slipped through the god's body easily, although the fish swimming in the robe looked most unsettled and darted away nervously.

'Cut it out, Tim,' said Kevin. 'You're flapping about in my god's body cavities. He doesn't like it. Doesn't like *you* much, either.'

Abandinus curled his lip at Tim. 'He shows no respect,' he stated.

'You could always smite him,' suggested Kevin.

'I could, couldn't I?' replied Abandinus and he raised his wooden staff high in the air above Tim's head.

'Wait!' called out Kevin. 'Not *real* smiting! I was only—'

But he was too late. Abandinus brought his staff down through the air and there was a crack, like thunder.

'—*joking*!' yelled Kevin, scared for Tim.

'Pwah!' spat Tim. He was engulfed in tiny white and grey feathers. 'Pwah! Where did all that come from?'

'Abandinus, of course!' said Kevin, laughing with relief that his friend was not a smoking pile of carbon. 'He just smote you!'

'Ummm—OK, if you say so,' said Tim, picking the feathers off his T-shirt.

'Didn't you hear the thunder?'

'No. Was there thunder? I was busy getting a face full of duck fluff.' Tim spat out a few more feathers.

'Well, that's how it starts,' said Kevin, eagerly. 'Abandinus!' He turned to face his god, who was inspecting the end of his staff as if it needed some maintenance. 'You need to do something to make him believe in you.'

'Do I?' said Abandinus loftily.

'Well—yeah—if you want me to sort out your shrine properly and get you a brand new hymn. Tim's been helping me. I definitely can't get the hymn without his help—he's got Grade Six piano! Come on! Do something goddy.'

Abandinus sighed and then blew out another cloud of feathers. The feathers swirled around and around in a mini cyclone. Kevin grinned. 'Make them go into the little alcove thing in your shrine!' he urged. 'Tim—watch this. Abandinus is going to get the feathers into the shrine.' He grabbed Tim and made him look in the right direction.

The god blew harder, his brow furrowing with concentration. The feathers flew in formation, spun once around the stone and then all piled into the alcove, where they compressed themselves into a perfect sphere.

'See?' said Kevin. 'Did you see that?'

Tim *had* seen it. For the first time since Kevin had revealed his secret, Tim's face had lost that '*Yeah—right!*' look. All that day he had just been humouring his friend, but now he gulped and stared at the shrine with wide eyes. 'I saw it,' he whispered.

'Do you believe me now?' said Kevin, bouncing excitedly on the balls of his feet. 'Do you believe in my god?'

Tim's eyes moved from Kevin's face to somewhere off behind his shoulder. There was another crack of thunder. Then Tim's eyes rolled up into his head and he went over like a felled tree.

'Your friend has the constitution of a *woman*,' observed Abandinus, as Kevin patted Tim on the cheek.

'Don't be sexist,' said Kevin. 'Tim! Tim! Wake up. It's OK—you get used to it.'

Tim groaned and his eyes opened. 'What—who—what?' he burbled, getting up onto his elbows.

'Take some deep breaths,' advised Kevin. 'Just look at me and take some deep breaths.' Tim did so, getting up into a sitting position. 'Yes,' said Kevin. 'You *did* just see a living, breathing superbeing in my garden. Like I said—I've got a god. But it's nothing to be scared of. He only smote you a bit for being disrespectful. Don't diss my god again and you'll be fine.'

Tim took another deep breath and then looked around at Abandinus, who was sitting on the small shrine, balanced easily upon it, and gazing back at him with mild interest. 'You—you're really a *god*?' breathed Tim, gripping two knots of tall grass in his fists as if anchoring himself into some kind of reality.

'I am,' said Abandinus. 'Do you wish to worship me?'

Tim gaped. 'Yes,' said Kevin, nudging him. 'Yes, you do!'

'Er . . . yeah. I can . . . worship you if you like.'

'Then bow down, dark one,' instructed Abandinus.

'Whoa—watch it. That's racist,' chipped in Kevin, as Tim dropped forward onto his elbows, dipping his forehead into the grass.

'I speak of what I see, blemished one,' said Abandinus, rather cuttingly, thought Kevin. He had noticed a
few spots on his chin this morning but 'blemished one'
seemed a little harsh.

'What?' went on the god, glaring at Kevin. 'Am
I not apparent at your shrine? Do you not bow and
pray? Do you not offer up a hymn?'

'Ah, well—we haven't got the hymn sorted yet,'
explained Kevin, getting down into a bow. 'But we can
do the praying bit if you like. Can't we, Tim?'

'Eeeyaup,' whimpered Tim.

'OK. Dear god Abandinus,' began Kevin. 'Um . . .
we pray for . . . um . . . peace on earth and blessings on
our families and all that . . . and . . . ' He glanced up at
Abandinus who was standing now, behind the shrine,
holding his staff high in the air and lifting his firm, dec-
oratively bearded jaw in noble pride. ' . . . and, well, I
think you remember the list?' He dug out the crumpled
napkin which he had dried out on his bedroom radiator last night, glad that the ballpoint pen ink hadn't
washed out of it. He didn't read it all; he didn't want
to come across as greedy. Just two or three for now.
'Um . . . Nintendo Wii, Emma Greening to finally
notice me? Oh—and my gooey toe to clear up. That's
really annoying me. And . . . er . . . well, for everything
else I refer you to the list which you've already seen.

Whatever you can manage will be great!' He paused and looked over at Tim. 'What about you, Tim?'

'I'm fine, thanks,' squeaked Tim, into the grass.

'Oh, well . . . in that case . . . I suppose it's just *Amen*, then,' concluded Kevin. He nudged Tim and Tim also mumbled, '*Amen.*'

Kevin got up onto his knees and watched Abandinus with great anticipation. The god continued to hold aloft his staff and gaze away into the trees.

After a while Kevin gave a polite cough. 'Ahem—was that OK then? Any good? Will it do for you?'

Abandinus continued to gaze away, as if his two worshippers weren't even there.

'Well?' persisted Kevin. 'We've got you a shrine . . . although we haven't put a candle in it or anything yet. But we will. And we've had a bit of a worship . . . any chance of a bit of prayer answering now?'

Abandinus suddenly snapped his attention back to Kevin. He looked aggravated. 'I am not,' he snipped, 'a bloody magician. I am a god. As such *I* choose if and when I answer prayers. In my own time. Now be gone. I wish to preside upon my shrine undisturbed.'

Kevin hauled Tim to his feet. 'Well, thanks a bunch,' he muttered, and guided his dazed friend back down the garden. When he glanced back, Abandinus was still at the shrine, but wafting back and forth in the air above it, on a cloud of feathers, his wooden staff laid across his lap, making swirly shapes with his hands.

'What's he doing?' whispered Tim, not looking back as they reached the shed. 'Is he gone?'

'No, he's still there,' said Kevin, glancing back one last time. 'Moving in a mysterious way.'

Chapter 6

Kevin walked Tim home. Tim was still in shock and might step out in front of a car if he went alone. He didn't say much as they made their way along the street past the youth and community centre. Every time Kevin checked with him on whether he really believed in Abandinus now, he just grunted, 'Yeah,' and kept walking, his hands deep in his pockets and his eyes on the pavement ahead.

Of course, he *had* to believe now that he'd met the god. Kevin just wished he'd cheer up about it. He left Tim at his gate, realizing that his friend probably needed to get away from him for a while and get his head together.

Walking back, Kevin noticed there was music coming from the youth and community centre and a few people coming and going around the single storey red brick building. Of course—this was where the

American students were hanging out together. They had been placed with families all around the village but would be meeting up for social events here. Kevin had asked Mum if they could have one to stay with them but she'd said no—she couldn't really manage that on her own. Mike Mears, of course, had one staying with him. He'd been boasting about it all last week.

Kevin smiled to himself. As it turned out, he was looking after a guest at his place after all. And this guest was a bit more impressive than someone from a different country. This guest came from a different *realm*! Or whatever it was you called the places where gods hung out. Or dwelt. Yeah—they definitely *dwelt*. He was a bit disappointed that Abandinus had got narky about delivering on his prayer list, but he supposed the god was right. It wasn't very respectful to treat him like he was a Father Christmas down at the local shopping centre. He would try to be a bit more subtle about it in tomorrow's prayers. Maybe not ask for anything at all apart from world peace and all that.

Ping! Something hit his nose. Kevin blinked and looked round.

'Hello again, shrine boy!' called a voice. It was the American girl from the bus. She was sitting on the wall of the youth and community centre car park with a couple of mates—one boy and another girl. One

48

of them had thrown a screwed-up sweet wrapper at him.

'Shrine boy?' asked the blond, well-built boy next to her, in a similar accent, looking at Kevin as if he was a specimen in a biology lesson. 'What's *that* about?'

'Ah, nothing,' said the girl, to Kevin's relief. He didn't really want all the American students to have him down as 'the boy with the shrine' when they got to school tomorrow. 'Just me being weird. Hi—how you doin'?' She jumped off the wall and walked over to him. 'Manage to haul that hunk of rock back home, OK?' she asked, more quietly.

'Yeah,' said Kevin. 'It wasn't that heavy.'

'No—like you're always purple and dripping with perspiration when you ride the bus!' she said.

'Well . . . it was hot,' shrugged Kevin.

'Hot? You've got to be kidding me! It's *freezing* here!' She shivered and rubbed her arms. It was late May and really warm for England, but he guessed she came from a hot part of the States.

'Where are you from?'

'LA,' she said. 'You know—Los Angeles?'

'Yes, I know what LA stands for,' laughed Kevin. 'I guess it's a lot hotter than here.'

'It's warm,' she said. 'Here is *freezing*. I had to put my coat on!' He saw she had a jacket on now. 'But that's

49

good. That's what England's like, right? And raining all the time too? Except we haven't had that yet. Where's your umbrella? I heard everyone in England carries an umbrella all the time.' She smiled widely as she said this, teasing him.

'Oh yes. Or a bowler hat,' said Kevin. He liked this girl. She talked as if she *wasn't* a girl. All the girls in his school spoke to boys as if they thought they were not just a different gender, but a different species.

She chuckled. She knew he was winding her up. 'You go to Amberton Secondary?' she asked, pronouncing the 'ary' like 'hairy'.

'Yep—I'll see you there tomorrow I expect.'

'And your friend, too?'

'Yeah, Tim will be there.'

'OK—I'll see you shrine boys in the recess!'

'Um . . .' said Kevin, and she looked back as she moved away. 'Can you do me a favour? Can you not—?'

'Not mention the shrine thing? Sure. I wouldn't have anyway,' she said and ran back to her friends on the wall.

When Kevin got home he was surprised to find that Dad was there. He could tell he was there even before he got inside, because Mum opened the door and had *that look* on her face. The look she always had

50

when Dad came. Smiling too tightly. Trying too hard to be a grown-up.

'Hello, Kev! Give your old man a hug then,' said Dad, knuckling his son's head and giving him a clumsy squeeze as Kevin walked into the sitting room. He was wearing some new gear, Kevin noticed. And he'd had his ear pierced like he'd said he was going to. Nan had muttered something like '*Midlife crisis*' when she'd heard about that. Mum hadn't said anything. Her eyebrows said it all.

'Dad! I didn't know you were coming!' cried Kevin.

'Nor did I,' said Mum, super-brightly. 'How nice, eh? Cup of tea, Jason?'

'No—no, I can't stop,' said Dad. 'I only dropped in to give you this.' He turned and picked a large plastic carrier bag off the sofa. 'I've been meaning to get it for you for ages—and I just got a bonus through at work, so . . . ' He turned round and presented Kevin with the bag.

In it was the answer to his prayers. Well, one of them.

'Oh my *god*!' marvelled Kevin. 'A Nintendo Wii! Thank you so much!'

* * *

51

'Dear god,' said Kevin, that night, kneeling beside his bed. 'Thank you for the Wii, Abandinus. It's brilliant! I can't believe you came through with it so fast. I'll sort that hymn out for you as soon as I can, I promise.' He fell asleep quickly, dreaming of the amazing game he'd been playing on the new console and shrines and storms of feathers and also a woman with a big egg in her hands and a man with a lion's head. But that's dreams for you.

Chapter 7

' . . . such a bore. Moping about like there's no tomorrow. Pretty bad luck considering there are *endless* tomorrows for *her*. And for the rest of us. She really does make eternity drag, that one!'

Kevin felt the hairs prickle on his arms and neck as he crept up the back garden early the next morning, before school, towards the high hedges which screened Abandinus's shrine. Someone was *there*! Someone female was talking there. Was it a friend of his mum's? Had Mum asked a friend in for a chat over an early coffee and then hotfooted it up the garden with her to chat about women's stuff? He had thought Mum was in the bathroom still, but maybe he was wrong.

'I know what you mean,' said another voice. A male voice. Kevin stood still in surprise. That was *definitely* Abandinus. He would recognize that self-important tone anywhere. 'I think she takes that title far too seriously,' went on Abandinus. 'I said to her, "Saitada, love. They called you Goddess of Grief for *half* a century! That's all! And you just can't let it go, can you? So it's *weep* here, *rock and keen* there, beat your breast today, gnash your teeth tomorrow. And you *wonder* why nobody invites you over?".'

'Hah! What did she say to *that*?' asked the female voice.

'Nothing. She just started crying.'

'Well—obviously!' sneered the woman. 'She's a one goddess irrigation project, that one.'

Kevin rounded the hedge and stared. Abandinus was sitting on his shrine again—quite a feat, considering he was the size of a tall man and the shrine was the size of a traffic bollard. In fact, he was seated in the air *above* the shrine, Kevin noted. And he was managing it quite gracefully, as if an invisible armchair supported him. More importantly, someone else was standing next to him. A woman whose flowing hair was the colour of the sea at dawn. She turned to look at him, with silver eyes and the same superior expression that Abandinus habitually wore. She was rather beautiful, in a slightly see-through way, thought Kevin, with her pale oval face, a long, straight nose and a full pink mouth. He realized that, like Abandinus's clothes, her *hair* was full of tiny fish, swimming daintily down from her crown and out of sight as soon as they reached the curled tendrils which hung to her waist. She wore an elegant long white robe—Roman toga style—and a bronze, plaited belt around her slender waist. Matching bronze bracelets encircled her wrists. Her feet were bare and her toes, like Abandinus's, were webbed.

'Oh-ho!' she said. 'You must be the worshipper!' She poked at Abandinus with one finger. 'Aren't *you* the clever one?' she chortled.

'Kevin,' said Abandinus. 'I would like you to meet Ancasta. She is my cousin. River goddess of the Itchen. Protector of the turn. Deity of fin, scale, and fast flowing current—'

'Hi, Ancasta,' said Kevin, with a little wave, cutting Abandinus off in all his grandness. The god twitched with annoyance. Kevin grinned. 'What are you doing here?'

'I am visiting,' said Ancasta. 'Do you wish to worship me?' She smiled and raised her eyebrows as if she was offering him a bag of toffees.

It seemed rude to say no. 'Um . . . yeah. Why not?' said Kevin. He flicked a glance at Abandinus. 'If that's all right with you, of course,' he said, with a little bow of the head.

Abandinus wafted his left hand imperiously and

nodded. 'She is my cousin. This is allowed. I am your principal god, of course, but you may worship Ancasta also, as a show of respect for me.'

'O . . . K,' said Kevin. He sank to his knees and dipped his head a bit. He hoped they wouldn't insist he went flat out on the ground this time. The grass was quite wet.

'Dear goddess—Ancasta. Um . . . I offer you my . . . worship . . . ness. And ask . . . er . . . for your blessing.' He paused. He didn't want to rattle off his wish list again, not after he'd already started that with Abandinus. After all, Abandinus was his *main* god, and it wouldn't be right to start asking for the same stuff from another god. That would be kind of two-timing. He flicked a glance up at Ancasta. She was looking distinctly unimpressed.

'And I ask that you guide my passage safely through fast flowing water,' he added, with a touch of inspiration, he thought. '*Amen.*' When he looked up again she seemed more satisfied. She gave him a little nod and then turned back to Abandinus.

'So . . . this is your shrine?' she said to him, pushing him backwards in his mid-air seat, so that she could see the shrine more clearly. She brushed her fingers around the domed top of the stone niche and curled her lip. 'Is this *it*?'

'It isn't finished yet!' protested Kevin. He pulled two small round candles out of his pockets, each in a little glass cup. 'I was coming to put these in!'

'Oh *look*, Dino!' cooed Ancasta. 'Your little worshipper has brought you some teeny tiny candles for your tiddly little shrine! How *sweet*!'

Abandinus frowned and dropped into a standing position next to her, allowing his staff to land with a thud on the slate base beneath the shrine. 'It is a work in progress!' he hissed. 'And let's not get too uppity about size, eh? *Your* shrine is only two feet high!'

Ancasta glared at him and her sea-coloured hair turned a shade of grey. 'My shrine is of huge importance,' she said. 'With Latin inscription, displayed for all to see in an ancient building named for me.'

'Hmmm,' said Abandinus, folding his arms and nodding exaggeratedly. 'Yes—let's see now—God's House Tower museum. *God's* House Tower. Not *Goddess's* House Tower, I notice.'

Ancasta bared her teeth at him.

'I wonder,' he went on. 'If they really *were* thinking of *you*, when they built God's House Tower! I wonder!'

'Um . . . thanks for the Wii, by the way,' said Kevin, trying to lighten the atmosphere. He didn't like to think what two scrapping minor gods might end up destroying if they got really annoyed. The glass in the greenhouse was a bit old and brittle.

'The wee?' Ancasta broke off from her teeth baring and stared at Kevin, looking revolted. 'He gave you his *wee*? Oh really, Abandinus. Is there nothing you won't do to get a worshipper?'

'Well, I notice *you* are hanging out around my tiddly little shrine rather a lot right now!' snapped back Abandinus. 'You're not above trying to get a piece of my worshipper, are you? And I even let you *have* a bit—but now I'm thinking that was a mistake.'

Ancasta suddenly switched on an angelic smile and her hair grew calmer and bluer. 'Oh, Abandinus! I was only teasing, my love! I think your shrine is adorable. And look . . . ' She bent over and ran her fingers along the edge of the stone plinth. 'There are feathers inscribed upon it!'

Abandinus took a deep breath and nodded stiffly, his arms still folded. 'There are.'

'And it must have been awfully heavy for you, getting it here,' said Ancasta, now smiling warmly at Kevin. '*Such* devotion.'

'Well, my friend helped,' Kevin explained. 'Tim helped me find it and then get it back here on the bus. I couldn't have done it on my own.'

'Tim? Your friend, Tim?' Ancasta suddenly looked

rather excited. She glanced at Abandinus and then narrowed her silver eyes. 'You mean to say there are *two* worshippers?' He shrugged and looked 'airy' about it.

'Well, there weren't until yesterday. Tim took a while to convince,' said Kevin. 'But he believes now, all right.' At least he hoped Tim still believed. His friend might have woken up that morning and decided he'd just had a blow to the head or something.

Ancasta was still looking excited. She stepped behind Abandinus and wrapped her arms around his chest. A calculating look wove across her fine features as she rested her cheek on his shoulder. '*Two* worshippers, Abandinus! This could be the start of something big!'

'Yes. Two. Both. Mine,' snipped Abandinus. 'Get your own worshippers, Ancasta!'

'Oh, don't be so selfish!' she said, unwinding her arms and stomping away from him. 'You *know* it's not that easy! Nobody in Southampton even knows what I *look* like! How can they visualize me? There are no carvings! No etchings! Not even a finger painting! If they can't even *think* about what I look like, how can they offer up even a flicker of a half of a whisper of a prayer, eh? *Nobody* has asked for my protection for six centuries! Apart from that one . . . ' She tailed off, looking rather dreamy and lost. 'But that was just a tiny exception. No. I am all but forgotten!' Her voice cracked theatrically as she added: 'It's no wonder I have faded.'

Kevin sat down on the grass, careless of the damp patch he'd have on his backside. He was beginning to understand something quite amazing. He had always thought that religious people *needed* their gods. But apparently, the *gods* also needed *them*! He was being *fought over* by a god and a goddess! It was just like when his mum and dad got going about who would have him at Christmas or Easter or on his birthday. All that power and influence . . . and yet still squabbling over who got the hugs!

He started to laugh.

Ancasta and Abandinus broke off from their spat and stared at him.

'You need worshippers,' chuckled Kevin. 'To feel like proper gods. Is that it?'

Abandinus was not happy. Ancasta was positively incensed. A whirlwind began to spin around her as she glared at him, until she was completely engulfed and then the whole mini storm vapourized into wisps of grey mist, which blew down the garden and evaporated somewhere over the greenhouse.

'Oops,' said Kevin.

'You have no respect,' rumbled Abandinus. 'I think I shall abandon your shrine and desert you.'

'Oh—look—don't be like that!' said Kevin, getting up and moving closer to the god. 'I didn't mean to disrespect you, honestly. I *like* having you around.'

'I am not a pet cat,' said Abandinus. 'I am a god. You humans are merely my playthings, do you not know? I could smite seven bells of hell out of you right now, if I chose to.'

'OK—fine—I understand,' said Kevin. 'I'm sorry I laughed. I didn't mean to be rude. But it seemed like you *need* worshippers. To feel OK about yourselves. There's nothing wrong with that. We all need . . . validation.' He wasn't sure this was the right word. His mum used it and he heard it on talk shows a lot.

Abandinus was looking thoughtful.

'I can help you,' said Kevin. 'I've already got Tim to believe in you, haven't I? And that's good, isn't it?'

Abandinus looked at him, and seemed to be considering something. At length he said, 'Sit with me,' and dropped to a cross-legged position on the grass. Kevin sighed. His school trousers were green and soggy enough already. He sat.

'Gods *do* need their worshippers,' admitted Abandinus, picking at his wooden staff. 'We are powerful, mysterious, potent, vengeful, magnanimous, and strange. But without anyone noticing . . . well, it's kind of hard to keep it up. After a few centuries of nobody noticing, it's difficult to keep momentum. We tend to sleep more. Some of my cousins are gone for good, I think. Sleeping so deeply that they will never wake. Nobody calls for their blessing or their curses or their protection any more. Nobody calls.'

Kevin nodded, feeling rather sad for the sleeping gods. It sounded a bit like being left in the old folks home with no relatives left to visit.

'Those of us who are fortunate to have some form of relic or shrine . . . even a mention in a book . . . we have some small hope of growing great once more. At least there is a record of our existence. Somebody *might* decide to start worshipping us. But this is an ungodly world. Few people think to worship any more. Apart from *EastEnders* or *Coronation Street*. These are worshipped regularly, at the television altar. Or in *Heat* magazine.'

Kevin gaped. A *god* knew about soaps and *Heat* magazine? 'You mean the *Cult of Celebrity*,' he murmured. It was something his mum referred to a lot. She couldn't stand *Heat* magazine and others like it. Although she occasionally 'researched' them—for her job.

'Yes,' said Abandinus. 'That is what I mean. So

you see, when somebody chances to throw a prayer upon your waters, it's . . . rather a novelty. You do what you can.'

Kevin took a deep breath. 'Look . . . would it help if I got more people to believe in you?'

'It would make me stronger,' nodded Abandinus. 'The more we are believed in, the stronger we are. The more able we become. It is an equation. You believe. I believe. We all believe,' he explained, sounding a bit like a '*Learn English in three easy steps*' CD. 'The belief germinates more belief. The power of belief is greater than you can comprehend, Kevin. And with that power,' he leaned in closer, 'I can do things for you. Make things happen. *Good* things.'

Abandinus grinned. A shrinestep salesman from the god realm. All he was missing was the clipboard and pen, but he was definitely selling.

And Kevin was buying.

Chapter 8

'You should probably put your tongue back in,' said Tim. 'You look like a poodle with heatstroke.'

Kevin grinned, leaning back against the wide trunk of the beech tree. 'Don't worry. She never looks at me. She never notices me at all.'

Emma Greening flicked back her long glossy dark hair and laughed with her friends. She was in school uniform like everyone else, but she still looked like a model with her perfect skin, her expensive shoes, and her effortlessly graceful pose against the wall of the gym block. Her school bag was 'designer' according to Zoe Spencer, who sat next to him in geography.

'Well, she doesn't notice you *yet*,' said Tim. 'But now that you're a chosen one, she's going to. That was on your list, wasn't it?' He adopted a high-pitched, breathy voice: '*Please* let Emma Greening notice me . . .'

Kevin jabbed his elbow into Tim's ribs, but he laughed. 'I don't think Abandinus is powerful enough to make the best looking girl in school notice a nerd. She walks around with a permanent "nerd filter" in place. She just doesn't see us.'

'Speak for yourself,' said Tim. 'I'm not a nerd. I can play football, remember? And you're not all that bad in goal. You're not *really* a fully paid up nerd. You've just got . . . nerdish tendencies.'

Kevin was pleased that Tim was back to his usual self. After meeting Abandinus at the weekend Tim had been so shocked that Kevin half expected him to be in complete denial by Monday morning. And that would not have been good, because he needed Tim. He needed him in the way that everyone needs a best mate, of course—but he needed him also because of Abandinus. Abandinus wanted followers. Worshippers. People to *believe*. He'd made that clear. The more believers, the greater his power. And with just one puny kid with nerdish tendencies believing in him, Abandinus wasn't going to be packing much voltage, was he? OK—so he'd got Kevin a Wii, but that was easy stuff. The rest of the list was still waiting.

'So—you still believe in my god then?' he said, watching Tim for signs of fear or shock.

'Yup,' said Tim, with a quick gulp. 'Tried to

believe it was all a big trick. Didn't work. You've got a god. Congratulations.'

'*We've* got one!' corrected Kevin. 'I'm going to share with you!'

Tim didn't look keen.

'Tim! Don't you get it? If we believe in Abandinus *really thoroughly* and worship him with hymns and candles and stuff—he's going to get stronger and then . . . you know . . . *phenomenal cosmic power* and all that! Wishes . . . coming *true*!'

'What—for just the two of us?' Tim screwed up his face sceptically.

Kevin sighed. He had to agree. Two of them wasn't enough. No self-respecting god was going to be impressed by *two* followers. 'We might have to introduce him to a few more people,' he said. 'We'll have to make a list. You know, people we know who would make good worshippers. People who won't freak out when they see him.'

'Well, that's a short list then,' said Tim.

Kevin sighed again. Tim was right. Abandinus was scary. He pictured a stampede of wild-eyed kids tearing back down his garden, screaming and frothing at the mouth, Abandinus floating along behind them, looking offended. 'Well—let's see how far we get with just you and me for a while, then. If we get the hymn done, that might power him up a bit. Have you made any progress?'

'Well—kind of,' said Tim 'But it's hard. I write *good* songs—not dreary old hymn things.'

'Some hymns are nice,' said Kevin. 'I like "Hills Of The North, Rejoice".'

Tim stared at him. 'Yeah. Right. Don't forget to tell *that* one to Emma when she starts noticing you.'

'Oh, come on! One measly hymn. You're the musician—you should be able to do this.'

'Well . . . mine keep coming out hip-hop style,' said Tim. 'You know . . . rap and that.'

'Rap?' queried Kevin. 'Since when did you get into rap? You told me it was a black teenage stereotype. That's why you played Chopin at the last school concert when all the other kids were doing rap!'

'I know,' muttered Tim, shoving his hands in his pockets. 'It *is* a black teenage stereotype. But I do quite like it anyway. And I tried to do a piano thing with the hymn but it sounded too drippy.'

'OK . . . rap away then,' said Kevin, with a shrug. 'Just promise me this won't involve "*innit?*" at any point.'

Tim started making percussive beat box noises with his teeth and throat, while his hands began to make the stabby-pointy downward gestures of a street rapper from the Bronx.

'Yo, *Abandinus, god of the river*
Get down with the groove
And be a wish giver
Respect, Abandinus, cos you is de **man**
We worship at yo feet
And we pray when we can . . .
Amen . . . '

In the silence that followed, Kevin didn't know
what to say. It was like no hymn *he'd* ever heard.

'You is . . . *de man*?' he echoed, eventually. He bit
his lip.

'Yeh.' Tim rubbed his nose. 'Actually, now I've
done it out loud, it is a bit . . . '

'Black teenage stereotype?'

They both snorted with laughter. 'You're a disgrace
to all your homies,' said Kevin. 'Get back to Chopin.'

Then someone close by giggled. Tim and Kevin
jumped and looked round. They'd thought they were
alone by the beech tree. The nearest kids were Emma
and her posse over by the gym block.

'It wasn't all that bad,' said a voice up above
them. 'Not sure about the hand movements though.
Looked like you were gardening.'

They stared up, blinking in shock. Some way
above their heads was Gracie, the American girl from

68

the bus. Kevin felt his face go scarlet. How much of their conversation had she heard?

'Are you spying on us or something?' said Tim, hotly. He also looked very self-conscious.

'No! I've been spying on *them*!' she called down, pointing across to the gym block. Her hair was still in plaits but she had no hat on today and seemed to be wearing some kind of uniform, presumably from her school in America—a blue sweatshirt with a motif on the front and black trousers and black lace-up train-ers. 'I was here first,' she added. 'Before you got here. Just checking out how the popular girls stay popular in England. Looks pretty much the same as in the States.'

'Why don't you go and talk to them?' said Kevin, playing for time while his brain desperately replayed the discussion he and Tim had just had. 'They'd love it.'

'They might,' said Gracie, beginning to climb down from the tree. 'For a little while.'

She swung down from the lowest bough and then dropped to the concrete, bouncing down to her knees and then up again, sending her arms out wide, like a circus performer. 'You don't have to look so worried,' she said, 'I really couldn't *hear* you mooning about over Little Miss Gorgeous—the leaves were rustling too much.'

'So how did you know I *was* mooning . . . I

69

mean . . . how do you—I mean . . . ' spluttered Kevin, both relieved that she probably hadn't heard all the god talk and embarrassed that she'd worked out the mooning bit.

'Ah, c'mon! Of *course* you were. I could tell by looking at the top of your head! Even your *hair* was mooning.' She laughed, slapping him hard on the shoulder. 'Why don't you go say hi?'

'Why don't *you*?' asked Tim. He gave her a sarcastic look.

Gracie smiled and nodded at them. 'OK—sorry. I'll butt out.' She backed away, with a little wave of both her hands. Kevin felt bad. He actually wouldn't mind her staying. She was fun. 'You two get back to your hymn practice.'

'WAIT!' called Kevin, and she stopped her waving and backing away and raised an eyebrow at him. 'So you *did* hear us!'

She shrugged. 'Not all of it. Just the bit about needing a hymn for your god. To go with your shrine, I guess. Jeez—you really are holy around here, aren't you? I mean—good for you! We all want God on our side.'

'You don't understand,' said Kevin. 'We're not talking about *the* God. We're talking about *a* god! An ancient English god called Abandinus.'

'Whoa . . . ' breathed Gracie, hooking her hands into her trouser pockets. 'Are you Pagans? Wow! I heard there were Pagans in England. Do you, like, put on white robes and dance around Stonehenge at dawn?'

'No we do not!' snapped Tim.

'Our god doesn't require dancing,' explained Kevin. 'We don't dance around *anything*. We've only just met him. Give us a chance!'

Gracie stopped giggling and gasping and tilted her head to one side, narrowing her eyes and measuring them up, trying to work out who was kidding who. After a few seconds she said: 'You've *met* him? You think you've met a *god*?'

'Keep it to yourself,' said Tim. 'Everyone will want one.'

'Hey! Gracie! You gotta come!' called an American voice and they looked round to see the blond-haired student waving at her by the entrance to the school hall.

She raised a hand and yelled, 'Right there!' before looking back at Kevin and Tim. 'Are you serious?' she asked, her smile hovering about her lips. 'You really think you've got an actual *god* hanging out at your little shrine?'

Tim and Kevin looked at each other. They didn't say anything.

'Can I meet him?' she asked, smiling broadly now. 'I'll be respectful! Might even be able to work out a little hymn for him myself, y'know.'

'OK,' said Kevin, as Tim turned to him and made urgent *'are you mad?'* faces. 'Come round my place. Four o'clock. Forty-two Swift Close.'

'Gracie!' yelled the blond boy again.

'OK—it's a date!' said Gracie and then turned and ran to the hall.

'What are you *doing*?' hissed Tim, as soon as she'd gone. 'Are you nuts?'

Kevin shook his head. 'We were just saying we needed more followers.'

'Yes—and *then* we were just saying how they'd freak out and we should just keep it to ourselves for now! Remember?'

'Yeah,' said Kevin. 'But I think she might not. I mean . . . they're a bit more, you know, open to stuff, Americans. Don't you think? They're not all negative like we are in this country. She might be good for Abandinus—or Ancasta.'

'Ancasta?' repeated Tim. 'Who is Ancasta?'

Kevin grinned. 'Ah yes . . . you've not met her yet, have you?' The bell went to signal the end of the lunch break, so he told Tim about the arrival of the goddess as they headed back into school.

Tim was taking steady, deep breaths as they reached the science block corridor. 'A god . . . *and* a goddess. This is getting weirder by the day. And you, like, worshipped her *too*?'

Kevin shrugged. 'Well—a bit. She seemed to want some worship. It would've been rude not to.'

'And Abandinus didn't mind?'

'Not at first. But then they had this row about me—about her trying to nick his worshipper. Turns out, they haven't been worshipped by anyone in centuries and they're kind of . . . needy.'

Tim shook his head, a grin spreading over his face. 'You're kidding.'

'Nope. It's true. So you'd better work on a proper hymn. Abandinus *needs* it. To feel good about himself.'

The flow of students in the corridor began to bottleneck because a girl had dropped her bag and was trying to retrieve it. In the crush, it got scuffed across the floor to Kevin's feet and as he picked it up he recognized the designer label. It belonged to Emma Greening. She was even now trying to look through the many legs of her classmates and calling out, 'Hey! My bag! Where is it?'

Kevin picked it up and held it high so she could see it above the throng of students pushing along the narrow strip of floor in two directions. He threw an excited smile to Tim. 'Abandinus at work, I think,' he said, struggling to stand still in the human river.

'Here it is, Emma,' he called, above the babble.

Emma's perfect profile turned, her long dark lashes rising as she opened her eyes wide. Her soft pink mouth curved into a smile of appreciation, and angels began to sing in harmony in Kevin's head as she fixed her lovely gaze upon . . .

Mike Mears.

A large, strong, suntanned hand grabbed the handles, and smoothly whipped the bag away as if Kevin's fingers were made of butter.

'Here you go,' said Mike, and the sea of students seemed to part as if he was Moses. He swaggered over to her and pressed the bag into her grateful hands.

'Hey!' protested Kevin, unable to stop himself, even though he knew sounding like a whiney kid was hardly going to impress.

Emma didn't even glance in his direction; she was busy smiling up at Mike Mears and gushing her thanks. Mike, though, glanced over his shoulder, pushed his fingers through his floppy fringe, and made a fake sympathetic face at Kevin. Kevin ground his teeth. As Emma finished her thanks and walked on to class, Mike turned and walked back past them. He thwacked the flat of his hand hard against Kevin's shoulder as he went. 'Bad luck, Muttley,' he grinned. 'But you've got to know, you're *way* out of your league there. Don't torture yourself.'

Kevin was speechless with rage.

'Ah get back to your shampoo adverts,' yelled Tim. 'Poser!'

Kevin found it hard to unclench his teeth as Tim shoved him along the corridor. 'With any luck he'll flop that stupid fringe over a Bunsen burner in Chemistry,' Tim was saying. 'He puts so much stuff in his hair it's bound to go up like a firework. Oh—I'd love to see *that*. Hang on—that's got to be worth a quick prayer, hasn't it?' He put his hands together. 'Dear Abandinus, please make Mike Mears's hair catch fire in Chemistry! *Amen*.'

Chapter 9

At five to four Kevin was having serious second thoughts about inviting Gracie over. Partly because Tim kept shaking his head and sighing, with his arms folded and saying 'It's a mistake!' but also because his mum had now got completely the wrong end of the stick and seemed to think it was a 'boyfriend-girlfriend' kind of thing. She was even making cakes for the occasion. And she hardly *ever* made cakes.

'No, that's fine, Kevin,' she had said. 'I'll just whip up a few fairy cakes. She's American—she'll love fairy cakes.' Tim was nearly rupturing himself, laughing in the hallway, as Kevin stood in the kitchen doorway, cringeing.

'Mum—really—it's no big deal,' said Kevin as she put the little cakes on a cooling tray twenty minutes later. 'She's just dropping in to talk about some . . . English culture stuff. They're all studying it while they're here.'

76

'Well, there you go then,' beamed Mum, raising her eyebrows as if to suggest that she knew the *real* story and was just going along with him. 'Fairy cakes are part of English culture. She'll love them. What's her name?'

'Gracie,' muttered Kevin, feeling hot and bothered.

'Lovely name,' smiled Mum, nodding encouragingly. The doorbell rang. 'Oh! That'll be her now then. Well . . . don't just stand there. Go and let her in.'

Kevin trudged down the hallway, Tim sniggering behind him.

Gracie was wearing another hat—a straw one— and pale lemon shorts and T-shirt, as the day had warmed up. But her feet were in brown suede walking boots, not sandals. She was holding a spiral bound notebook and pen. 'Hi!' she said, pointing to the notebook. 'I bring a hymn!'

'Shhhh!' said Kevin, glancing back over his shoulder. 'Mum doesn't know about my god!'

Gracie looked stricken, but not entirely serious. 'Sorry!' she whispered, and bit her lip, trapping a giggle.

They introduced her and Kevin's mum was very friendly and fussy and insisted on making her some proper 'English tea'. Then out came the fairy cakes.

Gracie was exactly what any mum would want in a visiting friend. Clean, presentable, polite, and enthusiastic. 'These are just wonderful!' she said, with a mouthful of warm fairy cake, having peeled it out of its little flowery paper case. 'You are *such* a good cook! And—let me get this right—you only call these muffins when they're much *bigger*. And *English* muffins are completely different—more like bread, right?'

'That's right,' smiled Mum. 'Next time you come we'll get some in. You have them toasted with lots of butter and a cup of tea . . . of course.'

Kevin and Tim at last managed to get Gracie away. 'If we'd stayed in that kitchen any longer she'd have started talking like the Queen,' said Kevin.

'Oh no! Your mom's lovely!' protested Gracie.

'Yes, she is,' said Kevin. 'Just a bit over-excited. And very English all of a sudden.'

'Have you really done a hymn?' asked Tim, as they stepped past the hedge and reached the little shrine at the end of the garden. He glanced anxiously around, but there was no sign of Abandinus.

'Ya-ha!' said Gracie, opening her notebook with a flourish. 'You did say his name was Abandinus, right?'

'Yes, that's his name,' said Kevin and he noticed Tim glancing around again, looking nervous, as if speaking the name aloud would in itself bring the deity to them. Which it might, he supposed. If Abandinus was in the mood.

'OK—well, I got to thinking about rhymes and stuff on the way home, and so I wrote a few things down . . . and then I set it to "Amazing Grace". Well, you know, I've always kind of liked that one, for obvious reasons!' she chuckled.

'O . . . K,' said Kevin. 'Go on then . . . '

'Are you sure?' She suddenly looked all bashful.

'Yes!' said Tim. 'You heard mine—now let's hear yours!'

'OK.' She took a deep breath and then sang out in a surprisingly sweet, clear voice:

> *'Aban-dinus—O English god.*
> *How great your grace must be.*
> *A-aban-dinus, oh come to us*
> *And blessed we will be.'*

She paused. 'There's more if you like it,' she said, rather pink in the face.

Tim and Kevin looked at each other and nodded. 'It's good,' said Tim. 'Better than I would've thought of.'

'He might kick up about the tune,' said Kevin. 'He said he didn't want any second-hand hymns. But changing the words might be enough. Go on,' he added, noticing Gracie looking at more handwritten words further down her page.

She took a deep breath and sang on:

> *'Aban-dinus, you have seen us*
> *And found us small and weak*
> *Your majesty and holiness*
> *We ever more shall seek.'*

'It's brilliant!' said Kevin. 'It doesn't really *mean* anything. Which is just what we want. Because, let's be honest, we don't want to say he's the best god *ever* and we'll give up our lives and stuff, do we? Just, kind of, that he's a pretty cool god and we'll, you know, pray and stuff. I mean—a hymn is really a kind of *god compliment*, isn't it?'

'Not sure about saying we're small and weak,' said Tim.

'Well, it rhymed well with seek,' said Gracie. 'I wanted to get "seek" in. Because I *do* seek. All the time. I seek new experiences, new friends, new ideas . . . '

'You're not kidding,' said Tim, but he was less grumpy at her now.

'So—shall we all sing it?' said Gracie. 'By the shrine. And hey, maybe I'll get to meet your god, too?' She was joking, of course, at this bit. She had no idea what she was getting into.

80

'Conference,' said Kevin, grabbing Tim's arm and leading him away from Gracie, who was running through the hymn again, singing softly to herself. 'What do you think?' he said. 'Will she be OK? We don't need a fainted American girl in the back garden. How would we explain it?'

Tim shook his head. 'I told you I thought it was a bad idea. I mean—*I'm* freaked out enough, thinking about seeing him again. Look at me!' He held out his hands and showed Kevin the trembling.

'*Aban-dinus . . .*' sang Gracie behind them.

'But she seems quite . . . tough,' ruminated Kevin. 'And she'd probably get on well with Ancasta—another girl.'

'*You have seen—aa-aah!*' sang Gracie.

'Ancasta? Oh, please—one god at a time! I'm really not sure . . . ' hissed Tim.

'Aaa-aaa-aah!' repeated Grace. 'Oh . . . my . . . god!'

'I think,' said Kevin, 'we don't need to argue any more.'

'OH . . . MY . . . GOOOOOOOD!' squeaked Gracie.

'Hi, Abandinus,' said Kevin, stepping over Gracie. 'Did you like the hymn?'

'It pleased me,' said Abandinus, standing tall

81

and holding his wooden staff aloft in a very majestic way. Kevin could tell he was doing it for effect. A girl was lying at his feet, gaping up, shocked and over-awed, and he knew the gods liked that kind of thing.

'Omigod, omigod, omigod,' she kept gasping.

Tim stood stock still behind them, gulping and trying to stay calm. 'It's OK. It's fine, it's fine,' Kevin heard him murmuring to himself.

'Fish . . . there's *fish* . . . ' squeaked Gracie, pointing to the shoal swimming around Abandinus's robe.

'Yes,' said Kevin, grabbing her arm and sitting her up. 'I know. He's a walking sea life centre. You get used to it. Um . . . Abandinus.' He looked up at the god, who was still holding his staff aloft and wearing an expression of ethereal greatness. A decorative swirl of white mist was moving around his head. 'Would you mind just taking the godliness down a notch? Just for a bit. Just until they've both stopped hyperventilating?'

'Oh, all right,' said Abandinus, turning off the swirly cloud. He moved into his familiar crossed-legged position, floating above the shrine, his staff laid across his knees.

'How are you?' asked Kevin, keeping an eye on Gracie and Tim, who, although they were swaying a little bit, seemed as if they might stay conscious.

82

'I am divine,' said Abandinus.

'Yeah, well, if you say so,' said Kevin. 'You've met Tim already. Say hi, Tim.'

Tim waved a shaky hand and croaked, 'Hi!'

'And we'd like you to meet a new believer. This is Gracie. She's from America. Say hello, Gracie.'

'H-hello!' whispered Gracie. 'Are . . . are you *real*? Or did Kevin's mom put crack in those fairy cakes?' She looked as if she fervently hoped it *was* class A drugs.

'I am as real as you wish me to be,' said Abandinus, effecting a charming smile.

Gracie got to her feet and edged closer, her mouth a little 'o' of amazement. She stretched out her hand and Abandinus regarded it with amusement as it moved towards his chest.

'Uh!' she gasped, as her fingers passed straight through his pale skin. She snatched her hand back and clenched it into a fist, against her chin. Her greeny-blue eyes looked huge in her face, which had gone several shades paler, despite the golden tan.

'Now try again, Grace,' said Abandinus, in a deep, rumbly voice.

She gulped and put her fingers to his chest again and this time, to Kevin's immense surprise, they did not pass through. The god's skin simply pressed in a little, like human skin. 'You—you're *real*!' gasped Gracie. 'This time you're real.'

'I was real the first time,' said Abandinus. 'What I am *this* time, is more substantial. I can be as substantial as rock. Or as insubstantial as air, if it pleases me.'

'Oh my . . .' murmured Gracie. She swayed a little and Kevin grabbed her arm.

'It's OK,' he said. 'You get used to it. It's weird, I know. But he's a good god. You don't need to be afraid.'

'And . . .' Gracie's wild eyes fixed upon his, 'you—you're his chosen one?'

'Well, I think so . . . maybe. Abandinus,' Kevin turned back to the god, 'am I your chosen one?'

Abandinus shrugged. 'If you like.'

'Yes,' said Kevin, rather smugly. 'Chosen. That's me.'

Gracie stared at Kevin as if he'd suddenly morphed into a superbeing himself. Then she shook her head. 'No,' she said. 'No—this isn't possible. This is a trick.'

She stood up straight and walked towards Abandinus, who was watching her with a benign smile, greatly amused. She pressed her fingers against his chest again. 'You're warm,' she said. 'You've got a heartbeat. You're as real as me.'

'I am,' agreed Abandinus.

'So—you admit it? You're just some . . . out-of-work actor. They've hired you, right? To play a trick . . . or . . . or maybe it's part of the Culture Course. Maybe all of us get to meet a "god". Th-that's cool. Yeah—that's just fine . . . '

'I am real,' said Abandinus. 'And I am a god. Do you need proof?'

Kevin gulped and shared an uneasy glance with Tim. He hoped Abandinus would just do the flying feathers show again . . . or another swirly cloud . . . but he could see from the god's expression that he was building up to something a bit more impressive.

'Sure,' said Gracie, with only a slight wobble in a voice striving to sound brash. 'Knock yourself out!'

Rain began to fall. Big ploppy drops. Out of a blue, cloudless sky. Big, ploppy, *green* drops. Big ploppy green drops with *legs*.

Gracie let out a scream and then clapped her hand to her mouth. A shower of small frogs tumbled all around them, pinging off the greenhouse with loud pops and splattering wetly across their heads and shoulders. The frogs didn't seem to be harmed by their adventure and hopped away into the leafy undergrowth as soon as they had recovered from their journey. The shower only lasted twenty seconds or so.

Then Abandinus twirled his staff like a majorette and smiled. 'Did that help?' he asked.

'N-n-natural ph-ph-phenomenon,' whispered Gracie, picking three small amphibians out of her T-shirt. 'They get sucked up out of a pond in a water-spout and pulled up into the atmosphere in a tornado and then rained down . . .'

'Ah—a tornado,' said the god, lifting up his staff.

'Abandinus . . .' said Kevin. 'No . . . not a tor—'

But the last two syllables were wiped out by the rising wind and suddenly Gracie was swept up into a vortex of spinning air. She didn't even have time to scream. Abandinus watched her, holding out the staff, to which the bottom tip of the vortex was tethered.

'Abandinus! Stop!' shrieked Kevin, as Gracie spun round higher than the top of the apple tree, her face a blurred mask of terror. 'You'll hurt her!'

'She is quite safe,' said Abandinus, still smiling.

'Cut it OUT! Or we'll *never* worship you again!' yelled Kevin.

Abandinus shrugged, drove his staff into the ground, so it stood up alone, and then rose up into the air and snatched Gracie out of the tornado. He held her as if she was a small child and she sagged against his shoulder, her eyes half closed and her limbs dangling. Kevin felt fear grip his throat. What if she was hurt?

Really hurt? He realized he'd been taking this whole 'personal god' thing much too lightly. Abandinus was unpredictable. Dangerous.

As he descended, Abandinus switched off the tornado. Kevin and Tim ran to collect the semi-conscious girl from his arms and allowed her to slip down onto the grass.

'Grace! Gracie! Are you OK?' breathed Kevin, slapping gently at her cheek. Her eyes opened and she stared at him in confusion. Tim crouched beside them, muttering and breathing hard. He'd been right, Kevin realized. This had been *such* a bad idea.

'That's the last time I bring you a new believer!' Kevin said, getting up to glare at Abandinus. The god merely smiled back at him, sitting suspended over the shrine once more.

'Your friend will be fine,' he said. 'She is strong and healthy—and has a great heart. She is merely overwhelmed by me. It is often this way with females,' he added, stroking his neat beard and looking incredibly smug.

Gracie sat up, shook her head a few times, caught her breath and then narrowed her eyes at Abandinus. 'OK, you otherworldly creep! I believe in you. But you do that to me one more time and I'll make up a hymn about you they won't even allow on the internet!'

Abandinus threw back his head and laughed. He was still laughing as he faded from view. Gracie got unsteadily to her feet. She looked furious. 'Your gods,' she muttered, 'your gods have got NO manners!' And she stalked off down the garden, back through the house.

Kevin and Tim tried to catch her before she went, but didn't really know what to say. Gracie opened the front door, called 'Goodbye, Mrs Rutley,' in a sweet voice and then glared at them both before stepping out and slamming it shut behind her.

'Well,' said Tim, as the crash of the door rang off the walls, 'that went well.'

'Oh dear—have you and your girlfriend had a tiff?' said Mum, putting her head round the kitchen door.

'Aaaaaargh! She is NOT my girlfriend!' bawled Kevin.

'I'm sure you'll make it up,' grinned Mum. 'God knows, I fell out with my boyfriends loads of times.'

'Trust me,' said Kevin, '*my* god knows—that's the last we'll see of Gracie.'

Chapter 10

Tim decided to go home not long after. He was very shaky and had obviously had enough. 'I'm really not sure about all this,' he said to Kevin, on the doorstep. 'We brought three of us together for him and his power shot up.'

'Well, yeah—that's what we want,' said Kevin. 'More power—more prayer answering. You should get your own wish list together now.'

'But what if he smites someone—properly? I mean, that tornado thing . . . that was seriously smitey, wasn't it? He could have killed Gracie.'

'But he didn't. He didn't,' said Kevin. He had been nervous too—but he had not believed the god would *really* hurt her. 'She'll be fine. We'll talk to her at school tomorrow.'

'Well—just remember—you can't control him,' muttered Tim. 'Just remember that. And also—how do you know he's answering your prayers?'

'I got the Nintendo Wii!' pointed out Kevin.

'Yeah—well maybe you were going to get that anyway,' said Tim. 'Maybe he's just yanking your chain! Maybe he's never going to answer any prayers. He's never actually *said* he would, has he?'

'Well . . . gods don't,' said Kevin. 'I mean . . . you're always getting told that, aren't you? It's a big get out for the vicar at Christmas. If you get what you want it's because God wants you to. And if you don't get what you want it's because God has other plans for you and it's all for the best. I bet Abandinus is signed up to the same "how to be a god" plan. But we can *talk* to him! We can offer him stuff too. Shrine, hymns, believers . . . we've got something *he* wants, remember!'

Tim shook his head. 'It'll all end in tears,' he predicted, like someone's mother, and then jogged away down the path. 'You should ask him to go,' he called back. 'Go back to his river.'

Kevin sighed. He didn't think Abandinus would just slope off like a guest who'd overstayed his welcome. He wasn't a genie. Kevin couldn't put him back in a bottle. And in any case, he didn't want to. It was exciting. Incredibly exciting, to have a real live god living in his garden.

But he would have a quiet word, maybe. See if he could lay some ground rules.

He went to make a cup of tea, and thought about Tim's words. Tim would cheer up a bit if Abandinus answered one of *his* prayers. Or if Tim saw one of Kevin's prayers coming true. He could mention that to Abandinus. Just something small, to encourage Tim. The phone ringing jolted him out of his plans. Mum, who had gone back upstairs to do some more work, called down, 'Can you get that, Kev?'

He went back into the hall and picked up the receiver. 'Hello?'

'Kev? Hi, mate—it's Dad,' came back a breathy, rather edgy voice.

'Hi, Dad. What's up?'

'Can you get your mum for me?' said Dad. He sounded distracted, awkward almost.

Kevin took the phone upstairs and handed it to Mum. 'It's Dad,' he said, and she pulled a surprised face as she took it.

'Hello, Jason,' she said, with a wary tone in her voice. 'What can I do for you?' She carried on tapping away at her keyboard with one hand while his dad talked into her ear. After a few seconds her hand stopped tapping and froze in mid-air. 'Are you serious?' she said.

His dad burbled on and Kevin, leaning in the doorway, wished he could hear what was being said

91

to make his mother's eyebrows shoot up behind her fringe and her mouth fall open.

'You've got to be kidding,' she said, at length. 'Are you sure? Haven't you talked it over? What . . . on the lawn? In bin bags? Oh, for heaven's . . . Well, haven't you got any friends who'll help you out? What about Derek? He's got room, surely?'

Kevin felt a prickly feeling on his skin. This sounded serious.

Now his mum was sighing and raking her fingers through her hair. 'Oh, Jason—you idiot! How could you let this happen? All right. All right—for *one night only*. Two at the most—do you understand? You'll have to kip in with Kevin on the bottom bunk. OK. See you in an hour.'

Kevin was speechless. He stared at his mum as she put down the phone and turned to look at him.

'Your dad and Lorna have had a row,' she said. 'She's chucked him out.'

Kevin gaped. Lorna—small, blonde, giggly Lorna, whom Dad had met at work and then started going out with and then moved in with last year—she was chucking him *out*?

'But . . . why? I thought she was nuts about him.'

'Really?' said Mum. 'I just thought she was nuts.'

'You said she was nice. You said you liked her!' said Kevin, remembering how Mum had broken the news to him last year that Dad had found someone to share his life with. She had been very upbeat and smiley at the time. She had told him it was a 'good thing' that his dad was 'moving on' with his life.

'Of course I said she was nice,' snapped Mum. 'What do you expect me to say? That she was a ditzy trollop with candyfloss for brains? I thought you'd work that out for yourself.'

Kevin bit his lip. He quite liked Lorna, but she had a laugh that could crack glass and a way of saying her S's that made her sound a bit like a highly strung baby snake. She was always clinging on to some part of his dad, too, as if he was a life-raft. It was creepy to think of Dad having a girlfriend anyway. To think of his dad *snogging* anyone was just—well—against the laws of nature. But Lorna *had* been nice. She was kind to *him*, anyway, even when he'd been nasty and sulky with her for taking Mum's place in Dad's life. Even though both his parents had sat him down and explained that they had 'grown apart' and couldn't be happy together any more, he'd never really believed they were actually separated until Lorna arrived on the scene. He'd been a bit of a git for a while.

'So—so he's coming back home?' he murmured,

feeling rather dazed as he remembered '*Mum and Dad back together*' on his wish list.

'Just for a couple of nights, at most,' said Mum, turning back to her keyboard. 'Just until he sorts out somewhere to stay.'

Kevin grinned. 'OK,' he said. 'If you say so.' *Thanks, Abandinus!* he thought.

Dad arrived an hour later, carrying two bin bags of clothes and CDs and stuff. He grinned at Kevin, looking rather embarrassed. 'Hello, mate,' he said. 'Got a spare bunk for your old man, then?'

Kevin had cleared the lower bunk of all his Lego, books, and CDs and stuff and Mum had made up the bed with fresh sheets, pillow, and quilt cover. Dad dumped his bin bags in the hallway and took just a backpack up to Kevin's room with him. He sat on the edge of the bed, leaning forward to avoid hitting his head on the bunk above.

'Funny to be back,' he smiled.

Kevin smiled back. 'Is it really over—you and Lorna?'

Dad shrugged and twisted the stud in his ear-lobe. 'Don't know,' he said. 'It seems like it, but you never know . . . she was probably a bit young for me. Kept taking me down the clubs. I think I may have lost some of my hearing. If I never experience another half hour of drum 'n' bass it'll be too soon. It's like being hit repeatedly by a blunt instrument until your nose bleeds. And paying for the privilege.' He shook his head. 'And queuing for forty-five minutes for the whole adventure. I can't hear high, shrill notes now . . . which means I lose every other word Lorna says.' He chuckled, ruefully. 'So there's some benefit.'

Mum did cottage pie for tea and Dad's eyes went a little misty when it was laid before him. Lorna wasn't much of a cook, apparently. Mum was friendly but cool, Kevin noticed. But he beamed into his potato and mince, anyway. Abandinus was starting to deliver. It was only a matter of time before Mum and Dad fell back in love.

It was hard to sleep. Dad started snoring in the early hours. It sounded as if a warthog was snuffling for truffles. Kevin lay awake, staring at the ceiling and feeling excitement fizzing through him. It was all starting to come together. He'd got the Wii and now he was going to get Mum and Dad together again.

He sat up and pushed back the quilt so he could check out his toe. The gooey area by his nail had been sore and red and oozing yellow stuff for weeks now. He'd put ointment and plasters on it, but it just kept going. Switching on his little torch, he shone the beam of light onto his foot and peeled away the grubby plaster. The toe looked better. Definitely better. Still a little red but much less swollen and with no gooey stuff at all.

Kevin took off the plaster and chucked it down into the little metal bin beside the bookshelf. Then he switched off the torch, tucked it under his pillow, and lay back to get to sleep.

'Waaaaaaarffff-leeerrrrg,' went his father. 'Waaaaaaarffff-leeerrrrg.'

Kevin pulled the quilt up around his ears to muffle the sound. It didn't help.

'Waaaaaaarffff-leeerrrrg,' went his father. 'Waaaaaaarffff-leeerrrrg.'

He leaned over the bunk, swung his arm down and prodded his dad's shoulder. Dad snuffled loudly and turned over. The snoring eased down in volume and frequency and at last Kevin managed to drift off to sleep.

In his dreams he went to the window and saw a man with a lion's head standing in the garden by the light of the moon. A woman was weeping loudly somewhere nearby. The lion-headed man smiled at Kevin in an eerie way, revealing long white fangs.

'Pray to the dark,' he said.

The woman's weeping grew louder. Her head was in her hands, so he couldn't see her face, and her long lank hair dripped around her like rain as she hunched, on her knees, in the middle of the lawn. 'Sorrow—aye, tha wilt sorrow,' she warned, between sobs. A pool of tears grew wide around her.

Kevin woke up at seven thirty to find himself lying on the bedroom floor. Dad was sound asleep and no longer snoring. He got up, feeling his limbs aching from the unusual sleeping position. How had *that* happened?

Downstairs, Mum was making toast. 'Dad awake yet?' she asked and he shook his head. He'd tiptoed about the room, getting his school clothes together, and then got dressed, after washing, in the bathroom.

'Sleep OK?' she asked.

'Yeah—sort of,' he muttered, helping himself to a square of hot wholemeal as it sprang up out of the slots. 'Dad snores though.'

'I know,' she laughed, filling the kettle. 'I could hear him from my room. Sorry about that, love. It won't be for long.'

'Did he tell you why they broke up?' asked Kevin, spreading first butter and then dollops of marmalade on his toast.

'I didn't ask,' she said, putting milk and coffee in a mug. 'You want some tea?'

'Yes please. But why? Why didn't you ask? Don't you want to know?' he demanded.

'It's none of my business,' she said. 'Your father's love life is nothing to do with me.'

Kevin bit into his toast. He couldn't believe she really didn't want to know. 'He told me he thought she was too young for him,' he said.

Mum snorted and shook her head, a tight little smile on her face. But she said nothing. As she waited for the kettle to boil she looked out of the window at the back garden. After a few seconds she leant across the draining board and stared harder. 'What is *that*?' she murmured. Kevin stood up and followed her line of sight. 'There's a huge great puddle on the lawn!' she said. 'I didn't think it rained last night! Where did that come from?'

'Maybe there was a little shower,' said Kevin, although something was stirring in his mind. *Something weird . . . in the night.*

They opened the back door and went out into the garden to see the puddle. It was more like a small lake, lying dead centre of the lawn. It had a bluey, rather milky look to it. A dragonfly skittered across the surface, gleaming red in the morning sun.

'Where did that come from?' said Mum, again.

'Um . . . lump of ice falling off an aeroplane?' ventured Kevin. 'Landing here and melting? You do hear of that. We're lucky it didn't hit the house. Could've smashed the roof in.'

'We'd have heard it land,' said Mum.

'Dad was snoring, remember.'

Mum folded her arms. 'I suppose,' she said, patting the toe of her sandal on the surface of the water and sending ripples across it. She sighed and went back indoors. 'I guess it'll just seep away,' she said. 'Come on in—you've got to finish breakfast and get off to school.'

Kevin knelt down by the strange pool. He felt a shiver rise from the base of his spine and wash up his back and over his shoulders. Something about last night . . . *what* was it? A woman weeping. It must have been a dream.

He put out a finger and touched the water, sending another saucer of ripples across it. Then he touched his finger to his tongue. He took a deep breath and exhaled it with a long, nervous, whistle. It was as he had expected.

The water was salty.

Chapter 11

'I think she's avoiding us,' said Tim, in lunch break that day. Gracie was at the end of the sports field with her American friends. There were about twelve students from LA at the school, all wearing shorts and high school T-shirts and sneakers. All tanned and healthy looking. A handful of their classmates were with them— including Mike Mears, of course, who had one of them staying with him—the blond sporty looking guy who was called Chad. Mike kept ostentatiously doing a 'high five' with Chad every time they passed in a corridor. Now Mike was lounging near the girls. All week he'd been perfecting his accent and an extra foppish flick of his hair. He'd never sounded so English. Still, at least Gracie wasn't paying him any attention, thought Kevin. She was talking to some of her fellow Americans.

He sighed and chewed on a stem of wiry grass

as they sprawled beneath the perimeter hedge. 'It's not *our* fault our god was rude. We can't control him!'

'Maybe she's telling them all about it,' said Tim, squinting under his hand at the group. 'I'm sure she looked across at us just then.'

'They'll think she's nuts. They'll never believe her,' said Kevin.

'No, Kev. They'll think *we* are nuts. They'll start calling you The Chosen One and both of us Shrine Boys. And just wait until Mike Mears gets hold of that. It's better than Muttley, isn't it? *Chosen One!*'

Kevin grinned. 'I don't care. I've got a god. It's only a matter of time now before he smites my enemies for me.'

Tim shook his head. 'You still think he's making all your wishes come true, don't you? But you've only had one computer game console out of it—and you might have got that anyway.'

Kevin lay back in the grass. 'Ah. But you don't know the news. Dad's come back.'

Tim gaped at him. 'What . . . back with your mum? You're kidding!'

'Nope. He's back. Came back last night just after you left. He and Lorna have split up. He slept in my room last night.'

Tim looked seriously impressed. 'You really think that was Abandinus?'

'Well, yeah—of course it was.'

'So—if he's back with your mum, how come he slept in *your* room?'

'Well, it's early days. They haven't had a chance to . . . I mean . . .'

'Is your mum all happy and lovey-dovey?' persisted Tim. 'Is she giggling and staring at him and stuff—like Emma Greening does with Mike Mears?'

'Oh come on—they're too old for that!'

'So—he's staying for ever?' prodded Tim, beginning to rather annoy Kevin.

'Well, at the moment he's just stopping over a couple of nights until he gets something sorted. But that's just how it starts. They'll fall back in love again—you wait and see!'

Tim compressed his lips and raised his eyebrows. He didn't look convinced.

'And I hope they do it soon, because I could hardly get any sleep last night for Dad's snoring,' added Kevin.

'I had a rubbish night too,' said Tim. 'Mad dreams.'

'Yeah—*I* had mad dreams,' said Kevin, but as he furrowed his brow, trying to remember, only a creepy feeling of unease returned to him. No images. No detail.

'Not surprising,' said Tim. 'All this god stuff is enough to give anyone nightmares. How are we supposed to get people believing in him? We thought Gracie would be cool but she freaked out—and if *she* did, so will everyone else. They'd be sending round exorcists before you know it. I think Abandinus may just have to make do with you and me.'

Kevin spat out the grass stem and sat up. 'I've been thinking the same,' he admitted. 'But if he doesn't get more believers he's never going to have enough battery power to grant our wishes, is he? And I *really* want a dog. And better skin.'

'You're so shallow,' said Tim. 'Do you think he'd get me a new Yamaha keyboard?'

'Not without a whole lot more worship and belief,' said Kevin. It was a knotty problem. 'And I just can't see how we can do it.'

'Well, you're not thinking creatively enough,' said a new voice and they both jumped. Gracie had skirted the field and was right there, standing above them.

'Whoa! Do you always have to do that?' squawked Tim. 'Have you not *heard* of waving and shouting hello? You're an American! What happened to loud and brash?'

'Well, you're a Brit and I can *see* what happened to tight-assed and repressed,' she snapped back and Kevin laughed. She sat down next to them and pulled something out of the slim brown satchel she was carrying. A small, silver rectangle, which she opened like a book.

'Hey—nice laptop!' marvelled Kevin. 'They let you bring it in to school?'

'Uhuh,' she said, pressing a button and making the small screen ping into silvery life. 'I can't connect it up here, of course, and I haven't gone live yet. But I will, later today. I worked on this in the night, when I couldn't sleep.'

She moved her fingers across the inbuilt cursor touch pad and tapped twice over an icon on the screen which read 'Abandinus'. At once a bright page filled the screen, entitled:

ABANDINUS—a god for *you*!

Beneath it was an image of a river and a mill. 'Hey!' cried Kevin. 'That's Houghton Mill! That's where I picked Abandinus up!'

'Yeah? Truly?' asked Gracie. 'Well, that makes sense because the River Ouse is where he's based. I did some research. I found this picture on the National Trust website. He's actually from just down the way in

Godmanchester, apparently. There used to be a Roman temple there dedicated to him. But I guess he gets about a bit. C'mon—read on!'

Beneath the river picture were glowing letters, animated to move slightly whenever the cursor ran across them.

> Join with us in worshipping the ancient British river god we have come to know—and see the blessings in your life multiply. Simply look to the east as you read this now, and say 'Abandinus, please bless me and guide me'.
>
> Go right ahead—say it now. What can you lose?
>
> We know you have much to gain.
>
> Then say it each day, at dawn or at sunset.
>
> For extra blessing, do this at your local river whenever you are passing.
>
> You have been given great good luck by receiving this message. Please pass it on to seven people who deserve to share in your good fortune. There is no catch and no money involved. Abandinus's blessing is free.
>
> The Chosen Three of Abandinus

'The chosen *three*?' said Kevin. 'So—you're joining us, then?'

Gracie nodded. 'I was a bit freaked out yesterday—and he *was* very rude! But hey—it's not every day you get a chance to hang out with a god. Also,

I figured you two could use some help. You seem a bit . . . lacking in direction.'

'So—how will this help?' asked Tim. 'It's a website, yeah? How are we going to get people to look at it?'

'No—it's not a website,' said Gracie. 'We'd have to buy a domain and leave our details and stuff—and we can't do that! No. This is a chain email. We each email it out to seven people and they email it to another seven people and so on, and before you know it, *thousands* of people are praying to Abandinus, and they don't even have to meet him.'

'What makes you think anyone's *actually* going to do that?' said Tim, looking very sceptical.

'Superstition!' grinned Gracie. 'The world is *full* of superstition. And what is it going to cost just to say "*Abandinus, bless me and guide me*" out loud while they're looking at this? Nothing. I bet you at least half the people who get this will do it. And then mail it on. I won't say bad things will happen if anyone breaks the chain—but I don't need to.'

Kevin and Tim looked at each other and excited grins began to spread across their faces.

'And even if they only say it once, it's got to help, right?' Gracie went on. 'Abandinus is going to like this! We've got nothing to lose by trying.'

'So—let me get this straight,' said Tim, raising his hands. 'We're going to start a new religion.'

Kevin and Gracie looked at him and then at each other. Gracie bit her lip and then giggled. 'Well, I guess so! But this is harmless—nobody else will get thrown into a twister, will they? Or have to drag a heavy shrine home on the bus. And when Abandinus feels really powered up by all this, we can hit him for world peace. How's that?'

'You might want to start a bit smaller than that,' advised Kevin.

'OK—so he can cure my asthma,' she said, pronouncing it 'azzma'.

'You've got asthma?' asked Kevin. He was surprised. She didn't seem the type.

'Yep. Never without this!' She pulled a blue L-shaped inhaler out of her pocket and waved it at them. 'But it's not so bad. I went into hospital with it when I was six, but these days I hardly ever get a real attack. Still, would be great not to have to worry about it.'

'So—when do we send these out?' asked Kevin, staring at the glowing message on the screen.

'Give me your emails—you both got one, right?' she checked. They nodded. 'So give them to me and I will send this to you and we can all start after school today. How's that?'

'It's brilliant,' said Kevin, and spelt out his email as she typed it in. Tim did the same.

'So,' said Kevin, getting up as the bell rang for afternoon classes. 'After school today. Get home. Have a cup of tea. Tidy my room. Start a new religion. Seems like a plan.'

DOOF! Kevin felt all the air leaving his body as the hard leather ball punched into his belly. Even though he couldn't breathe he still scrabbled for the ball, tried to stop it glancing off him and into goal.

But he wasn't fast enough and—of course—he was at exactly the wrong angle. The ball ricocheted off its first target and bounced into the corner of the net. The whoop of joy from his team mates morphed instantly to a groan of disappointment. Kevin fell to his knees, his hands in the mud, arching his spine and trying desperately to suck some oxygen back into his lungs. He was horribly winded. It was nearly half a minute before the first trickle of air was allowed back in. By this time, the game had already carried on. Someone had retrieved the ball and run back down the pitch with it.

'Hey! Muttley! Still trying to impress the ladies? Take a tip from me. They don't like it when you crawl.'

Mike Mears ran past in his striker's shirt, flicking back his fringe and sparing a wave for a line-up of girls at the edge of the pitch. Some of them were on a free period. They sat against the steep grassy bank that framed the school field, trying to get a suntan on their legs. As Kevin got to his feet, gasping and dizzy, he noticed that Emma Greening was among them. Oh great. Just great.

'Come on, Abandinus!' he muttered, angrily. 'I could really do with a bit of prayer answering here! Remember—number seven on the list. Make me sporty!'

It didn't look good. The action was heading back in his direction again now, led by Steve Pitt, the hardest boy in school, who possessed a kick so vicious he was sometimes called 'Buckeroo'—when he wasn't in earshot. He was about to unleash it now, and the ball would fly like an Exocet missile. It would probably take his head clean off, or at least break a couple of ribs, if he didn't get out of the way. Kevin even found himself wishing that Mike Mears, on his own team, would get a successful tackle in. He'd have Emma and all the bare-legged girls gasping with admiration and that would burn a hole in Kevin's insides—but it wouldn't be as big as the hole that Steve Pitt's strike was about to make.

So—to save or to dodge? Be a hero? Or still able to pick up a pen?

Emma Greening was standing up, watching closely, her shining hair blowing in the breeze and her elegant hand shielding her eyes from the late afternoon sun.

Save or dodge? Hero or zero?

'Oh god!' moaned Kevin.

'To your right,' said Abandinus, leaning on the left goalpost.

Kevin screamed a little and then leapt to his right, stuck both hands into the air, and nearly broke his wrists catching the ball. He swiped it into his chest, dimly aware of his team bawling with delight, as he gaped at Abandinus.

'What the—what? Why are you here?' he squeaked.

'You seemed to need some help,' said the god.

'Muttley! Muttley! Muttley! Muttley!' Mike Mears was leading the chant. Everyone on his team was jumping about. Rob White—a really good player—ran over and clapped him on the back. Kevin dared to glance across to the edge of the pitch and saw Emma Greening also bouncing up and down with two or three friends.

'OK, let us have it back then,' said Rob White, and wrestled the ball out of Kevin's frozen grip.

Seconds later they were all haring back down the field.

Mike Mears paused long enough to laugh, 'Fluke, Muttley! Lucky fluke!'

'Did—did *you* make me do that?' muttered Kevin, turning to his god who was still loitering beside goal.

Abandinus looked smug. 'Number seven on your list,' he said.

'Wow! I didn't think I'd worshipped enough for that. And how come you're here? I thought you'd only show up at the shrine. Can you be anywhere?'

'I can be wherever I choose,' said Abandinus. 'I am most at home in my river, and at my strongest there—but I can travel.'

'And they can't see you, right?' Kevin waved towards the twenty boys tearing around the pitch and Mr Chapman, the tired looking PE teacher at the touchline.

'Not unless they choose to believe in me,' said Abandinus. 'Do not worry yourself about such things. Best that you stop talking to me. They're coming back and you look like a lunatic. *Left*.'

Kevin snapped his attention round just as the ball flew at him again. Filled with godly power, he launched himself to the left and struck the leather missile away from the goal. Another roar of appreciation rose from

111

his team, although this time Mike Mears slowed down almost to a halt and stared at him. He didn't look quite so pleased.

'You mean—you mean I am sporty? I'm actually—*sporty*?' Kevin could feel his rapid heartbeat dancing around in his chest and he felt lightheaded with the thrill of such a thought. Maybe they'd even let him out of goal one day . . . maybe he'd be able to play properly! Tackle! Score! Now he could see a group of girls walking down beside the pitch, getting closer to his end. Emma was there among them. She was smiling at him. He was sure of it. Number three on his list! Number three!

'Left again,' said Abandinus.

Emma Greening was *noticing* him!

'LEFT!'

CRUNCH!

Kevin stopped the ball again. With his face.

What he remembered most, later on, was the way Emma Greening's look of admiration and excitement snapped into shock and revulsion. Possibly because his face had suddenly become a geyser of blood.

His head had thwacked backwards and forwards like a plastic ruler with the force of the strike—and helpfully sent the ball back out towards Mike Mears. But Mike did not seize his chance to dribble it back

112

down the pitch. He stopped it under his boot and stood still, staring, like Emma, looking revolted.

'Oh man!' said Steve Pitt, who had kicked the ball. 'That is disgusting!'

Kevin stood for a few seconds, feeling a warm spattering sensation down his chin and chest. And then he sank back down to his knees. The pain in his nose was beyond anything he'd ever felt. He really thought it might have been flattened right into his skull. He imagined he looked a lot like the cat in *Tom & Jerry* just after it had been walloped with a flat-iron.

Mr Chapman elbowed his way through the crowd of boys, all groaning and marvelling at the mess in goal. He hauled Kevin to his feet, offering him a scratchy school towel to stop the flow. Kevin went 'Aaa—aa-aah!' in a girly, high-pitched voice, when the material flapped against his face.

Staggering away, supported by the teacher, Kevin noted that Abandinus was nowhere to be seen. He had delivered number seven on the list. And, as it turned out, number three too. As he lurched past her, showering blood onto the grass, Emma Greening put her hand over her eyes and turned away from him, towards her friends who were squealing with disgust. 'Oh—yuck!' he heard her say.

Yes. Emma Greening had definitely noticed him.

Chapter 12

Kevin's nose stopped bleeding about half an hour later. The school receptionist, who doubled as an unqualified nurse, had pinched the bridge of it and wiggled it, ignoring his whimpering.

'No,' she said, 'I don't think it's broken.'

'How cab you be dure?' squawked Kevin, clutching a mound of blood-spattered tissue in his lap. 'Idd hurtz!'

'I'm sure it does, love,' said the receptionist. 'But if it was broken you'd be screaming like a Year Three.'

It got less painful as the last hour of school wore on—easing down to a dull, numb ache, as if he had a heavy cold. The receptionist gave him cotton wool and sent him to the toilets to clean himself up. Over the row of grimy white stone sinks with their single taps and plugless chains, Kevin peered into the mirror. His face looked as if he'd been in an explosion in a jam factory—and his nose was swollen out wide, making him look like a boxer. An unsuccessful boxer.

He sighed and set about cleaning up. The cold water made his nose feel a little better—but it was going to be a long time before he could breathe through it again. The water gurgled musically in a small twisting torrent from the old tap. Gurgled and giggled.

Kevin stopped mopping and froze. Giggled? He heard it again, behind the gurgling water. Someone was in here and giggling. Must be one of those little Year Sixes up on a visit from the junior school, hiding in one of the cubicles. 'Yeah—it's hilarious!' shouted out Kevin. 'Thanks for your concern!'

There was a pause and then more giggles. The toilet wasn't well lit. Only thin shafts of light came in through high shallow windows, and the dark-blue painted walls created a gloomy atmosphere, designed to discourage pupils from hanging around in here too long. In the shadows between the cubicles and the urinals he saw someone small run across, reflected in the mirror.

'Oi!' he shouted. 'Cut it out!'

There were more giggles. Plural! There was more than one Year Six in here, definitely. Why couldn't he see them?

Kevin spun round. He went to the cubicles and

began to bang open the doors. BANG! *Empty*. BANG! *Empty!* BANG! *Something nasty floating in the toilet—but empty*. He threw his soggy pink cotton wool in the paper towels bin and stood still, his heart beginning to pick up speed and a cold shiver rising up his back. 'Who's here?' he whispered.

There were more giggles. He ran to the second set of cubicles and crashed all the doors open. Nothing. And yet behind him he heard and sensed small figures running from the sinks to the door. He spun round again and saw three kids—in a split second—dressed in robes with hoods. They reached the door, turned to laugh merrily at him, with a flash of blue eyes. And then they vanished.

Kevin staggered back against a cubicle door, which opened inwards, sending him flailing back onto the toilet. He slumped on the seat and tried to catch his breath. What *the hell* was *that*?

Come on, said a voice in his head. *You're the boy who's got his own god. Don't tell me you're freaked out by some little ghosts!*

But he was. Incredibly freaked out. Shaking, and covered in a sheen of cooling sweat, he pulled himself up and moved dazedly back to the sink to lean against it and run cold water over his wrists. It was something his mum had taught him to do if he felt sick and it worked well. It seemed to help a bit now as his shaking eased off and the sweat dried on his skin.

Kevin stood up and looked into the mirror. A woman was looking back at him. She had braided brown hair and blue eyes and was smiling gently at him. She seemed vaguely familiar in her woven green robe. A daisy chain lay around her neck and across her ample bosom. She was holding a large white egg in her cupped hands.

'Who are you?' he whispered, aware of his own reflection somehow merged with her face.

'He comes,' said the woman, and her kindly smile faded and tears welled in her eyes. 'And I do not know if you can be helped.'

'I can be helped, all right,' said Kevin, suddenly finding his voice and a shred of confidence. 'I have a god!'

She smiled again, sadly. 'The lion, also. And thou wilt sorrow.'

And then she was gone.

'You look like death,' said Tim when he met Kevin at the school gate at three o'clock.

'Thanks,' said Kevin and trudged out onto the pavement.

'I heard what happened in sports,' said Tim, falling into step with his friend. 'You did three *brilliant* saves! *You!*'

'Well, you don't have to sound *that* surprised,' grouched Kevin. 'I have caught a ball before, you know.'

'Yeah, but . . . three saves. *Good* saves! They were calling you Golden Gloves!'

'Were they?' asked Kevin, feeling a grin spread across his face, in spite of the nerves still jangling through him. It made his swollen nose tickle and sting.

'Well, one of them did. The others were calling you The Nose Of God.'

'Ah,' said Kevin.

'So, was it Abandinus? Did he answer your prayers?' Tim was quite breathless with excitement.

'Well—yeah. Sort of,' said Kevin, and he related what had happened.

'So—he was just leaning on the goal? Just like that? No little hurricanes or storms of feathers or anything?' probed Tim.

'Nope. He just showed up. Ping. Like that,' said Kevin.

'So—why aren't you . . . you know . . . pleased? I mean, I know you've got a flattened conk, but hey!

He actually *did* answer your prayers! Man! That is so *cool*! I'm going to work on a better hymn now. Can I come round to yours now? Can I come and worship?'

Kevin shrugged. 'If you like.'

Tim stopped and made Kevin stop too. 'What's up? This is good, isn't it?'

Kevin leant against the low wall outside the community centre. He tried to think straight—but he was still shaking from seeing the little hooded figures and the woman in the toilets.

'Yeah. It's good. Making those saves was just amazing. Brilliant. Getting noticed by Emma wasn't so good . . .'

'Oh, she'll get over that,' said Tim, with an encouraging punch on Kevin's shoulder. 'She'll be well impressed with those saves. Don't worry.'

'That's not what I'm worried about,' said Kevin. 'It's what happened afterwards.' He related the next bit of the afternoon's events and this time Tim got quieter. They sat together on the low brick wall, trying to make sense of it.

'So she was, like, carrying an *egg*?' he queried. 'Like an egg for breakfast?'

'Bigger,' said Kevin. 'Like an ostrich egg.'

'And what did she say, again?'

'She said "He comes". And she said she didn't

know if I could be helped. I said I *could* be helped—and then about having a god and that. She didn't seem impressed. She said I've got a lion too.' Again, something flickered in his mind. A grey image . . . the garden . . . the pool of salt water . . . and it flitted away again.

'A lion?' echoed Tim. He looked thoughtful. Then he took a breath, 'Any chance you got concussion?' he asked.

'You mean you think I was just seeing things?' snapped Kevin.

'Well . . . you never know.' Tim shrugged. 'The mind plays tricks. And all this stuff with Abandinus is going to make you believe in mind tricks a lot quicker, isn't it?'

'Hmmm,' said Kevin. He could taste blood in his throat and something darker shifted uneasily in his chest.

'So—this woman,' went on Tim. 'Long brown hair, daisy chain round her neck, quite busty, eh?' He grinned. Kevin nodded. He didn't grin. 'And three little hooded kids running around her—and she was carrying . . . an egg!'

'Cuda,' said an unfamiliar voice. They both jumped violently. They'd been so caught up in their discussion, they'd forgotten they were out in public.

A man was in the car park, his keys in one hand,

opening the door of a rather aged Fiat parked just by the wall. He was around thirty-five, guessed Kevin, and had a warm, easy smile, green eyes and thick, close-cropped dark hair. 'Cuda,' he repeated, his smile turning slightly self-conscious. 'Mother goddess. That's who you're describing.'

Kevin and Tim gaped at the man. They were speechless.

He pulled his jacket out of his car and shut the door before wandering over to them. 'Sorry to eavesdrop,' he said. 'I just heard you talking about a woman with an egg in her hand—and little hooded figures. Not kids—*cucullati*, by the way. They accompany Cuda. Are you studying ancient deities at school?'

'Um . . . sort of,' gulped Kevin. 'So . . . how do you know about . . . Cuda?'

'Oh, I love this stuff,' grinned the man. He stuck out his right hand and added, 'Greg McCrae. Ancient British culture geek. I'm here to work with the American students and make sure they get to learn the really good bits about England.'

Kevin shook his hand and so did Tim. They mumbled their names back and then found themselves staring at him.

After a slightly awkward pause, the man said, 'So . . . Cuda, eh? Unusual one for school kids to study

121

these days. Usually it's all Greek and Roman gods and legends. Apollo, Zeus, Aphrodite . . . the old Celtic deities rarely get a look in.'

'Well . . . it's more of a . . . private project,' said Kevin. 'What do you know about her? Cuda, I mean?'

'Well,' said Greg McCrea, pulling on his jacket and wrinkling his brow. 'She's a mother goddess. She's usually shown with an egg—or sometimes a loaf of bread—in her lap. And she has cucullati with her. They're little hooded creatures—dwarves, maybe. You never really get a proper look at them in the inscriptions.'

'They sounded like kids,' muttered Kevin, and Tim kicked his ankle and shook his head.

'They do sound like kids when you hear them described,' said Greg McCrae, apparently not noticing. 'And some people see them as kids—but they're not really. Cuda is all about fertility and prosperity, so they *could* be kids in her case. But most people think of them as men. Truth is, we'll probably never know for sure.' He sighed. 'There's just not enough evidence left of all these ancient gods and goddesses. People didn't write much down back then. All we've got are some weathered inscriptions and the odd reference on a map or in an old book. Shame.'

'Have you heard of Abandinus?' asked Kevin, suddenly keen to hear more.

'Abandinus . . . ah . . . let me think,' said Greg McCrae, rubbing his hand through his hair. 'River god. Over in Cambridge, I think.'

'That's right,' said Tim, looking at Kevin and nodding.

'Is he a good god?' asked Kevin.

The man chuckled. 'Gods and goddesses don't fall into goody or baddy camps. They were meant to be changeable, capricious—moody. Some were broadly helpful, like Cuda—all about prosperity and fertility and mothering. But you could just as easily call upon her to put a curse on someone.' He chuckled again. 'I think you chose your god or goddess and then just hoped they'd be on your side and help you out. Sometimes they might pop up in a vision and warn you of impending trouble by talking to you or just by weeping loudly in the night—that was usually before a death occurred. Sometimes it was thought they'd sent a storm to protest that you were doing the wrong thing. When things went wrong, people would think they'd maybe angered their gods and then they'd have to make some kind of sacrifice and hope it would all be forgiven.'

'Sacrifice? What kind?' breathed Tim, transfixed.

'I don't know . . . a few children maybe,' shrugged the man. Then he laughed again. 'I joke! No, more likely an animal or maybe just some food left on an altar. It's so far back it's hard to know for sure.'

'HEY!'

All three spun round to see Gracie haring along the road towards them. 'Hey! I see you've met our professor!' she beamed.

The man shook his head with a rueful smile. 'I keep telling you, Gracie, you don't have to call me "professor". Just Greg is fine.'

'I see you've met Greg,' she said, with a little nod and smile to the man. 'He's running our culture course. He's our professor. Maybe you should ask him about little gods.'

'Ah, we've got there already,' said Greg. 'We've covered Cuda and Abandinus so far. Are you doing this project too?'

Gracie glanced quickly at Kevin and Tim, trying to read what was happening. 'Well, I've been kind of helping out. They're really into their ancient history these two.'

'Well, tell me some more about it sometime soon,' said Greg, 'I've got to head into town now. See you later, Gracie. See you, Kevin, Tim.' And he headed back to his car.

'Wow!' said Gracie. 'Didn't expect you to start picking our professor's brains.'

'We didn't either. He just overheard us and joined in the fun,' said Tim.

Gracie's blue-green eyes widened. 'You told him? About Abandinus?'

'No, of course not,' said Kevin. 'Just asked if he'd heard of him. Anyway—we've got another one to worry about now. Cuda. She popped up this afternoon in the boys' toilets. I think she was trying to warn me about something . . . '

'Cuda?' echoed Gracie. Kevin sighed and repeated the story and at the end of it Gracie was also sitting on the wall, looking concerned.

'Why do you think she was warning you about a lion?' she muttered, hugging her knees to her chest and bumping her chin on top of them.

'I don't know! Maybe there's a circus in town and a big cat's going to escape.'

'Circuses don't have big cats any more,' said Gracie. 'Animal welfare won't let them.' She fidgeted on the wall, hugging her knees still tighter. 'Um . . . you guys will probably think I'm nuts or just making this up, but . . . '

'What?' prodded Tim, looking uneasy.

'I've been having some funny dreams,' she said. 'Not funny ha-ha, y'know? Kind of funny-scary.'

Kevin felt goose pimples rise up his spine again. 'What about?'

'Well . . .' said Gracie, examining her nails. 'A man with a lion's head, for one.'

Kevin jolted. The dream about the thing in the garden—the lion-headed man and the crying woman—suddenly crashed back into his mind as if it had been released from a spring-loaded box. Tim had stood up and was looking nervous too.

'And . . . a woman. Knelt down . . .' went on Gracie.

'Crying,' said Tim, his hands clenched into fists.

'Saying . . .' whispered Gracie, 'thou wilt . . .'

' . . . sorrow,' croaked Kevin.

All three stood up and looked at each other.

'We *all* dreamed this?' said Kevin.

They exchanged amazed glances. Then Tim shook his head and let out a nervous laugh. 'OK—OK. But . . . they're only dreams,' he said.

'Are they, though?' said Kevin. 'Or do we just *think* they are?' He was remembering finding himself waking up on the carpet below the bedroom window. In his dream he had been staring out of that window, seeing the weeping woman and the man with the lion's head.

Gracie shivered. 'They *are* dreams. That's all.' She bit her lip.

'Except . . .' began Kevin.

'What?' said Gracie and Tim, together.

'The woman—she was crying so much there was a big pool of tears around her.'

'Yeah,' nodded Tim. 'She was in mine too. She was well creepy.'

'And when I went into the garden this morning,' went on Kevin, 'there was a big puddle of water on the lawn. And it was salty.'

Tim looked really edgy now. 'I'll look in my garden when I get back.'

'Well, I don't *have* a garden!' said Gracie. 'She was weeping all over the community centre hall floor!'

'Have you been in there today?' asked Kevin. She shook her head. They all turned and walked through the car park towards the centre. The single storey brick building had a double glass door, leading through to a lobby. Off the lobby there were several small rooms and another set of glass double doors into the main hall. The hall's floor was polished woodblock, set down in a herringbone pattern and kicked and scuffed by generations of people.

They pushed open the second set of glass doors and then stood still, staring at the floor. A little yellow CAUTION sign, on a metal stand, stood in the centre of a large bloom of discoloured wooden blocks.

Kevin had never been afraid of a floor before.

'Your professor,' he whispered to Gracie, as a group of American kids began unstacking chairs at the far end of the hall. 'He told us that the gods used to send messages. Crying in the night. A warning.'

'Of what?' she whispered back.

Kevin and Tim looked at each other.

'Of death,' said Tim.

Chapter 13

'Hello, mate? How was school?'

Kevin jumped. He was used to wandering into the house quietly, making himself a cup of tea or getting some juice from the fridge, grabbing a couple of biscuits and then pottering upstairs to say hello to Mum, who was always either bashing away at her laptop, writing press releases, or on the phone to someone, interviewing them. If she was on the phone she would make flapping 'sshhh, I'm on the phone' motions with one hand and then grab his arm and pull him in for a quick hug while she kept up the conversation. Kevin knew better than to interrupt. This was his mum's job and she took it seriously. She had to. They needed the money.

So it was a shock to find Dad in the kitchen, reading the paper, with a cup of tea in one hand and an empty biscuit tin on the table.

'Hi, Dad,' he said, remembering, with a jolt, what Abandinus had done. Dad was here because of his prayers. He grinned. 'Not bad,' he said.

'Not *bad*! You look like you went three rounds with a kangaroo!' spluttered Dad, noticing his fat, bruised nose.

Kevin shrugged. 'One round—with a football.' He had almost forgotten the sports field incident. He and Tim had walked on home after the revelation at the community centre, trying to work out whether they should be scared. Whether they should or not, they both *felt* scared. Gracie did too, Kevin could tell, although she'd been breezy enough as they left.

'Forget it! We've got a god to protect us,' she'd said. 'Now, remember we're starting Project Believer after tea. I'll phone you both. Let's all send out the chain email together at the same time! Choose your seven people and hit the button. We can sing the hymn while we're doing it,' she'd added, getting rather carried away, Kevin thought. 'This time tomorrow we could have *hundreds*—even *thousands* of Abandinus believers!'

'Tough match, eh?' Dad was saying, with a sympathetic smile, peering at the damage on his son's face. He knew Kevin wasn't great at sports.

'No—actually—really good,' said Kevin, remembering the thrill of his sudden god-given ability. 'I did some great saves and got cheered and everything. But then I took one in the face. I saved that one too. Just ended up spouting blood everywhere.' He prodded the empty tin. 'All the biscuits gone, then.'

'Um . . . yeah. Sorry,' said Dad. 'I expect your mum will get some more in later. What does she normally do for tea on a Monday?'

'Um . . . curry, maybe,' said Kevin, forlornly checking the cupboard for hidden digestives. There were none. He sighed, emptied some school letters and stuff out of his schoolbag onto the kitchen table and then went to the fridge. He picked up the carton of orange juice and found it empty. He looked accusingly at his dad as he dropped the carton into the pedal bin.

'Sorry,' said Dad, again. 'Got a bit thirsty.'

'Why aren't you at work?' asked Kevin, trying not to sound annoyed. It was brilliant to have Dad at home again, even if he had been through the fridge and the cupboards like a swarm of locusts.

'Aah, decided to take a day off,' said Dad. 'A bit of recovery time. It's not easy getting dumped, you know.'

'Has Lorna called?'

'No,' said Dad and his smile was thin. He looked quite upset behind his cheeriness, Kevin realized. But soon he'd be back with Mum and everything would be great. 'You putting the kettle back on?' asked Dad, holding out his empty mug with a hopeful grin.

Kevin took a cup of tea upstairs for Mum too, and found her sitting, bashing away at the laptop as usual. She had shut the door to her room and looked around edgily as he came in. When she saw who it was she relaxed. 'Thanks, love,' she smiled, taking the tea. 'Ooh—what happened to your nose?' She reached out to touch it but he dodged away.

'Football hit it!' he explained. 'It's not as bad as it looks.'

She made a sympathetic face and then turned back to her keyboard. 'Your dad still downstairs?'

'Yeah—with an empty biscuit tin,' muttered Kevin.

She sighed. 'It won't be for long. He's only staying one more night,' she said, as if Kevin didn't *want* his dad to stay.

'I don't mind,' he said, quickly. 'He can stay as long as he likes . . . can't he?'

'Well . . . not really,' said Mum. 'He has to sort himself out.'

'Don't you . . . you know . . . *want* him to stay?' asked Kevin.

Mum looked back round at him. 'Kevin, there's not enough room! It's not fair on you.'

She didn't seem to be getting the point. But that was how it went sometimes. Kevin had seen enough romantic comedy films to know that at first the woman didn't like the man—or didn't seem to—and by the end of the film she'd be madly in love with him. Usually because fate had thrown them together. Well, fate was throwing. Or, rather, he and Abandinus were. It was just a matter of time.

'What's for tea?' he asked, as he edged back to the door. 'Curry?'

'Mmm? Um. Yeah, if you like,' said Mum, lost to her latest press release.

Kevin took his mug of tea into his bedroom. He nearly fell over a pile of his dad's clothes which had spilled across the floor from one of the black bin bags. The other bin bag was on the lower bunk. The room smelt like Lorna and Dad's flat. He hoped Mum and Dad would fall back in love soon so he could get his room back. He would have to do a bit more worshipping, probably. He glanced out of the window, down into the garden. The pool of water on the lawn had gone now. Further down the garden, among the trees, Kevin could see the leaves shaking and a small cyclone of white fluffy stuff. Abandinus's feathers. Obviously the god was *in*. He set down his mug and went downstairs. He could tell Abandinus about the chain email thing they were doing. Would Abandinus know about the internet? Maybe he should just say they'd found a good way of collecting many more worshippers around the world, very quickly. That ought to please him. And then he could throw in a quick prayer and so on—maybe sing the hymn.

By the time Kevin reached the greenhouse he could hear that Abandinus had company again. And this time it was more than one friend. Three of them were lounging on the grass beside the shrine and it looked as if there was one more somewhere further down, among the trees. Kevin approached quietly. He should probably watch his step. That was quite a few gods, even if they were lesser deities. Ancasta was there again, reclining against the trunk of an apple tree in a very decorative way, looking as if she was in a painting.

'Oh yes, *very* full of herself these days,' she was saying, with a languid wave of her elegant hand. 'I mean, she was just Diana, your average hunting goddess, full moon, bow and arrow, ya-de-ya-de-ya ... and she was bad enough then, what with being Apollo's sister. It was always "Oh, Apollo says *this*, Apollo says *that*"!' Ancasta breathed, in a high, girly voice. 'Anyone would think she had a lot more than *six* tiddly inscriptions to her.'

'Well, it's five more inscriptions than *you've* got,'

pointed out Abandinus, who appeared to be eating grapes as he draped one arm across the shrine.

'The point *is*,' went on Ancasta, with a flick of her oceany hair and a flash of her beautiful eyes, 'she carries on these days as if she has her own *temple*. Ever since that wretched princess died, it's all gone to her head. All it took was one comparison and there was no stopping her. She's even started wearing her hair the same way. It's so tawdry! You can't have an ageless deity going around with a mid-nineties blonde hairdo. It's unbecoming.'

'Well, *I* know Apollo quite well,' said the third god, who was young, with long golden hair and wistful dark eyes. He was wearing a lilac coloured robe, holding a delicate silver harp, and had a small shaggy brown dog at his feet. 'I have played for Apollo,' he added, tracing his long fingers across the strings which let out a torrent of gorgeous notes in response.

'Yes, Maponus,' sighed Ancasta. 'We *all know* you're in with the superstars. But when did you last get a gig out in Greece or Rome?'

'Had one at Rudchester,' muttered Maponus.

'In 231,' said Ancasta, crisply. 'Getting on for eighteen centuries ago. Maponus, your agent hasn't called since 1239. Move on.'

Kevin took a deep breath, walked past the three

deities, and went to light the candles on Abandinus's shrine. 'Mind yourself,' he said, as Abandinus removed his arm from the stone plinth. The two candles lit nicely, and fluttered gently in the little stone niche.

Kevin turned and bowed to the assembled company, casting a glance further along the garden to try to see who else was there. He could make out another male figure, short and stocky, and glowing *yellow* as far he could tell. 'Good afternoon, everyone,' he said, like a teacher in assembly. The gods did not slowly chant back 'Good afternoon, Mr Rutley'. Abandinus, though, nodded at him with a rather knowing smile, peering at his nose, Ancasta preened her hair and gazed coldly at him, and Maponus cocked his head to one side and raised one eyebrow with mild interest. His dog lifted its head off shaggy paws and regarded Kevin with a very similar expression.

'Um . . . glory to you all . . . ?' offered Kevin.

Ancasta and Maponus exchanged a glance. 'He's not very good,' said Ancasta. 'But he is enthusiastic, which counts for a lot.'

Kevin decided to let this remark go. He knelt down, to be on the safe side, and inclined his head towards Maponus. 'I am pleased to meet you,' he said. He flicked a glance at Abandinus. 'Aren't I?' he checked. Abandinus waved graciously once more.

'Kevin,' he said, 'meet Maponus—musician, poet, Divine Youth, pet handler . . . ' He curled his lip at the shaggy dog (a border terrier, thought Kevin, who'd spent many hours leafing longingly through a dog breeds book) and the dog curled its lip right back at him.

Maponus struck a few chords on his harp and gave Kevin a little nod. 'So, you are Abandinus's chosen one,' he said, with a gentle smile. Maponus was, without a doubt, what some of the girls at school would call 'well fit', Kevin acknowledged to himself, grudgingly. But hey—he *was* a god.

'Um—yes—I think so,' said Kevin. 'Along with Tim and Gracie.'

'Gracie?' said Maponus, pausing in his harping and stroking a silver pendant that hung around his neck. 'There is a *female* follower too, Abandinus?' He raised an eyebrow at his neighbouring god and added, 'Well, you old *dog*, you!' His terrier made an affronted noise and dropped its nose back on its paws.

'Gracie. Yes,' said Abandinus. 'I fear she is slightly smitten by me.'

'Smitten?' echoed Kevin. 'What—like, you think she *fancies* you? Oh come on! She called you a creep!'

'I smote her,' said Abandinus. 'Slightly. Hence—she is slightly smitten.'

137

'Ooh—*that* kind of smitten,' said Kevin, with some relief.

'Both kinds,' grinned the deity, smugly.

'Oh, get over yourself,' said Kevin.

There was a crackling and then a thudding noise among the trees. 'Who *is* that?' said Kevin, trying to peer past Abandinus's very distracting robe, which was bubbling with some kind of crayfish today.

Ancasta cast her eyes heavenward. 'Oh don't even *ask*, boy! It's *too* tiresome. I didn't ask him along. Did either of you?' Abandinus shook his head but Maponus looked a little guilty.

'I might have *mentioned* I was coming here, in his hearing,' said the Divine Youth.

'Oh well, that's enough, isn't it?' said Ancasta, getting to her webbed feet, wafting up alongside Kevin and peering down the garden. 'Hey! Semitas! You'd better not be doing tarmac!'

'Tarmac?' gasped Kevin. 'What—you think he's messing around with tarmac?'

'Or bitumen,' said Ancasta. 'Or flagstones. Bricks, blocks, cobbles, gravel . . . whatever. Depends what mood he's in. Never get too close when he's on the pea shingle. It can turn nasty.'

'Who is he?' Kevin could now make out a stockily built man with short dark hair. He appeared to be

138

in a short tunic and leggings, with boots like a Roman soldier's. And over it all, most bizarrely, he was wearing a fluorescent yellow tabard. Like the ones workmen wore.

'Oh, he hasn't really got a proper name,' said Ancasta. 'His title is Deo Qui Vias et Semitas Commentus Est. We call him Semitas for short.' Kevin gaped at her. 'What—don't you know *any* Latin?' she demanded and then rolled her eyes and tutted. 'It means *The God Who Invented Roads and Pathways*. Catchy, isn't it?'

'Roads and pathways?' murmured Kevin. 'Does that mean . . . ? Hey!' He ran down through the trees as the god pounded something into the earth. What was he doing? Laying a road or something? Mum would have a fit!

There was laughter from the other gods as he bashed through the low, prickly branches towards the Day-Glo-vest-clad immortal. 'Hey!' he yelled again and Semitas turned round. He appeared to be holding a metal thing—a bit like a road drill in shape, but without the engine attachment. His face was covered in a short grizzled beard, and his eyes were black and baleful.

'You got a problem?' he asked. His skin was tanned a leathery brown and rippling with muscle. Kevin saw that the thing in his hand was some kind of heavy metal tool—possibly to pound some chunky red clay tiles into the soft muddy earth. There was a neat narrow path of them, about two metres long, along the perimeter fence at the very end of the garden.

'Um . . . um . . . no . . . ' murmured Kevin, rather admiring the path which was laid beautifully flat and with perfectly even gaps between every tile. 'I just . . . wondered what you were doing.'

'I am the god of roads and paths,' said Semitas, with a South London accent. 'It's what I do.' He didn't sound very happy about it.

'Oh,' said Kevin. 'Well . . . it's very nice. Thanks.'

'Are you being sarcastic?' snapped Semitas.

'No!' said Kevin, alarmed. 'No! It *is* very nice.'

'It's not easy, you know,' said Semitas. 'River gods and earth gods and mountain gods—*they've* got it easy. No shortage of happy little prayers for *them*. It's all, "*oh bless me, please*" and "*grant me safe passage*" and "*do make my crops flourish*" and it's little candles and food offerings and even your own temple if you play your cards right.'

'Ummmm . . . ' said Kevin, not really knowing what to say.

'And what do *I* get?' peeved on Semitas, rubbing his tarry fingers through his hair and glaring at Kevin. 'Town planners whingeing at me day and night. "*For* god's sake, let this new four lane motorway get through planning!" "I hope to god there'll be no banner wavers stopping us carving a trunk road through this ancient forest!" Or it's just the motorway drivers stuck in jams. And blaming *me*. "God, I hate this road! Whoever invented this road? I'd like to spatter him over the central reservation!"'

'Oh,' said Kevin. 'I see what you mean.' Semitas did seem to have drawn the short straw. If you were going to be an immortal being, presiding for ever over a mountain or a river would be quite agreeable. Being anchored to a network of motorways wouldn't be so great.

'Semitas, do stop whining,' said a crisp voice in Kevin's right ear. He jolted as he realized Ancasta was leaning on his shoulder, making his skin feel as if cool water was flowing across it. 'If you're joining the party you could at least try to be better company.'

Semitas glowered at Ancasta.

'Stop paving and come and take part in the conversation,' said Ancasta. 'Or do us all a favour and disappear up your own junction.'

Kevin gulped. He thought Semitas might hurl balls of boiling tarmac at Ancasta, or something. But the god just huffed a bit and then laid his metal pounding thing aside and followed the goddess back down to Abandinus's shrine. The roads and pathways god sat down next to Maponus and his dog and started laying little stones out in a neat line while the gods talked on.

Kevin sat down near to Abandinus. He wished the others would just go. He wanted to talk to Abandinus about the weird dreams and Cuda and the cucullati and everything that had been happening. He needed a bit of reassurance from his god, but he didn't want to talk about any of it in front of Ancasta and the others. They would probably laugh at him.

'So, Kevin,' said Ancasta, after they'd finished speaking rather unkindly about another goddess who was said to have the feet of a rabbit (rich, thought Kevin, when at least two of them had the feet of a duck), 'sing us your hymn.'

Kevin looked nervously at Abandinus. 'Well . . . it's to him,' he said, nodding towards his god. 'Not to everyone.'

'So? No matter!' trilled Ancasta and clapped her hands. 'Come! Entertain us!'

'But,' said Kevin, reluctantly, and then found himself standing up on his tiptoes and waving his hands in the air. He was astonished. He had not planned this at all—but his limbs seemed to have suddenly developed their own ideas. 'HEY!' he shouted.

'Sing!' commanded Ancasta. 'And dance! Dance for your gods!'

And Kevin danced. His left leg stuck out daintily, the toe pointed like a ballerina's, and then he skipped lightly across the grass and twirled through the air, before opening his mouth and singing, in a rather high voice:

> '*Aban-dinus—O English god,*
> *How great your grace must be . . . '*

He leapt up, turning gracefully mid-leap and grazing his head on a low bough of the apple tree. He was too affronted to notice. He was being *controlled*!

'*A-aban-dinus, oh, come to us . . . and blessed we will be,*' he sang on, shooting a look of fury at Ancasta who was clapping her hands and laughing. Maponus and Semitas were also laughing and clapping and the little dog was up on its paws, barking enthusiastically, its shaggy fur standing out.

'More! More!' Ancasta cried, wiping tears of merriment from her eyes. 'Faster! Faster!'

And Kevin began to dance and spin and sing faster and faster, the second verse of the hymn forcing itself out of his unwilling throat. He wasn't just angry now. He was scared. This goddess could *make* him do things he didn't want to do. She could make him backflip down the garden and straight into the glass of the greenhouse if she so chose. He danced and spun and sang in sharp cries and began to feel sick and appalled. He had been so stupid. He had thought this gods business was *cool*! His arm struck the tree again, and Ancasta shrieked with laughter. His head whacked into another branch and now blood was dripping into his eyes. The garden was becoming a blur of pink and red and still he was singing between gasps for air.

There was a deafening crash of thunder. As suddenly as his fit of dancing had begun, it ended. Kevin slumped into the grass amid a shower of hailstones. Abandinus was standing up, holding his wooden staff aloft and shouting something at Ancasta and the others. He heard Ancasta begin to argue and then there was another crash and she screamed and then . . . there was silence.

Kevin rolled onto his back and opened his eyes despite the well of blood in one. The world was still spinning and the hail had turned to rain. He gritted his teeth and tried to calm his breathing.

Abandinus leaned over him as the rain eased to a light shower and then stopped. The god's face was grave. 'Kevin?' he said. 'Are you all right?'

Kevin struggled up to a sitting position as the

spinning slowed down. He stared at Abandinus, feeling hurt and angry. Abandinus should have protected him.

Abandinus looked ashamed, much to Kevin's surprise. He didn't think gods ever needed to do that. 'Ancasta believes humans are the playthings of the gods. She plays too roughly.'

'And what do *you* think?' said Kevin, wiping the blood from his eye.

'I do not share her enthusiasm for this game,' said Abandinus. 'Although it can be amusing to play with humans, I think it is unseemly to damage them. This is why I halted her game, when I saw you were hurt.'

'Well . . . thanks,' muttered Kevin. He was still furious about being used like a puppet. 'Feel free to step in a bit sooner next time!'

Abandinus sat down beside him. He touched his hand to Kevin's brow and at once the stinging and swelling on it subsided. Kevin felt his swollen nose improve too. And also a sense of calm and wellbeing and . . . what? What was that? A swell of emotion. Gratefulness, he supposed.

'You should know more about the gods,' said Abandinus. 'Most of those I move among are benign— but they are unpredictable. You cannot assume they will help you. Even the benign ones have bad days and are as likely to smite you as bless you. If you get

145

caught up between two warring gods it can be very bad news.'

'Oh. Are you warring with Ancasta now?' said Kevin, feeling a little edgy again, remembering the crack of thunder and the shouting and screaming.

'What 'Casta? No! I just put her in her place. She's a drama queen,' said Abandinus, making Kevin grin by using one of those modern phrases again, as if he was born in the 1990s. 'We will make it up and she will be more respectful to you in future. She likes you, in fact.'

'Hmm, well she's got a hilarious way of showing it,' muttered Kevin. 'So—where have they gone back to? Where do gods hang out?'

'At their rivers, their mountains, their roads, their forests, caves, lakes or seas . . . ' listed Abandinus. 'We may dwell in any place we choose but we have our own cradles—the places we were born into. Here we are most at ease and at our strongest.'

'So . . . when you're not here you go back to the River Ouse?'

'I do. It is a river of great reach,' he said, with pride in his voice. 'But I am fondest of the stretch where we met. Ancasta's river only runs through a single county.' He smirked.

'Well, as long as it's not in *this* county,' muttered Kevin. 'I'm glad she's gone now. I'm glad they all are. I

146

wanted to talk to you on your own. I need to tell you things.'

'KEVIN!'

He jolted with shock. 'Oh no! That's Mum!' Abandinus raised a finely sculpted eyebrow but did not look in the least bit concerned.

'KEVIN! Your American friend is on the phone!' yelled Mum, her voice getting louder as she walked down the garden, presumably carrying the walk-about handset.

'She can't see this!' hissed Kevin, staggering over to the shrine and blowing out the candles.

'KEV! Are you down here?' called Mum, reaching the hedge by the greenhouse.

Kevin leapt to his feet and raced to meet her. 'Here, Mum!' he called and then hissed back to Abandinus, 'I'll come back to talk to you soon!'

But his god had gone, leaving only a few feathers drifting through the smoke of the extinguished candles.

Chapter 14

'OK—have you checked your email?' said Gracie as Kevin took the phone back into the house.

'Hang on,' said Kevin, switching on the rather elderly computer in the little study area under the stairs. Mum didn't let him have a computer or a TV in his bedroom, and he had to ask for a special key to get on the internet browser, but he could log on to email friends. The machine switched on with a familiar jingle of notes and the monitor screen illuminated.

'Are you OK?' asked Gracie. 'You sound kind of weird.'

'I know,' said Kevin. His teeth had begun to chatter. He guessed it was delayed shock after being Ancasta's puppet. 'I'll tell you later. Right—here it is.' He clicked on his inbox icon and found the email entitled 'Get yourself your own personal god'. Gracie's message was there, laid out neatly with the picture of the water mill. 'OK. So I just forward this to seven other people.'

'That's right. Get it ready to go in ten minutes. I'll call back with Tim on the other line and we can count down and hit the send button at exactly the same time.'

'OK,' muttered Kevin. 'Why do we need to do it all at the same time, again?'

Gracie made an impatient noise. 'Kevin, you have no sense of theatre! I want this to be cool! We want people to pick these up and do as the message says and then send it on, and if we all *believe* they will, just as we're sending, it will probably work better.'

'Gracie,' said Kevin, after a short hesitation, 'how come you *want* Abandinus to get more powerful? I mean . . . didn't he freak you out with that mini tornado thing?'

Gracie paused too and then she said, 'Yes, he did. But . . . well . . . when he picked me out of it again and put me down, it felt . . . '

'What?' said Kevin.

'I don't know . . . like . . . he cared. Like he was sorry. I was too angry to really notice it at the time but it came back to me later. Now I kind of . . . trust him. You know?'

Kevin nodded at the phone, even though he knew Gracie couldn't see. 'I do know,' he said.

Gracie phoned back ten minutes later, with Tim on the landline of the house where she was staying. She put both phones on speaker mode so they could all hear each other. 'Ready to send, both of you?'

'Yep,' came back Tim's voice, tinnily, through his phone and Gracie's.

'Me too,' said Kevin.

'OK—so—dear Abandinus,' said Gracie, 'we're doing this for you—to get a whole load more believers, so you can be strong and powerful. Amen. OK, guys—*believe* . . . and SEND!'

Kevin clicked on SEND and watched his email go out to seven friends. He had chosen people who didn't go to his school. Some he'd met at a summer camp last year, two of his cousins in France, and a bloke he'd bought a book from, on line, and had a few funny email exchanges with. That ought to do it.

'Now what?' said Tim.

'Well—we wait and see,' said Gracie. 'Kevin, check in with Abandinus in a couple of hours and see if he's feeling anything. You know . . . like a bit more powerful.'

'OK,' said Kevin, although he was feeling very tired and thought that maybe he would just leave it until tomorrow. The scent of Mum's curry was drifting out from the kitchen and all he really wanted to do was eat it and then go to sleep.

'Kevin! Come and get plates out will you?' called Mum, peering round the kitchen door with a spatula in one hand. 'What were you up to on the computer?' she added, as he came in.

'Ahh, nothing really,' said Kevin. 'Just starting a new religion.'

'Fair enough,' said Mum.

Dad was at the table, reading *Men's Health* magazine. It was strangely familiar. He always used to read at the table years back when they all lived together. Back then it drove Mum nuts. She said it was the height of rudeness when she was preparing him a meal. She wasn't saying that today though. Kevin watched her expression as he got the plates out. She looked . . . *restrained*. He wished his dad would put down the magazine and talk.

'So, have you had a good day off, Dad?' he asked, as he put the plates out and Mum began dolloping spoonfuls of rice onto them.

'Not bad, Kev, not bad,' said Dad, his eyes still fixed on a feature about getting a six-pack.

'Found somewhere else to live yet?' asked Mum in a bright—*glaringly* bright—voice.

'Give us a chance, Lor—er . . . Kate,' said Dad. He went a little pink and Kevin took a deep breath. He'd just nearly called Mum his ex-girlfriend's name. This was not good.

'Plenty of flats out there for rent,' said Mum and her tone had gone a little colder. She poured the curry from the pot onto the rice.

'Yeah—I'll get on line this evening and see what's out there,' said Dad, hiding behind the magazine.

'Will you? And will you call Derek and see if he can make some space for you tomorrow night?' asked Mum.

'Yessss—I will. Can you stop nagging me now?' Dad pulled a face at Kevin, as if he was sharing a joke.

Mum didn't say anything, but she clunked his plate of curry in front of him with some force.

They ate in silence for a while. The atmosphere was thick with tension. Kevin tried again. 'Dad—do you think you could fix my drawer in my bedroom, while you're here?' he asked. 'It's coming apart.'

'Of course, mate,' said Dad.

'Or I can,' said Mum, giving Kevin a look. 'I'm quite capable of a little drawer fixing, Kevin.'

'Yes, your mum's good at everything,' said Dad, giving his ex-wife a sarcastic smile.

'Well, I *have* to be good at quite a lot of things,

152

don't I?' she snapped. 'It's not like I can ever rely on *you*.'

'No—I didn't mean . . . ' said Kevin. This was going badly wrong. Abandinus really wasn't delivering on Number 5.

'Oh, don't start all that again!' said Dad, glaring across his food.

'No—no, of course not,' said Mum. 'Wouldn't want to put you off your dinner.'

Dad stabbed his fork into the curry and his left hand went up and twiddled with his new earring. He did that a lot when he was aggravated or anxious, Kevin had noticed.

'You'll go septic,' said Mum, eyeing her ex-husband's puffy red earlobe.

'Yeah, well, that'll make two of us,' muttered Dad, shovelling down chicken and rice.

'Kevin,' said Mum, ignoring his dad, 'why didn't you give me that letter from school before now?' She waved towards the kitchen worktop where a bit of green A4 told of upcoming events at his school. 'You've got a school disco on Thursday! And I've only just found out. It must have been in your bag for two weeks!'

'Sorry, Mum,' mumbled Kevin.

'You'll need something decent to wear,' she went

on. 'And I might not have time now to take you to get something.'

'I can take him,' said Dad.

'No you *can't*—you'll be at work. Or flat hunting,' she said, pointedly. 'You see, Kevin? I need to have time to plan these things! Don't just leave school letters in your bag!'

'Oh, give it a rest, Kate. You're giving us all indigestion,' groaned Dad.

'Well, if you don't *want* to join us for tea, you really don't have to,' hissed Mum. 'There's a perfectly good McDonald's up the road.'

Kevin felt an ache in his chest. This sounded familiar too. Mum and Dad had always argued over meals. Some days it had felt as if the dining table was a battle ground with cutlery and salt cellars and plates being crashed around in open warfare. He'd forgotten how much easier it had become when it was only him and Mum, and maybe Nan, sitting down to dinner. Tiredness swamped him. Today he had become brilliant at sports, nearly broken his nose, attracted Emma Greening's attention in the worst possible way, seen a ghostly goddess and three creepy childlike things in the school toilets, discovered that his nightmares were being shared by his friends and might actually be *real*, got turned into a puppet by a viciously playful goddess, started a new religion by email . . . and now he'd witnessed a time loop of his parents' old bickering.

It was time to go to bed.

Kevin excused himself, but by now Mum and Dad were in full flood, their argument getting louder and louder. They seemed to have forgotten he was even there.

As he got into his pyjamas, Kevin wondered how the seven emails he had sent were doing. Had they multiplied, seven times seven times seven times seven, all around the world? Were hundreds or even thousands of people now shrugging and offering up a quick prayer to Abandinus, just because they were superstitious, or thought they might as well? Would it make any difference? Would Abandinus suddenly fill up with a huge delivery of extra power? And if so, what would he do with it?

Curling into his quilt, Kevin went through his prayer checklist. He'd got the Wii and the sportiness . . . and Emma Greening's attention, although none of these things was really making him happy. He hadn't really had time to play the Wii. More important things were going on. His toe was better and Mum and Dad were back together. Sort of. And right now, as their highly strung voices crashed off the walls downstairs, nobody was happy about *that* . . . Kevin sighed heavily. There was still being cool, a dog, better skin, not getting car sick, and world peace to go. He wondered if he could change the list. Could he amend it and add to it . . . or take things off? Re-pray everything in a better way? He wanted something else now, after the day he'd had. All day he'd had a feeling in the pit of his belly that wouldn't go away.

11. *He wanted to be less scared.*

'Waaaaaaarffff-leeerrrrg. Waaaaaaarffff-leeerrrrg.'

Kevin opened his eyes and stared into the dark. Beside his bed his digital clock glowed green—00.43. Dad had come to bed around 11, waking Kevin as he tripped over one of his bin bags and dropped heavily into the bottom bunk. Kevin had drifted off again soon after but now the snoring was back.

'Waaaaaaarffff-leeerrrrg. Waaaaaaarffff-leeerrrrg.'

He got up to go to the toilet. He didn't bother switching on any lights. As he washed his hands he glanced out of the open window and up the street. There was a ping, and the nearest pale orange street lamp suddenly went dark. Then another ping, and another street lamp, across the road, also died. Kevin felt the hair stand up on the back of his neck. He leant further

156

out of the window and saw a third lamp go dark. Then a fourth . . . and a fifth. The lamp at the far end seemed to glow brighter for a second before it too, blinked out. The street was shrouded in darkness. Kevin realized that the lamps in the surrounding area must also have gone out. There was no city light glow reaching his road at all. But there was *some* kind of glow. A little moonlight, yes . . . but beyond that . . . by that furthest lamp, now just a dim post at the turn of the pavement, there was a different kind of light. A pulsing blue-red-grey light. A kind of . . . *dark* light . . . Kevin shivered again. He ran out of the bathroom and down the stairs, keeping as quiet as he could in the sleeping house. At the door he scuffed into his trainers and unlatched the chain, before opening it and letting the night air in. In with the air slithered a mournful wail. *Oh no*, some part of him whimpered. *Oh no, don't no don't no don't go out there don't . . .*

Kevin went out. The mournful wailing came from the woman, doubled over in the middle of the road, her hair dripping around her head and hands as before. 'Maaaw-oooooh,' she keened. 'Ooooh. Thou wilt sorrow . . .'

'What about?' asked Kevin, although he was peering up towards the dead street lamp at the corner, trying to make out the meaning of the dark light.

157

'Thou wilt sorrow . . . ' she said again. He glanced back at her but her head was still in her hands.

'Yeah well, thanks for nothing,' he said, in a voice much steadier than his heart. She stopped wailing and just hitched her breath in raggedly as he walked past her and towards the corner.

As he grew closer the source of the dark light gradually came into view. It was a mouth. A wide, deep-throated mouth, from which the blue-red-grey intensity of light streamed out. Kevin felt his knees begin to shake. He slowed his walk and tried to get control of his breathing. His lungs had suddenly crushed away inside his chest. He struggled to get air in. The mouth slowly closed and the dark light streamed through a grinning clench of jagged white teeth as the face around it swam into view. It was the lion-headed man. His body was clad in a dark leather jerkin, revealing muscled arms as thick as tree trunks. The hands on the end of them were human, but the viciously sharp curved yellow claws on each finger certainly weren't. At the waist was a belt with a dagger and a curved short sword tucked into it, above trousers of a similar dark leather which creased into black metal boots.

'Pray to the dark,' said the creature. 'Follow the dark light. All manner of things may be yours . . . Take what you *want*. Not only what is *given*.'

Kevin was rooted to the spot, on the pavement, his lungs still clenched shut like flattened bellows. Over the creature's shoulder he could see two figures. One was Tim, wearing only his boxer shorts and a bewildered expression. The other was Gracie, in green silk pyjamas, her hair in plaits, looking sick with fear.

The lion-headed man smiled at Kevin, his eyes glittering red, and then opened his mouth again. *Oh no no oh no not the dark light no* . . . whimpered that voice again. Dark light streamed out between the teeth, reaching for him. Kevin closed his eyes and felt the world tip over into a dark light abyss and the little voice began to scream.

'Waaaaaaarffff-leeerrrrg. Waaaaaaarffff-leeerrrrg.'

Kevin shot up in bed, drenched with sweat and gasping for air.

'Waaaaaaarffff-leeerrrrg. Waaaaaaarffff-leeerrrrg,' went his dad in the bunk below.

Kevin sank back under the quilt, too scared to get up to go to the bathroom and wash himself down. Too scared to even look out.

Chapter 15

'*You* don't look too great,' said a friendly male voice as Kevin trudged to school. 'Been having trouble with your gods?'

Kevin spun round in shock and saw Gracie's professor ambling along towards him, wearing a rather crumpled linen suit and holding a battered cardboard folder full of old papers.

'Um . . . ' said Kevin. His mouth was dry and he felt as if he'd been awake all night, even though he knew he hadn't been.

The man stopped, fished his spectacles out of his inside pocket, put them on, and peered at him more seriously. 'You really *don't* look well, Kevin,' he said, putting Kevin to shame because he couldn't remember the professor's name. 'Greg,' he said, helpfully. 'Greg McCrae. We spoke in the car park the other day, about Cuda and her cucullati.'

'Oh yes,' said Kevin. 'Sorry. I just didn't sleep too well last night. Funny dreams.'

'Hmmm,' said Greg, tilting his head to one side and narrowing his eyes at Kevin. 'Do you suffer from insomnia a lot?'

'No—not really. Just a bit recently.'

'Maybe you should take the day off,' he said. 'Go and catch up a bit.'

'Nah,' said Kevin. His bedroom was full of Dad's stuff, and quite possibly still full of Dad too; he'd still been asleep when Kevin left. There was nowhere in the house where he could really relax after the night he'd had. The dream still had a nasty grip on his belly and he'd only been able to eat half a bit of toast for breakfast. The dream should have faded by now. He should be laughing about it. But he wasn't.

Greg turned round and joined him as he walked on towards the school.

'I found out some more about your mother goddess,' he said, taking his glasses off again and tucking them back inside his jacket. 'Of course, Cuda was just one of a number of them. The three best known were Cuda, Cernunnos, and Suleniae—they used to hang out together in the Cotswolds. Cuda's my favourite though.'

'Why's that?' asked Kevin, interested in spite of his sick stomach and tiredness.

'Easiest to pronounce,' grinned the professor. 'She was worshipped mostly in a little village near Cirencester—Daglingworth. Which *isn't* so easy to pronounce.'

'So,' hedged Kevin, 'if you were to *meet* a god or a goddess today, from all those ancient Celtic ones—would you be happy to meet Cuda?'

Greg peered at him and then blinked and laughed. 'Nice question. Um . . . yeah. Cuda would be good. At least, I'm pretty sure she wouldn't mean me any harm. She was a protective type of goddess. The one who would warn of danger—just like your own mother. Or maybe that you were going to have a lot of babies. Fertility goddess too, remember.'

Kevin gulped. Babies were *definitely* not in question, so that could only mean that Cuda was warning him. And she had, hadn't she? About the lion.

'How would you feel about meeting a god with a lion's head?' he asked, pausing as they reached the corner of the road his school was in.

Greg looked at him, narrowing his eyes again, as if he was trying to read his mind. Kevin shuffled and stared at his shoes.

'I would feel . . . uneasy,' said Greg, quietly.

Kevin heard Tim calling for him at the gate. He stepped away from the professor but looked back over his shoulder.

'And what would you *do*?'

Greg's face was serious and his brows were drawn together with something like concern.

'KEV!' yelled Tim, waving. 'C'mon!'

'What would you do?' repeated Kevin, still watching the professor as he backed away towards his friend.

Greg tilted his head to one side. 'I would run.'

Tim looked OK. Cheerful, even, as they headed into tutorial. 'I'm going to be DJ!' he said. 'At the disco on Friday. Me! Behind the decks!'

'But . . . isn't that always Mr Simmonds?' asked Kevin, foraging through his bag for a pen. 'He always does school discos.'

'Yeah—he's doin' it. But he's letting me do half an hour!' grinned Tim. 'ME! And you know what—it's all because of our god!' He dug in his pocket and pulled out a crumpled bit of lined notepaper and waved it in Kevin's face. Kevin grabbed it and peered at the list on it.

1. Yamaha keyboard
2. Better singing
3. To be a master DJ

4. Get money—lots of it
5. Better teeth

'Better teeth?' he snorted. 'What's wrong with your teeth?' He squinted at Tim's mouth and Tim grinned widely at him and then looked embarrassed.

'They're too big,' he said, prodding at his incisors with distaste. 'They could be a little straighter, too,' he added, like one of the women on cosmetic surgery TV shows. Kevin shook his head in wonder. He had never noticed Tim's teeth *at all*. He read on down his friend's list.

6. Pass all my exams without doing work

'Ah—that's a good one,' said Kevin. 'I should have thought of that.'

7. World peace and all that
8. TBC
Amen.

'TBC? What's that?'

'To be continued,' said Tim. 'I can't think up *everything* all at once, can I? So! Let's go to the shrine after school today and see if all the email worshippers have juiced up our boy Abandinus!' He grinned, drumming his fingers on the desk top excitedly. 'He could be packing ten times more power now!'

'He's not a battery!' muttered Kevin. 'And don't call him "our boy"—it's disrespectful. He won't like it.'

'What's got to *you* today?' said Tim, giving him a shove.

Kevin stared at him. 'Did you have any dreams last night?' he said.

Tim shrugged. 'What, more weepy waily lady dreams? Nah. And there was nothing soggy in the garden when I got back yesterday either.'

'Are you sure? You didn't have a dream last night?'

'Yeah, I had a dream,' grinned Tim. 'About jelly. And tambourines. You still freaked about the salty puddle and all that? Just a coincidence! Don't worry!'

Kevin said nothing. The grip of unease inside him was as strong as ever.

'Why—did you dream?' asked Tim, his grin fading.

'I'll tell you at break.'

They got to talk properly at break, in their usual haunt under the beech tree. First, Kevin told Tim about the thing with Ancasta.

'She *made* you? She like—possessed you and made you dance?' marvelled Tim. 'Man, that is *cool*.'

'Cool? Are you kidding? It was *horrific*!' Kevin spluttered. 'You have *no idea*. She could have made me do *anything*. Smash through a window. Bash my head against a wall. I got smacked about on the trees as it was. I was covered in blood and bruises!'

'So . . . how come you're not bruised now?' asked Tim, squinting at his friend's face for signs of injury.

'Abandinus took them away,' said Kevin. 'I think he was sorry about it. Although he'd never exactly say it. Gods don't apologize. He stopped her, though, and sent her packing.'

'So—your god protected you. That's cool,' said Tim, with a shrug. There was no way, Kevin realized, that he could get across to his friend quite how awful it was to be controlled.

'Yeah, he did. Eventually. But not before the rest of them had had a good laugh.'

'The rest of them?' Tim looked startled. 'Who else was there?'

Kevin told him about Maponus and his dog and harp, and about Semitas and his bad-tempered path-laying.

Tim was awed about yet more gods arriving. Then he sniggered. 'A god of *roads*? How lame is that?'

'Yeah, I think Semitas has got issues with that too,' said Kevin. 'Lays a good path, though.'

'So, is this what's made you all moody today?' asked Tim. 'Being the plaything of the gods?'

Kevin was getting aggravated. Tim, picking at the bark of the beech and chortling, just didn't seem to be taking this seriously.

'Well, how would *you* like it if some uppity female suddenly bashed *you* into a tree?' he snapped.

'OK, OK—not much!' Tim put up his hands. 'But you're all right now. And it'll never happen again.'

'YOU!' snarled a furious voice. Gracie appeared, as usual, out of nowhere. But without her usual happy greeting. She stomped up to them and then grabbed Kevin by the shoulders and whacked him hard against the tree. 'YOU! Don't you DARE!'

The back of Kevin's head actually cracked audibly against the trunk. 'WHAT?' he squawked. 'Have you gone *nuts*?'

'I'm telling you—DON'T YOU DARE!' she repeated, pink in the face, her eyes glittering, her hands still gripped on Kevin's shoulders as he tried to bat her away.

Tim pulled Gracie off him and Kevin gaped at her while checking the back of his head for blood. A few other kids were standing around watching and nudging each other.

'What are you *doing*?' hissed Tim. 'Have you lost your mind?'

'He—' Gracie pointed a shaking finger at Kevin. 'He *knows*!'

'What?' yelled Tim. 'What are you on about, you nut job? What do you want to go smacking him against a tree for?! He's had enough of that kind of thing!'

Gracie looked from Tim to Kevin and then seemed to notice the attention she was attracting from the growing crowd of agog students. She shook her head. 'Come with me somewhere quieter and I'll tell you,' she muttered.

They headed for the playing fields and the perimeter hedge, Gracie sat down, cross-legged, and bit on her thumbnail as Kevin and Tim sat down with her.

'What's going on, Gracie?' asked Kevin, rubbing the tender spot on the back of his head.

'Did you dream last night, Kevin?' she asked, looking at him very directly.

'Yes. I was just about to tell Tim about it when you attacked me.'

She glanced over at Tim. 'Did *you* dream?' she said.

Tim shrugged. 'Can't remember if I did,' he said. 'Why?'

'What was in your dream?' she asked Kevin.

Kevin took a breath and allowed himself to remember, even though it made his insides clench again. 'I went outside because of the dark,' he said. 'And the weeping woman was there again and so was this . . . this . . . guy, with . . . with a—'

'Lion's head,' finished Gracie, sending a cascade of coldness down his back. Kevin stared at her and then nodded.

'And there was this light . . . ' he went on. 'This . . . *dark* light. I don't know how to explain it. Sort of blue and red and grey and . . . dark . . . at the same time.'

'It came out of his mouth,' said Gracie. 'It came right at you.'

'It did?' whispered Kevin. He couldn't quite grasp all the details any more. Just the horrible feeling in the dream. 'Yeah . . . it did.'

'And who else was there?' asked Gracie, her face pale and tense.

'You were,' said Kevin. 'And so was Tim.'

'That's right,' said Gracie. 'Tim was there too.'

They both turned to look at him but Tim shook his head. 'Look, whatever weird his 'n' hers nightmare thingy you two had going on last night—I was *not in it*. I don't remember any of this.'

'You were there,' repeated Gracie. 'This lion-headed thing asked you to pray to the dark light.

You said no and then you tipped over and disappeared.'

Tim narrowed his eyes, staring at the grass, and
then shivered and caught his breath, raising his hands
to the back of his head. 'OK, *thanks* for reminding me
of that. Really wish you hadn't.'

Gracie turned to face Kevin, her face deadly serious.

'And then he asked you the same thing, Kevin.
And you know what?'

'What?' said Kevin.

'You said yes.'

Chapter 16

'I did *not*!' retorted Kevin.

'You did!' said Gracie. 'I *saw* you! You got down on your knees and you said *yes*!'

Kevin shook his head. 'I did *not* say yes to any stupid lion-headed thing about anything, Gracie! I *did* dream about him—and you were there and Tim was there, but I didn't see Tim disappear. When he asked me to pray to the dark light I fell over and then I woke up. I didn't *ever* say yes! Not ever!'

Gracie looked at him, her finger on her lips, trying to work out if he was lying.

'It was a *dream*, Gracie! Not real. I mean ... weird, yes. Weird that we saw each other in it. But still a dream. You weren't seeing exactly what I was seeing, were you? I mean ... what was I wearing in your dream?'

She shrugged. 'I don't know ... jeans and sweatshirt, I guess.'

'I was wearing pyjamas last night. So, that wasn't quite right, was it? And you were in green silk pyjamas in my dream.'

She made a face. 'I don't have green silk pyjamas.'

'There you go then,' said Kevin. 'Tim, did you wear boxers to bed last night?'

Tim raised one eyebrow. 'I don't think you should ever ask me that again,' he advised. 'But, if you must know, I was in pants. Underpants. I don't do boxers—or pyjamas.'

Kevin raised his palms at Gracie. 'Well?'

She picked at the grass and looked a little ashamed. 'I—I guess I may have overreacted a little,' she mumbled.

'Well, duh!' said Tim. 'And you know what, Gracie? It's coming back to me now. That dream. And in *my* dream you were in a dress and he was in T-shirt and jeans . . . and I didn't see that lion-headed guy ask him anything. He asked *you*.'

Gracie folded her arms and tilted her head, with a sceptical expression on her face. 'Yeah right, now you "remember".' She did a little 'quotation marks' thing with her fingers.

Tim brought his face closer to hers and his expression was dark. 'Yes, I remember,' he hissed. 'I saw the lion-headed thing and the light that came out from behind its teeth was like the lamps of hell.'

Gracie gulped. So did Kevin. Tim's description was exactly right.

'And what did I say?' whispered Gracie.

'You didn't say anything,' said Tim. 'But you were on your knees . . . which can't be a good thing, can it?'

'I was never on my knees!' cried Gracie.

'In *my* dream you were!'

'OK—stop!' said Kevin. 'We need to talk to Abandinus about all this. He should know what's going on, shouldn't he?'

'Yes, I think you're right. We should ask our god,' said Gracie, looking stressed and not meeting his eye. 'Kevin . . . I'm sorry about bashing you against a tree.'

'Forget it,' sighed Kevin, getting up as the end of break bell went. 'I get it all the time.'

It was raining when they all gathered at the shrine that afternoon. There was no sign of Dad, although his stuff was still in the house, and Mum had gone out, so Kevin was able to get Gracie through the hallway and past the kitchen without fear of a sudden attack of buttered English muffins.

173

Now they stood under the dripping leaves of the apple trees and stared at the stone ornament, with its feather carvings and little candles. Kevin reached into the alcove to light the candles and they caught quickly, protected from the rain and the breeze. A pleasant smell of freshly struck match wafted around them.

'Dear Abandinus,' said Kevin, putting his hands together and staring up into the sky. 'Please come to your shrine. We need to talk to you. Amen.'

They waited, watching for little storms of feathers or small cyclones. Nothing happened.

'Abandinus!' called Kevin. 'Come on! Be among us and all that!'

Still . . .

. . . nothing.

'Maybe we should sing his hymn,' suggested Gracie. She led the singing and they chorused through her words to the tune of 'Amazing Grace'. Then they waited.

And waited. The rain stopped. Nothing else changed.

'Oh, just *great*. Isn't that *exactly like* a god? Never there when you need them,' muttered Tim.

Kevin folded his arms and blew out loudly, making a noise like an aggravated pony. After all the freaky stuff that had been going on over the last couple of days, he really could use a bit of godly guidance and comfort now. 'Maybe he's seeing to all his new email worshippers today,' he said. 'I guess we've only got ourselves to blame for *that*.' They waited for twenty minutes and then got cold and bored and decided to go back to the house for a cup of tea.

But as they walked away from the shrine there was movement in the trees. Kevin glanced back, narrowing his eyes. The leaves on the apple trees further down the garden were spinning in a frenzy.

Three figures—two walking tall and one slumped over and stumbling along behind them—were moving towards the shrine. It was Ancasta, arm-in-arm with Maponus, who was carrying both his dog and his harp in his other arm. The person behind them had long lank hair and very bad posture.

'Typical,' squeaked Tim, trying hard not to sound nervous. 'You wait ages for a god and then three turn up all at once.'

'Ancasta!' said Kevin. 'Maponus!' He dropped to his knees, nodding his head, to keep them sweet. But he shot Ancasta a wary look. He hadn't forgiven her yet for the dancing thing.

'Aaaaah, Kevin,' smiled Ancasta, detaching her arm from Maponus's. 'Dino's little chosen one! And his little friends, too! Hello!'

Gracie stared at Ancasta and then murmured: 'You are *soooo* beautiful!' She dropped to her knees beside Kevin while Ancasta preened and ran her fingers through her oceanic hair, which seemed to be hosting some glittery flying fish today.

'Now *this* girl I *like*,' said the goddess, with an approving smile. 'Would you like to worship me, American?'

'Uh . . . sure!' said Gracie. 'Ancasta, right? Would you like me to make you a hymn?'

Ancasta beamed even more widely and Maponus chuckled and ran his long musician's fingers across the harp, unleashing a cascade of notes. 'Do we have another musician?' he teased and Gracie looked at him and caught her breath. He *was*, Kevin reminded himself, seriously god-like in his lilac robe with his piercing eyes and golden curls.

'I—I'm not really a musician,' said Gracie, blinking up at Maponus. 'I can do the words, though . . . and Tim can do the tune.'

Tim, who had joined in with the kneeling, nodded, looking dazedly at Ancasta. He nudged Kevin. 'This is the one who made you dance?' he whispered. 'She's well fit.'

Kevin peered past Ancasta towards the third god and then clutched at Tim's wrist as a chill swept over him. 'Who—who is that?' he asked the god-dess.

Ancasta glanced over her shoulder and then wrinkled her perfect nose. 'Oh no! Not *her*! Maponus, did you invite her?'

Maponus shrugged. 'Not as *such* . . .'

'You idiot! You're completely useless at saying "no" to people, aren't you?' snapped Ancasta. 'And now she'll hang around us for *hours* like a bad case of flatulence. She's so hard to get rid of and she's *so* depressing.'

'Who is it?' asked Kevin, again, getting to his feet.

'Saitada,' groaned Ancasta. 'The Goddess of Grief—and oh, how she plays that part to the full. Just you wait and see. Ten minutes with her and you'll be seriously weighing up jumping in front of a truck. Saitada could make Ronald McDonald lose the will to go on.'

As they blinked in surprise at Ancasta's twenty-first century gag, right on cue Saitada began to wail. The sound sent a sensation of cold dread and hopeless-ness across Kevin's throat and shoulders. It was exactly the same noise he'd heard in his dreams. As soon as it rose through the air, the rain began to fall again.

'Oh my god—that's *her*!' murmured Gracie, clutching *Kevin's* wrist now.

'Yup,' said Tim. 'I'd recognize that whining any-where. It's the dream droner.'

'Why is she here?' Kevin asked. His fear was making his voice strident and probably not respectful enough for Ancasta, but the goddess just shrugged.

'How should I know?' she said. 'She's always drooping around the realm, attaching herself to any deity foolish enough to ask her if she's all right.' She poked Maponus's arm at this point, and the god smiled sadly and nodded. His dog whined at his feet as Sait-ada moved closer to them all, slumping along on her hands and knees.

'Ooowooooh,' she informed them all. 'Sorrow, sorrow. Thou wilt sorrow . . . '

'What *about*?' snapped Kevin. He'd been putting up with this for some while now and felt it was about time he got an explanation.

'Oh, don't mind her,' said Ancasta. 'She's *always* like this. She's just our little ray of misery, aren't you, Saity?'

Saitada paused in her wailing and for the first time she raised her head. Lank greeny-brown hair draped across it like a curtain of seaweed but Kevin could still make out her face which was long and wan with wide pale-grey eyes and a deeply grooved mouth which turned down, like the mouth of a cod fish. '*You'll* be sorry,' she warned Ancasta. She seemed to have a Geordie accent, Kevin noticed.

'Darling, I already *am*!' trilled the other goddess. 'Your mission is successful. Why don't you go and depress someone else? Surely your wellspring of tears is nearly dry now? Why don't you pop off and see Latis for a few beers?'

'Are you tryin' to get rid o' me?' said Saitada, swaying unsteadily on her knees.

'Not at all!' sang Ancasta. 'If you want to join in the fun, you're more than welcome. But you will *have* to promise not to cry for at least five minutes.'

Saitada glared at her. 'Stop cryin'?' she snapped. 'Stop cryin', she says. When the weight of the whole world's sorrows lies upon my breast! Stop cryin'? Why—I haven't even started!'

'Saitada,' sighed Maponus. 'You've been crying for 1,746 years. I think you've made your point now.'

'Made my point?' Saitada swung around to glare at the god. 'While you go frolicking about with your harp and your mongrel and she swans around like she's got a bullrush up her—'

'Are you *ever* going to tell me what I'll sorrow about?' cut in Kevin.

Slowly, Saitada turned her face upon him, like a baleful satellite dish. Rivulets of rain ran down her cheeks between the stringy clumps of hair. 'Aye,' she said. 'Aye. Thou wilt sorrow, boy. Tha'll all sorrow.' She swung her miserable gaze across Gracie and Tim too, and the three of them moved a little closer together.

'But *why*?' demanded Kevin. Saitada opened her mouth . . . and began to wail again. He looked at Ancasta. 'Can't you make her tell us?'

Ancasta shook her head. 'It is not my place or my power to force another god's actions. I can only persuade and suggest.'

Saitada was rocking again now and tearing at the muddy shreds of robe across her mottled grey chest.

'Oh yuck,' said Ancasta, clapping her hand over her eyes. 'She's going to start breast beating. Saitada! Stop it! Nobody wants to see your bony little cleavage. Put it away.'

Kevin flinched and kept his gaze on Saitada's face. He dropped back down to his knees, in case it might help. '*Please*, Saitada, goddess of grief—tell us what we will sorrow for . . . ' Saitada began to grind her teeth in rhythm with her wailing. They made a horrible muffled screeching sound.

'Oh big surprise,' intoned Ancasta. 'Here comes the gnashing.'

'*Amen*?' tried Kevin, still staring into Saitada's face.

She stopped the breast beating and gnashing and stared at him, a waterfall of tears streaming out of her pond-like eyes.

'The dark light will claim one of you,' she whispered. 'And the rest shall surely follow.'

Then she disappeared so suddenly it was as if a large water balloon had been burst in front of them. They were all splashed in salty tears and Saitada was nowhere to be seen.

'Eeeuw,' said Grace, spitting. 'I must learn to keep my mouth shut around gods.'

Ancasta stepped closer to Kevin and eyed him with fascination. 'Dark light?' she said. 'You are being seduced by the dark light?'

'No,' said Kevin. 'We are not.'

She drifted around the three of them and touched her hand to each of their heads. It felt as if a cool river was flowing through him, thought Kevin, as the goddess made contact. And from the way Tim took in a sharp breath and Gracie went 'Oh!' it was clearly the same for them. In a second Kevin forgave Ancasta for what she'd done the previous day.

'Which god?' she said, softly, as Maponus gathered up his dog and looked on.

'We don't know,' said Kevin. 'He comes to us in dreams.'

'Hmmm,' pondered Ancasta. 'Many do that.'

'He has a lion's head,' said Gracie.

Ancasta stepped back. 'Come, Maponus,' she said. 'I weary of this place. Let us return to our realm.'

'Wait,' said Maponus. 'Did you hear what she said?'

'Time to go,' said Ancasta, grabbing his arm again.

'But she speaks of Arimanius!' Maponus directed a look of compassion at Gracie. 'And you say we must go?'

'We will inform Abandinus,' said Ancasta. 'They are *his* worshippers, not ours.'

And then a ribbon of white light cut through the dank grey air and the god and goddess stepped through it. The dog ran after them, turning once to whine sympathetically at the three mortals by the shrine. A second later nothing moved in the garden but the rain.

Chapter 17

Kevin went out again the next morning, hoping to raise Abandinus before he went to school—but there was still no response at all to his prayers. He was beginning to feel like an ordinary worshipper—the kind that never really expected his prayers to be answered, but did them anyway, in forlorn hope.

'What were you doing in the garden, love?' said Mum as he trudged back into the kitchen.

'Oh, just needed a bit of air,' he said, not entirely truthfully.

'Yes, you do look a bit peaky,' she said, feeling his forehead with one hand, while she held her open pot of cherry yoghurt in the other. 'Have you got a headache?'

'No, just didn't sleep that well,' said Kevin. He moved away from her concern and got a yoghurt out of the fridge for himself.

At least he had not dreamed in the night. No

more dark light or lion-headed gods. But Dad was still in the lower bunk, and the snoring was beginning to drive him slightly mad. Whenever Dad *stopped* going *waaaaaaarffff-leeerrrrg* Kevin just lay there, holding his breath, waiting for the moment when it started again. And if it didn't start he would begin to wonder whether his dad had stopped breathing. Then—after up to a minute—there would be a sudden gurgle and a snort and the waaaaaaarffff-leeerrrrgs would be back. It was grimly mesmerizing, and the soundtrack to all his worries.

'I am sorry, love,' said Mum. 'I'll talk to your dad today—give him a shove to get out of your room.'

'Could he go in with you?' asked Kevin, unable to keep the hopeful tinge out of his voice.

Mum just gave him a *look*. She didn't seem remotely love-struck. The romantic comedy film plot really wasn't coming together. The conversation with Dad over dinner last night had been just as tetchy as the night before. His parents seemed to *wilfully* misunderstand each other and take offence at the slightest thing—and Kevin kept trying to defend first Mum against Dad and then Dad against Mum. He remembered now, how he'd been doing that for a very long time before they split up. It made his insides knot up—and after the run-in with the three gods in the garden, they were knotted enough.

'Well,' Mum was saying, 'I hope you're not too tired after school—it's your disco tonight! Will you be going with Gracie?' She couldn't help smiling in a 'knowing' way which made Kevin groan with annoyance. He wasn't the only one trying to will a bit of romance into someone's life.

'I'll be going with *Tim*,' he snapped. 'And we'll both see Gracie there. For the last time, Mum, she is *not* my girlfriend.'

'OK—OK!' Mum put up her hands, one holding a yoghurt pot and the other holding a spoon. 'Whatever you say! So, you still hung up on that Emma, then?'

Kevin grunted.

'Aaaah,' said Mum. But she didn't say anything else, happily.

Kevin *had* been looking forward to the disco in a way. He had been hoping that Number 2 on his list—*To be cool*—would have kicked in by now. Especially with Emma and her friends there, watching. He usually felt awkward and idiotic at discos—unsure about whether to dance or just lean against a wall all evening, trying not to look stupid. Usually he danced a bit alongside Tim, who didn't seem to care what anyone else thought while he wildly flailed his limbs about and bopped to the beat. But tonight Tim would be DJing some of the time and he wouldn't be able to shuffle about alongside him. Kevin had begun to think that maybe it wouldn't be so bad this year if 2. *To be cool* was answered in time. But after Abandinus had failed to show up yesterday and this morning, he wasn't holding out much hope. By now, thousands of people should have got the Abandinus email and the god's power ought to be rising all the time. Maybe he'd just gone off his chosen one and decided to be omnipotent for someone else more interesting, someone who'd started praying to him after getting the email. Gods were like that, he'd heard. Fickle.

'Cheer up,' said Mum. 'I've got you stuff to wear tonight. I picked these up in town yesterday. They ought to fit.' She showed him the contents of a carrier bag— soft blue jeans and a black T-shirt. They looked good.

'Thanks, Mum,' said Kevin, smiling at her. 'I'll try them on as soon as I get back. Got to go now.'

He felt a bit better, as he walked to school, remembering that the dream of dark light had not returned in the night, despite Saitada's dire warning. Maybe the lion-headed god—Arimanius—had given up on him. He hoped Tim and Gracie would also report a dreamless night.

'My serve!' yelled Rob White. *CRACK*! The yellow tennis ball flew low across the net.

Relax, Kevin told himself. *He has given up on us. We're OK now.*

CRACK! He hit the ball back without even glancing at it.

Gracie and Tim didn't dream of him last night, either, he continued in his head. *Probably Ancasta and Maponus told Abandinus that Arimanius was bugging us—*

CRACK!

—and he's gone in there with his staff blazing and scared old furry-face off. Yes . . .

CRACK!

. . . that's what's happened.

CRACK!

So now we can just get on with Plan A—boost up Abandinus's god battery and see what else he can do for us.

CRACK!

And the world, of course. I won't forget to ask for world peace and all that.

Kevin only really noticed what was happening when the crowd of other kids doing other sports went quiet. He was in the middle court, out by the field, and about seventy other students in his year were doing assorted sports and games or just mooching about with a ball or a bat in one hand, chatting and trying to avoid playing anything.

Kevin didn't much like tennis, but that was what he'd been told to do. Tim was off over the field doing high jump. Gracie and some other Americans and their host English students were playing rounders under the trees at the edge of the grass. But now more and more of the assorted sport activity was tailing off or slowing down and a small crowd was gathering at the side of the tennis courts.

CRACK!

Rob White smacked the ball back at Kevin, looking pink in the face and somewhat shocked.

CRACK!

Kevin hit it back. Without bothering to watch Rob at all. His feet and his arms just moved around fluidly, perfectly, dealing precisely with the yellow missile every time it returned, his racquet meeting it at the perfect angle and velocity, while his mind floated elsewhere. Only *now* he was beginning to pay attention, along with a growing number of his fellow students.

Kevin suddenly grinned and began to enjoy himself. He was *good* at sports now, he remembered. And it hadn't been a one-off fluke. Abandinus had *really* delivered on Number 7!

Rob was a good tennis player. Possibly the best in the school, even though he wasn't the oldest. He had groaned when Kevin got picked to play opposite him.

He'd been hoping for Mike Mears who was also pretty good, but he was playing with Chad on the court to their left. *Had* been playing. Now Mike had stopped and was staring through the wire mesh fence, his mouth agape, while Chad bounced the ball on his racquet impatiently, unaware of what a remarkable thing was happening in the next court.

CRACK!

CRACK!

CRACK!

The audience was now ooohing and aaahing. They had never seen anything quite like it. The nerdy, non-sporty kid who'd had those fluke saves in goal the other day was now having a fluke rally in tennis. Someone had started counting and now the crowd was joining in.

'36 . . . 37 . . . 38,' they all chanted. Even the American rounders players had come over now and were joining in. Gracie was grinning at him. Tim was walking over to join her, shielding his eyes from the sun, watching and laughing. They both knew what was *really* going on.

'39 . . . 40 . . . 41.'

Rob White was haring around the court, puffing in the afternoon heat, looking amazed and confused at what was happening. And a little angry. He was used to being the best. Kevin was also haring around his end of the court, but it didn't feel like hard work. He was hardly puffing at all, and he felt cool and focused. He didn't make a single wrong move; never overshot, never had to stretch too far. It was as if he knew exactly where to be before the ball was even hit back to him. He grinned. If sport was going to be like *this* from now on, he was going to start loving it.

'46 . . . 47 . . . 48,' the crowd chanted, the pitch rising with their excitement.

CRACK!

Rob White lunged at the ball as it hurtled across just beyond his reach. He howled with anger as it spun past the tip of his racquet and then he tripped over on his toes and fell flat on his belly. The ball bounced and rolled. Shouts and clapping erupted from the crowd. Rob lay gasping and furious on the gravel, his elbows grazed. The bell sounded from the school building and everyone began to wander away, looking back over their shoulders at Kevin and muttering to each other in amazement. Kevin walked over to Rob and held his hand out over the net to shake, but Rob ignored him. He looked shaken—scared almost—as if he'd witnessed something supernatural.

Which, of course, he had.

'Whoa! Mate! That was so *cool*!' said Tim, clapping Kevin's shoulder.

'That was a-mazing!' said Gracie. 'And you know something else?' She glanced around to be sure nobody was in earshot. 'I just did twenty minutes of rounders right next to a patch of wild grass—seeds and pollen blowing everywhere—and hey!' She dug the little blue L-shaped inhaler out of her shorts. 'Didn't need this! *No* wheezing!'

They all grinned at each other, aglow with excitement.

'Do you really think the chain email is working?' asked Kevin, as they walked back towards the school building.

'Must be!' said Gracie. 'I'm cured!' She held the inhaler up for a moment and then flung it into the litter bin by the double doors.

'Hey—is that a good idea?' asked Kevin, alarmed. 'What if you have an attack?'

'I won't,' she beamed. 'I have faith! How about you, Tim? Any prayers answered yet?'

'Well,' said Tim, also looking around to check for spies. 'How about this?' He pulled a thick roll of paper out of his pocket, grinning. 'Number Four on my list.'

'Is that . . . money?' Kevin gaped at the bundle of notes in his friend's palm.

'£165 in five pound notes,' muttered Tim, quickly

shoving the money away again. 'I found it lying in the road. It was just outside the school gates when I went out for morning break. I was out first and nobody saw me nip out and get it.'

'But . . . shouldn't you hand it in to the cops or something?' asked Gracie, looking a little uneasy.

'No way! Finders keepers. Abandinus sent it.'

Kevin grinned a bit more. 'This is getting good!' he said. '*And* I didn't dream of lion-head guy last night. Did you?'

Gracie shook her head. Tim did the same. 'Maybe we put him off, y'know?' said Gracie. 'By not giving in to him the last time.'

'You said I *did* give in to him!' pointed out Kevin.

'Yeah, well, I must have been wrong. You didn't in *your* dream and that's what counts. I think our own dreams were just about what we were scared of happening. That's all.'

'Yeah,' said Tim. 'And maybe Abandinus has gone round and punched his dark lights out.' He drove his fist up into the air. 'Go Dino!'

They all laughed and relief blew around them with the summer breeze.

'You going to the disco tonight, Gracie?' asked Kevin as they reached the science block corridor.

'Of course,' she said. 'You too, huh?'

'Yep.'

Tim nudged him. 'Still hoping for Number 3, yeah?' he laughed.

'Number 3?' asked Gracie.

'Emma Greening,' said Tim. 'Falling at his feet!'

Kevin shrugged, feeling his cheeks go pink. Gracie wrinkled her nose. 'Are you sure about that?' she asked. 'I mean . . . have you ever even *talked* to her?'

They stared at her. Tim shrugged.

'Hey—what do I know?' she said, raising her hands. 'See you later.' She ran off down the corridor to her next class.

'Jealous,' said Tim. 'Anyway—it's already in the back of the net, Kev. I can't wait to see the look on Mike Mears's face when you're dancing with Miss Super-model.'

'Ah,' said Kevin.

'What?'

'I'm *rubbish* at dancing.'

Tim looked at him for a few seconds. 'Hmmm—yeah. You are,' he agreed. 'Better get another prayer on your list as soon as you get home.'

Chapter 18

'Kevin . . . ' Mum had that irritating *knowing* smile on her face again as she handed him the phone. 'It's *Gracie*.'

Kevin shot her a *don't go there* look and took the phone. 'Hello. What's up?'

'Kevin, have you told stuff to Greg?' demanded Gracie, direct as ever.

'Who?' he furrowed his brow.

'The professor! Greg McCrae! He's just cornered me at the community centre, so he could find out whether you're self-harming or thinking about going postal and machine-gunning the school!'

'What?'

Gracie laughed. 'It's OK—he wasn't really serious. But he said you were talking to him about a lion-headed god and all that and he was worried about you. Wanted to know if I thought you were OK. So, obviously, I told him you were just another up-tight Brit who should get out more.'

'Thanks,' said Kevin.

'But what *are* you doing? Did you say you'd been dreaming about Arimanius?'

'No, of course not. He just met me in the street and was telling me more about Cuda. You know, the Mother Goddess, and the cucullati—those little guys that run around with her. The ones I saw in the school toilets. And I just wondered if he knew about any lion-headed gods.'

'And did he?'

'Well—yeah—I think so. He said if he ever met one he'd run.'

Gracie didn't reply for a moment. And then, 'OK. If that's all, we're OK. But you gotta be careful, Kevin. If he starts to think you're nuts he might say something to my English family and they might stop me hanging out with you guys. They're already a bit funny with me because I should be spending more time with their daughter.'

'Who are you staying with?'

'Chloë Carpenter.'

'Oh,' said Kevin, understanding. Chloë Carpenter was a very studious, rather dull girl who was given to reporting students for any rule breaking she spotted.

He couldn't imagine staying at the Carpenters' was much of a party.

'Anyway, I'll be coming with Chloë tonight, so you'll have to be careful what you say to me.'

'You don't think Greg *will* say anything to them, do you?'

'No. Not now I've told him you're OK. I think he's more *interested* than worried. He'll be coming tonight too, so perhaps you can talk to him as if you're normal. Can you manage that for five minutes? See you there.'

She hung up abruptly, not giving him a chance to answer back.

When he went into his room to get ready he found Dad there, sitting at his son's small desk—a cheap white thing with a rash of old stickers—and bashing away at his work laptop. 'Sorry, mate,' said Dad. 'Just got a bit of work to catch up on.' His briefcase and laptop bag lay across the floor along with several bits of A4 paper, and his mobile phone was charging on Kevin's pillow, the lead strung across from the socket by the skirting board, at an awkward angle for anyone trying to reach the wardrobe. Kevin felt a twinge of annoyance. His room was being slowly taken over by Dad stuff. He ducked under the mobile charger lead and picked his way across the cases and papers on the floor to reach the wardrobe. In it he found his new jeans and T-shirt, and quickly got into them. Normally he'd take his time. Maybe mess around with a bit of hair wax, hoping to tame his unruly thatch, but with Dad at the desk he couldn't get to the mirror and so he decided not to bother. The hair wax never helped much anyway. His distant image across the room, though, showed that he was definitely less spotty. Maybe Abandinus was seeing to that too!

He hurried out into the garden to do his daily stint of worship, the matchbox in his pocket so he could light the candles. Hopefully Abandinus would show up today and he could thank him for the tennis thing, and the money for Tim and Gracie's asthma cure. And maybe ask about the gift of dancing in a way that wouldn't make him look like a nervous donkey on rollerskates.

But as he turned the corner of the greenhouse he stopped dead. Standing by the shrine was his mother. She was holding an empty garden waste sack and staring at the little stone plinth and its candles with a mystified expression on her face. As he stood, gaping in surprise, she turned to him with one eyebrow raised.

'Kevin? What do you know about *this*?' she said.

'Ummm,' said Kevin. He didn't like lying, least

of all to his mum, so he tried to keep it as close to the truth as possible. 'Me and Tim brought it down here.'

Mum gaped now. 'Why?' she said. 'What on earth would you do that for?'

'Well . . . ' Kevin struggled for a plausible explanation. 'It was going cheap at the garden centre. They knocked a few quid off so it seemed like a bargain and—'

'Wait! Back up!' Mum held up her free hand, looking even more mystified. 'You're saying you *bought* this?'

'Well, me and Tim. Yeah.'

Mum shook her head and blinked several times. 'So . . . you're telling me that you pooled your money together with your best mate and—totally ignoring Warlord Of Oblivion Three for the Widdle or Spinescape or TurboHeadSmacking Five on X-CUBE—you thought you'd buy a *nice garden ornament* instead.'

'Well . . . yeah,' said Kevin.

Mum stared at him. 'Again . . . why?'

'It's . . . kind of a project,' said Kevin, his brain spinning wildly around all the explanations he could find. 'To do with English culture . . . to help Gracie.'

Mentioning Gracie definitely helped. A little understanding dawned on Mum's face.

'She—she wants to study some of the old gods

and stuff—you know, Celtic gods and all that. So we kind of did some role play.'

'O . . . K,' said Mum, tilting her head to one side. 'I can just about get my head around that. Americans do like the old stuff, don't they?'

'Oh yeah—Gracie's mad about Abandinus and Ancasta and Maponus and all that,' said Kevin, relief washing through him. Mum seemed to be accepting his story.

'Abandinus and Ancasta and Maponus?' she echoed, with a smile. 'Sounds like you really *have* been doing some homework!'

'Well, Greg—this professor guy who's looking after the American students—he really knows about this stuff,' said Kevin, warming up now, because this was all true. 'He was telling us about Cuda, the mother goddess, and the cucullati and all that.'

'OK, OK—you've convinced me!' laughed Mum, waving the empty garden sack at him. 'I still think you and Tim have lost your minds . . . but I suppose a pretty girl will do that to you.'

Kevin cringed. '*Mum!* How many times do I have to tell you. Gracie is just a *friend*!'

'Whatever you say.' She smiled and headed back to the house. 'Don't get grass stains on your new disco gear,' she called back.

Kevin waited for a few minutes before lighting the candles and kneeling down. 'Dear Abandinus,' he said, 'hallowed be thy name and so on. Thanks for the money for Tim and for Gracie's asthma cure and all the cool sports stuff for me. And for warding off Arimanius. Ummm . . . I hope you like all the extra worship we've got you with the chain emails. Hope that makes you feel good. Ummm . . . any chance you can give me some dancing powers? In time for tonight? Because, you know, I think the Emma Greening thing might be happening now. And after the tennis thing, I almost think I could ask her to dance . . . except that I'll probably step on her foot or elbow her in the face or something. I'm really rubbish at dancing.'

He paused as a breeze tugged at his hair and stirred the tall blades of grass around the shrine. He watched for little curly feathers and then the appearance of the god.

But Abandinus did not come.

'Are you there?' he called up into the air. 'Are you there, god?'

Nothing. Ah well. Abandinus probably thought he'd done enough for one day. And that was fair. With any luck, though, he would deliver dancing just in time for this evening.

'Oh! Look at *you*! What a handsome young man!'

Nan was in the kitchen with Mum as he went back in. She gave him a hug. 'All the girls will be queuing up to dance with you,' she said.

'Nan! Don't *you* start too!' complained Kevin, going pink. It was bad enough having his mum sniffing out romance in every corner of his life. Especially when there wasn't any.

'Shall we go into the sitting room?' Nan said to Mum, picking up her mug of tea from the table.

'Ah . . . no . . . best not to just yet,' said Mum. 'Jason's on the phone to Lorna.'

'Oooh,' said Nan, lowering her voice. 'Do you think they're going to get back together?'

'No!' said Kevin, before he could stop himself. That was *definitely* not part of his plan. Dad and *Mum* were meant to be getting back together, not Dad and Lorna.

'*Kevin!*' said Mum. 'Your dad misses her. It would be great for him if they made things up.'

'He doesn't miss her!' insisted Kevin. 'He said she was too young for him!'

Mum and Nan exchanged glances and Kevin stalked out into the hallway and stood by the sitting room door, trying to hear Dad on the phone. He couldn't hear anything. He knew it was wrong, but he eased the door open a crack. He still didn't hear anything, but he saw his dad sitting on the sofa, the phone cradled in his hands, staring into space. Dad looked miserable. He sniffed sharply and shook his head, as if trying to stop crying. Kevin felt his insides twist up. He hadn't seen his dad look this upset since . . . since that horrible 'we're splitting up and it's not your fault' talk three years ago, in this very room. Maybe he really *did* miss Lorna.

He eased the door closed again and stood still in the hallway, trying to think. After a few minutes of feeling uneasy and confused, Kevin took a deep breath and told himself it didn't matter if Dad was missing Lorna now. Soon his son's prayers would be answered and he and Mum would realize how much they wanted to be together again. Soon.

Nan gave him a lift to the school. 'How have you been?' she said, on the way. 'No more funny turns, eh?'

'Oh—*loads* more!' laughed Kevin. 'My life is *full* of funny turns!'

Nan laughed too, not taking him seriously, which was what he'd wanted. He did not want to worry her. Or Mum. Or anyone else. If he ever tried to tell any adult the truth they would have him carted off to the funny farm. Certainly, they would never *believe* him, which meant they would never *see* Abandinus and the other gods, which would only convince them more thoroughly that he was mad—or just playing a big trick on them, along with Tim and Gracie.

No. Far better to let everyone go on as normal. His small gods secret would have to stay just between him and Tim and Gracie. The Chosen Three. He smiled at that, remembering Gracie's chain email. The Chosen Three. It made them sound as if they had superpowers. And after the tennis thing, he was beginning to think that they just might.

'For heaven's sake!' said Nan. 'Get out of the road!'

Kevin snapped out of dreaming about the gods. 'What was that?' he asked, as Nan veered the car violently to the right and then drove on, muttering.

'Some stupid woman in the road,' she said, glancing in her rear-view mirror. 'Must have dropped something. She certainly wasn't paying attention to the traffic! She's gone now.'

Nan waved him off at the school gates and drove her little red Peugeot off round the corner. The windows of the school hall were aglow with multicoloured disco lights and the bass thud of a chart hit was already resounding through the building. Tim gave a shout and ran up the road to meet him. He was wearing skinny blue jeans and a dark blue and black two-tone T-shirt which looked as if it had been dipped in petrol. His hair had been teased into little black spikes all over his head. He looked good, Kevin had to admit. His cool mate.

'Shouldn't you be DJing?' he asked, as they filed into the school with a queue of other kids, all wearing stuff they were never normally seen in past the playground gates.

'Nah—not till eight thirty. Then I get half an hour to do my set,' said Tim as he handed in his quid and the little yellow slip at the door. Kevin was relieved. He needed to be able to hang around with Tim, getting his nerve up to ask Emma to dance.

The hall was decorated with red, white, and blue flags, some British and some American. In the disco lights it was barely recognizable as the dull, yellow-walled assembly room of the day. Mr Simmonds was running the disco, as usual. He wore a glittery wig over his thinning grey hair and a shiny silver waistcoat which didn't quite cover the words MAD FOR IT on his T-shirt. Kevin shook his head, laughing. Mr Simmonds still did quite a good job of the disco, though. He had CD players, an MP3 and twin decks, where you could mess around with tracks on vinyl, mixing tracks live, like Tim liked to do.

The music was loud and over by the canteen

hatch volunteer teachers and mums were selling cans of Coke, Sprite, and Dr Pepper and sweets and crisps. Clusters of girls were grouped around the room, looking strange and alien in their disco clothes, giggling together and glancing at the boys with a mixture of interest and scorn. Kevin leant against the back of a chair and scoured the room for Emma Greening. At first he couldn't see her and felt a stab of disappointment. Maybe he'd have no chance to talk to her at all, let alone ask her to dance. She wasn't coming. Then Tim nudged him and pointed. There she was, standing by the emergency exit doors with two of her friends. She was wearing a short red dress with red earrings and her hair up in a high ponytail. She had on high-heeled strappy sandals and golden bangles on her wrists. As he stared across the room, she turned her perfect face in his direction and smiled.

At Mike Mears.

Mike Mears pushed past, his beefy right shoulder knocking Kevin sideways, and strode straight towards Emma, who smiled up at him and giggled. Her two friends smiled and giggled too.

'You gonna stand for that?' said Tim, prodding him in the arm. 'Go on! Get over there!'

'Not yet,' said Kevin. 'I need a drink first.' And he went to get a Coke.

'Hello, Kevin,' said a friendly voice in the queue. He looked round to see Greg, the professor, wearing T-shirt and jeans and looking very un-professorial. 'How's the project going?'

'Um—good,' said Kevin, glancing around uneasily. He didn't really want to talk about Celtic gods with his classmates within earshot.

Greg seemed to understand. He grinned. 'No more run-ins with Arimanius, then!' he said, more quietly. 'I think that's his name, isn't it? Your lion-headed god?' It jolted Kevin until he realized that Greg couldn't be taking any of this seriously. He really did think it was just a quirky little hobby.

'Um . . . yeah . . . that's his name. And no run-ins!' he grinned. 'He wouldn't dare try to come in here anyway,' he added. 'Not with *that* going on.' He pointed to where a bunch of kids were energetically doing the actions to 'YMCA'.

Greg laughed and winced. 'Yep! *That* would hold back any number of underworld deities!'

But as Kevin turned, his Coke and his change in his hand, Greg leaned his head in so he could be heard against the barrage of teenagers yelling, '*Young man! There's no need to feel down!*' He put his hand on Kevin's shoulder and said, 'None of my business, Kevin, but if you ever need to talk about . . . anything . . . ancient god related or not, you *can* find me here at the school, or at the community centre.'

Kevin stared up at him for a few seconds, trying to read the man's face. What did he think was going on? Greg smiled back, his cheek patterned by oily blobs of disco light, patted him on the shoulder again and turned back to the refreshments bar. Kevin felt a sudden urge to tell him everything. It would be very reassuring to get an adult viewpoint. But there was every chance Greg would decide it was all a big wind-up. Or worse, that he was losing his mind, and professional help was called for. It was too big a risk to take.

For a person with several gods on his side, it was a bit pathetic, thought Kevin, twenty minutes later, as Tim headed over to the disco decks to get ready for his half hour slot. He still couldn't summon up the nerve to speak to Emma, even though Mike Mears was now gyrating on the dance floor to a David Bowie track, flicking back his floppy hair and posing with great concentration alongside Rob White and Chad, and Emma was just standing with her friends, curling her ponytail around her slender fingers.

'Oh, will you just go and *talk* to her!' Gracie suddenly arrived at his elbow. She was wearing a purple dress with a high, Chinese style collar, and shiny black knee high boots. Her hair was loose and a bit wild and she'd smudged some dark grey glittery stuff around her eyes, making them look astonishingly turquoise. She looked *nothing* like any of the girls here. Even the other American ones were all in the latest fashions, with little sandals and lots of bangles and dangly earrings but Gracie was a thing apart. He grinned at her. He *liked* the way she looked. Anything else just wouldn't be Gracie. He felt oddly proud of her.

'C'mon. You're never going to know if you never try,' she grinned at him, giving him a nudge. 'Go!'

'All right—I will—when the time's right,' he muttered, swirling the dregs of his Coke around in the can.

'Time's never gonna be right, shrine boy,' said Gracie and began to propel him across the dance floor.

'No, no, no!' whimpered Kevin as Tim made a thumbs-up gesture from the disco decks, where he was preparing to start his live mixing.

'O-K!' said Gracie, taking his can from him and putting it on a nearby table. 'Just dance with me for a while then. Kind of warm up to it.'

Kevin gulped and began to move to the music as best he could. He stepped from one foot to the other, rocking his arms from left to right.

'Oh my!' giggled Gracie, dancing in front of him

with perfect ease and easy rhythm. 'You really *can't* dance!'

'Well, thanks!' huffed Kevin, coming to a halt.

'No, no—you can't do *that*!' laughed Gracie. 'Now you look like a cranky toddler! Just—look—do this . . . '

She moved her shoulders to the music and her arms and hands just seemed to follow on naturally, then her hips joined in and then her feet.

'Well, it's easier for girls,' muttered Kevin, trying his best to copy her.

'What, in these heels? Are you kidding me? C'mon. Surely you've danced before.'

'The only time I danced,' said Kevin, 'was when Ancasta *made* me. *Then* I could have got into the English National Ballet!' He remembered the horror and the anger of the forced dancing . . . but also the astonishing nimbleness of his limbs as they had bent to Maponus's music with perfect timing and grace.

'Hmmm,' said Gracie. 'Wait here a minute.' And she dashed away, heading past Emma and through the emergency exit doors into the darkening evening.

Kevin sagged onto the nearest chair, feeling dejected. The dance floor was getting fuller and some boys had even got girls up to dance. How did they *ever* find the nerve? And yeah, now—of *course*—Mike

Mears was heading for Emma. He strolled through the dancers and went directly to the best-looking girl in their year, took her hand and led her out into the middle of the floor. Emma was giggling and looking a little self conscious but soon she dropped into an easy shuffle around the dance floor. It wasn't *proper* girl-boy dancing, Kevin told himself. It was just dancing about to fast music, kind of *looking* at each other. But even so . . . he sighed. He might as well give up.

Tim started doing his set and the floor got a bit fuller as more boys joined in. Tim's music was a bit blokey—lots of ska and hip-hop. Kevin wished Gracie would come back. At least he looked a bit less like a loser when she was talking to him. He remembered that she'd said she was coming with Chloë Carpenter. She'd probably gone to find her to hang out with, rather than be around *him*.

Emma was now back with her friends but Mike Mears and Chad were hovering around them like wasps at a picnic. Kevin realized that Number 3 on his list was probably never going to happen. He should just accept it. He shivered as a cool breeze wound around the sweaty fug of the disco hall. And he stood up.

He walked across the floor, avoiding Steve Pitt and two other boys spinning around on their backs, and headed straight for Emma. His steps were steady and confident, his head held high, his hips and feet moving in time to the music, his eyes fixed upon the prize.

Only problem *was*—it wasn't *him*. His body was in the grip of somebody else's control. Rolling his eyes to the right, with a little gurgle of horror, Kevin saw Gracie, grinning at him from the emergency exit doors. And leaning in the doorway next to her was Ancasta.

The goddess had taken control again, despite her promise to Abandinus, and now there was no doubt about it. He was going to ask Emma to dance. Whether he liked it or not.

Chapter 19

Emma looked surprised as he walked up to her. Possibly because there was a kind of fight going on across his face. Ancasta was forcing Kevin to smile and raise an eyebrow as if he was Roger Moore in a 1980s Bond movie and *Kevin* was desperately trying to stop smiling and pull the eyebrow back down.

'Hello, Emma,' he said, in a voice much more controlled than his face.

'Well, if it isn't the Nose of God!' sniggered Mike Mears, punching him on the shoulder in a fake friendly way. Chad gave a barking laugh, like a hyena.

'Well, if it isn't the face of *Smug* Magazine,' said Kevin, counter-punching Mike's shoulder so hard he flew backwards and ended up spinning on the floor next to Steve Pitt.

Emma gasped along with her two friends and the American student. 'Shall we?' said Kevin, taking her hand. Not waiting for a yes, he led her onto the dance floor, skirting Mike Mears, who was coming to a halt in his unexpected break-dance and looking thunderous. Emma gasped again as she was suddenly expertly twirled, the soles of her strappy sandals spinning on the hall floor, her ponytail and the skirt of her red dress marking two horizontal arcs through the air. Then Kevin pulled her into a dance where music pulsed through him from his shoulders to his hips to his toes and out to the very tips of his fingers. Once again, he was Ancasta's puppet, and even Emma seemed to be controlled as she spun and shimmied and raised her arms and flicked her hair. Over on the decks, Tim gaped across the whirling vinyl, his hand falling away and the headphone pressed to one ear tumbling over his shoulder.

A small circle of clear dance floor formed as more and more students stepped away and stood to watch. Kevin was somewhat conflicted. He was raging at Ancasta and Gracie and tried to shoot them an angry glare as they stood, unheeded by everybody else, in the doorway. Ancasta was wearing a look of intense concentration as she choreographed him from left to right. But even as he tried to glare, Kevin had to admit that winding around his fury was growing excitement and also a little snaking satisfaction. He was the centre of attention. And a part of him was *loving it*.

As the fast-paced track that Tim had been playing drew to its end, Kevin expected Ancasta to let him go, and allow the rest of the disco to continue normally. He expected wrong. With a deft flick of one wrist Tim suddenly flipped a larger disc from the cardboard box next to the decks. His eyes stretching with amazement, for this was not his plan, Tim threw the long player onto the spool, clicked the dial from 45 to 33 rpm and seamlessly mixed a new song into the set. As the staccato beat of strings, drums, and piano rolled from the speakers there were murmurs of confusion and amusement from the disco-goers.

Emma stared at Kevin as if she was in a dream, her large eyes round and dazed. She couldn't believe what she was hearing. Neither could he. 'Straight from the mean streets of downtown Argentina . . . ' whispered Ancasta, suddenly at his shoulder, her cool water hand on the back of his neck. 'Feel the passion!' It was a *tango*.

Therrrum-dum-dum-dum . . . thudded the bass, and Kevin, with a squeak of terror only just masked by the music, grabbed Emma by the hands and pulled her towards him as Ancasta floated away. Emma gave a little yelp of shock, her warm breath smelling of Dr Pepper, and then a wavering cry of astonishment as she found herself stepping out in Latin America's most passionate dance—with *Kevin Rutley*!

Gracie ran across the floor, and just as the couple executed a swift about turn, their arms and hands outstretched and rigid and their chins switching from left to right in perfect time, she tucked a long-stemmed red rose between Emma's teeth. Emma bit down upon the green stem, gathered from the school garden, her face a picture of utter amazement and her feet trotting along in perfect step with Kevin's and the Argentinian beat.

Even the teachers were transfixed now. Mr Simmonds stood with his packet of cheesy snacks frozen in the air, gaping. Mrs Bathwood and Miss Archer were shaking their heads and murmuring. Some of the boys were whooping and the girls were squeaking excitedly and applauding at every tango turn. The break dancers were now all on their feet, staring. Mike Mears stood motionless among them, his face dark with fury.

All this Kevin could see only in a blur as the goddess drove him and the girl of his dreams along the floor. The disco dancing was one thing. But a *tango*? He knew he should be enjoying the moment, but as the dance went on he began to feel increasingly uneasy amid the exhilaration. How could he *explain* this to everyone? How? That he'd been secretly attending Latin American and disco dance lessons for the past year? How would *that* go down next time he met Steve Pitt and his cronies in the toilet block? Amid the whirl of lights and music and the dizzying control the goddess had over him, he could barely see Emma in his arms. He had finally got exactly what he wanted. Yes! Number 3 on his list . . . but how could this possibly end well?

Yet it *was* ending. The last few chords of the tango were pounding out and suddenly he was sweeping Emma down in a low arc, holding her waist, her dark hair skimming the floor as she arched back with one hand outstretched, the other on his shoulder, one foot pointed out and the rose still clenched between her teeth.

Da—da—da—da-di-DAH! Daaaa-DAH!

A storm of whooping, cheering, and applause erupted around them. Kevin stood up, and helped Emma stand, smoothly leading her into a curtsey to fit within his bow. After this final flourish, Ancasta, back in the doorway, grinning like a goddess who'd got the cream, finally let go of him. As Emma's posse crowded around her, squealing with excitement and admiration, Kevin staggered backwards, all grace and balance gone.

He turned round just in time to see Mike Mears coming for him. His new sporty reflexes did not kick in this time. He took the punch full in the gut.

Kevin and Mike Mears shot out of the emergency exit, a tornado of fists, elbows, and knees. How the teachers missed it would be an absolute mystery to him for ever afterwards, but somehow not one of them spotted the fighting boys. Nor did any kids form an excited ring around them. As soon as Kevin had recovered from the punch in his gut, looking up from where he'd slumped against a wall to see Mike Mears curling his lip at him and promising more if he didn't stay away from Emma Greening, fury flooded through him and he'd sprung to his feet and thumped Mike on the jaw.

The fight had been coming for some time, he now realized. Probably since the football field thing.

Instinctively they took it outside into the cool evening air. No excited posse of onlookers trailed after them, shouting 'Fight!' It was almost as if they were cloaked in invisibility. Unnoticed, shoving and punching all the way across the grass outside the hall, they ending up scuffling in the dirt by the staff car park. Although Kevin had been turned sporty he was not any stronger, physically, than he had been a week ago. But he was angry—at Ancasta for controlling him again, at Gracie for calling her in, at Abandinus for just not showing up for the last two days, at his dad for crying for Lorna . . . so he fought like a demon; dirty and without rules. There was kicking and hair pulling and scratching as well as punching and shoving. It wasn't noble. He was getting as much as he was giving and it hurt a lot, but it was as if someone else was feeling the pain. Dimly, he knew he'd feel it all much later.

It might have gone on for minutes on end—because no teacher was coming and no mate was pulling him or Mike off, saying 'Leave 'im! It's not worth it!' Kevin felt a grim satisfaction in grabbing a handful of Mike's stupid poncey hair and tearing at it and Mike was getting similar kicks out of twisting his nose which was still tender since the football incident.

Kevin could smell and taste blood. His own, most likely, mixed in with the scented flowers in the hedge around the school garden, as they slid and scrambled towards it, and the gritty dust from the tarmac and the cheap aftershave which Mike had sprayed all over his neck and armpits earlier that evening. Neither one of them was for giving in.

But as he rolled over, trying to pummel his foe in the ribs, Kevin caught sight of something which shot hot, scared adrenalin through him, way beyond the violent acid already pounding in his veins.

He rolled over with double vigour and shoved Mike away from him. Getting to his knees Kevin glanced at the boy as he scrambled up onto his feet and readied himself for another attack. '*Stop*,' said Kevin, in a voice that came out low and croaky. Mike paused, unsure, wondering whether Kevin was going to give in. He started shaking twigs and grit out of his hair.

'Get back inside,' said Kevin. He was shocked at the cold steel in his voice. Because inside he was bubbling with terror.

'Yeah, right—like I'm taking orders from a snot-rag like you, cringeing in the dirt!' sneered Mike, although he looked uncertain, as if he was picking up on the terror. The *real* terror.

'You've won,' said Kevin. 'You beat me up. Go.'

And this time Mike did. He glanced around, trying to work out what was happening, and then he ran back towards the disco hall. Whether he looked back or not, Kevin didn't know. His own eyes were locked on the dark light streaming from the school garden undergrowth and the red-eyed silhouette inside it.

Chapter 20

The dark light cascaded around jagged teeth and the red eyes glowed like volcanic pits, but as his horrified pupils adjusted to the truth of what lay before them, Kevin saw that the lion-headed man was smiling at him. Grinning, in fact—like a gargoyle. And clapping its hideous clawed hands.

'Arimanius,' said Kevin, still on his knees. 'Why are you here?'

'This is my cradle,' rumbled the lion-head. 'You came to me. I knew you would. Pray, then. Pray to the dark light.'

'No,' said Kevin. 'You're not my god.'

'I am anyone's god,' said Arimanius. 'I am a god of the underworld. And anyone can meet me, at any time, if I deem them worthy. In you . . . I see so much potential. Did you not enjoy the sport? The sweet rush of pain? The taste of blood?'

'Get away from me,' gulped Kevin. The hair on his arms and neck was standing up so straight it was prickling all over his skin.

'But you called *me*,' protested Arimanius. 'With your anger and your violence. I am impressed. You fight well. You fight *dark*. So turn to me, and you can take what you wish for, not just accept what is given.'

'What's given is *fine*!' said Kevin. 'I don't want any more.'

'Are you *sure*, Kevin Rutley?' smiled Arimanius. 'You seem like a boy who seeks much in life. Will the meagre rations of pleasure that you can scrabble at in your mortal world be enough? I can bring so much more to you. The underworld is an endless sea of power for those who know how to use it.'

Behind Arimanius a cave-mouth had grown up out of the earth, leading down to a subterranean world filled with seething, shifting dark light. It repelled him. No. That was not true. It repelled *most* of him. Something in him felt tugged forward, fascinated, hungry. He thought, fleetingly, of a drug addict struggling against the endless pull towards one last destructive narcotic hit; the blistering hot joy followed by grimness and misery.

Arimanius was staring at him, his eyes like red

221

marbles, veined and glowing. Mesmerizing. 'You see. The dark light speaks to you. We both know it.'

'No,' gulped Kevin, leaning back. 'I don't want it. I don't want anything from you.'

'Are you sure?' Arimanius cocked his huge, horrifying head to one side. 'Is your world so perfect, Kevin Rutley? Are you *sure* you will want for nothing else tonight?'

'Yes—I'm sure,' said Kevin, getting to his feet. 'You've got nothing I want.'

Arimanius smiled deeper. 'Not yet,' he said.

And the dark light vanished, taking the cave opening and the underworld god with it.

Tim ran up to him the moment he stepped back inside the hall. 'What happened?' he shouted. The disco was still in full flood and Mike Mears was nowhere to be seen.

Kevin walked around the dancers, vaguely aware of Emma Greening and her knot of girls staring at him. He made for the boys' toilets, hoping he wouldn't find Mike and his friends in there already. He didn't. The toilets were empty. Tim followed him in.

'What *happened* to you?' he asked again, as Kevin washed his face, which mercifully—and strangely—was not covered in bruises. He'd scored only one red scratch under his right ear. He realized he'd taken most of Mike's blows around his ribs.

'Well?' demanded Tim. 'One minute you were tangoing all over the place like a championship ballroom dancer—the next you were gone!'

'Didn't you see Mike Mears thump me?' gurgled Kevin, through the water in his cupped palms.

'What? He hit you?'

'Yes! Right after the dancing stopped, and then we were outside scrapping. And *nobody* noticed! And you know what . . . ' He looked at Tim, getting ready to tell him about Arimanius and how he felt as if the underworld god had *made* the fight happen and *made* nobody come to stop it and *enjoyed* the violence.

But then he couldn't. He couldn't tell Tim because he couldn't admit the nasty satisfaction he *had* felt, hurting Mike. And he didn't dare think that maybe it wasn't Arimanius who had made that happen too. *You fight well. You fight dark*. No. *No*. Blood lust had never been on his wish list.

'What?' said Tim.

'I can't believe Gracie called Ancasta in,' said Kevin, abruptly changing direction.

'It *was* brilliant, though!' said Tim. 'I mean, she controlled *me* too—made me put that tango record on. It was well weird. But your dancing was so cool. Emma

Greening's out there now, just dribbling about *you*. Get out there! Bask in it!'

Kevin stared into the mirror, wondering if Cuda and her little cucullati might make a comeback, to warn him again about Arimanius. What was it she had said? '*You have a lion too.*' And '*I do not know if you can be helped.*' He shivered. No woman looked back at him through his reflection. Only Tim stood behind him, bouncing up and down on the balls of his feet and urging him back out into the disco to revel in his dancing glory.

Kevin followed him back into the thudding music and the wildly gyrating disco lights. He got himself another Coke, using the last of his money, and hoped Tim wouldn't see how much his hands were shaking as he opened the can. He had said no to Arimanius. He had said *no*. And that should be that. Had he passed a test? If so, it hadn't been a difficult one. Who would want to accept favours from a red-eyed lion-headed underworld god with a freaky dark-light show going on behind his teeth?

'Whoa—if it isn't Fred Astaire!' Gracie arrived at his side, grinning from ear to ear. Even Chloë Carpenter, pausing a few steps behind her in a long brown dress and gold hoop earrings, looked at Kevin with new respect.

224

Kevin gave Gracie a hard look. 'You shouldn't have done that, Gracie.'

'But it was perfect!' Grace dropped her voice to a conspiratorial whisper. 'You needed to dance and you couldn't do it on your own . . . so Ancasta and I just gave you a little help. What are gods for if not to help?'

Kevin turned on her so fast he spilt his Coke. 'You don't know *what* gods are for!' he said, in a hard, choked voice. 'You have *no idea*!'

Gracie stepped back and stared at him, the fun and teasing draining from her face. He felt bad at once, but something else flickered in him and made him add: 'Next time you want to start playing with the gods, just remember—they're a lot better at playing with *us*. And *they* never get broken.'

Gracie lifted her chin and then turned and walked back to Chloë without a word.

'A bit harsh,' murmured Tim.

Kevin slurped some Coke. 'I've just had enough of her interfering in my life.' He glanced over to where Emma and her friends were standing, talking to each other excitedly and glancing across at *him*. 'Let's go over,' he said.

* * *

225

As the disco drew to a close, Mr Simmonds put slow tracks on and now the intense emotional fog of fascination and fear descended as boys tried to summon up the nerve to ask a girl to dance a slowie and girls agonized over whether they would be asked and what to do if they were. Kevin and Tim had no such problem. Emma and her friends made it quite clear that the ballroom dancing champion was on their hit list and so was his disco-decks mate.

As Kevin led Emma out onto the dance floor for the second time that evening he expected to feel elated. Thrilled. He had diligently buried his experience with Arimanius at the back of his mind and now he was ready to see the benefit of Ancasta and Gracie's meddling. All he needed to do was shuffle around in a clinch with Emma to a cheesy seventies ballad. He'd dreamed of this for months.

'So . . . how did you learn to dance like that?' asked Emma, in her high voice, as they moved in a slow circle, holding each other's elbows.

'Oh—that wasn't me,' he said. 'I was temporarily possessed by a passing goddess.'

Emma giggled. For quite a long time. She anchored her hands around his neck and said, 'You're so *funny*!'

'But you danced really well too,' he said, putting

226

his arms around her waist and feeling extraordinarily awkward.

'Oh, I used to do ballet,' she said. 'But I got bored of it. It's really hard work. There are easier ways to be famous.'

'Oh,' he said. 'You're going to be famous, are you?'

She giggled and tossed back her hair. 'Well—yeah! Of *course*.'

'What for?'

She giggled again and shrugged, as if he should be able to guess.

'What . . . modelling or something?'

She giggled some more. She giggled a *lot*, Kevin was realizing. 'I've already sent pictures off to the London agencies,' she said.

'And what will you do if that doesn't work out?' asked Kevin, realizing too late that he sounded like a careers teacher.

'It *will* work out,' she said, looking at him as if he was an idiot.

'Yeah—yeah, of course it will.'

'What are *you* going to do?' she asked. 'To be famous.'

'Um,' Kevin wrinkled his brow. 'I'm not really planning to be famous.'

Emma looked astonished. 'But . . . *everyone* wants to be famous!' she said. 'Like—on TV and stuff. I'm going to be in *OK!* magazine and everything.'

'What for?' asked Kevin.

'Duh!' She looked at him as if he was simple-minded. 'Being famous!'

'Well . . . ' He really couldn't think *what* to say next. 'I'm sure *OK!* magazine will be all over you. And *Hello*. And *Heat*. And *Chit-Chat* and *Closer* and *Stalker* and *Now That's What I Call Famous* magazine.'

Her giggle went off again, sounding a lot like his digital alarm clock on a school morning. 'Oh, you are *so funny*!' she said.

'Three Times a Lady' was only halfway through.

'So she said to me, "You *never* will!" and I'm like, "I *so* will!",' giggled Emma into his neck as 'Three Times a Lady' went seamlessly into 'I'm Saving All My Love For You'.

'So . . . I did! Right there and then. It was just *amazing*. I *so* did it! Can you believe that?'

'Wow! You really *did*?' said Kevin. He hadn't the *faintest idea* what Emma had *so* done. His mind had drifted as he stared around the dance floor. Tim was dancing with Abby Wilson, one of Emma's good

228

looking friends, and looking very pleased about it, but he couldn't see Gracie anywhere—and he had to admit to himself that he was feeling bad about yelling at her earlier. She really had been trying to help.

He was also expecting Mike Mears to come lording it across the dance floor at any moment, too, having 'beaten' him—but there was no sign of the boy and this, oddly, was worrying him even more.

' . . . so nobody could, like, *believe* I'd done it. It was like, just *so amazing*,' Emma was trilling on. 'And they were *so* not going to say anything like *that* to me again. And you'll never guess what it was, after all that?'

There was a pause as Emma's lovely eyes narrowed into his own. 'Kevin! I said what do you think it was?'

'Ummm,' said Kevin. What? He hadn't a clue. What was he supposed to say? *Orange? A big square thing? Cheese flavoured?*

'Amazing?' he guessed, with a hopeful grin.

She giggled. 'You're making fun of me,' she said, and pouted.

'No—no I'm not,' he said. 'You *are* amazing. That's all.' *Yep. Amazingly boring*, said a voice in his head.

'So where's your funny American friend?' asked

Emma as they shuffled on round. His palms felt sweaty on her waist. He hoped she wouldn't notice. He wished he could feel what he wanted to feel. What he had always imagined he'd feel. Not what he *did*.

'I don't know. Around somewhere,' he said, looking about the room again.

'I *love* her look,' said Emma, with a snort and a smug twist of her pretty mouth. 'So . . . weird. Like . . . what are those black boots about? In the middle of summer?' She giggled again and shook back her hair. 'Maybe she's going fishing afterwards.'

'Ah,' said Kevin, abruptly letting go of her with a wave of both disbelief and relief. 'You've reminded me! She *is* going fishing. And I'm going with her. Seeya.'

As he walked swiftly away, Emma stood on the dance floor staring after him with her mouth opening and closing like a landed trout. She was absolutely staggered.

'Kev! Wait up!' Tim skidded up beside him in the corridor. 'Where are you going? You're not telling me you just dumped Emma Greening on the dance floor! You've got to be kidding me!'

'I just remembered there was somewhere else I had to be,' said Kevin, still walking.

'Where? Are you *nuts*? You've waited for this moment since Year Seven!'

'Have you seen Gracie?' he asked, looking up and down the corridor which stretched from the school hall to the main reception entrance where teachers and PTA members were counting up the takings and having a glass of wine. Some of the younger kids' parents were coming in, too, to collect them.

'No, not since you had a go at her,' said Tim.

'Mike Mears?'

'No, not since your tango. Why?'

'Oh . . . look, I don't care about him,' sighed Kevin. 'I just wanted to say sorry to Gracie.' He paused by the girls' toilets. Chloë Carpenter was just coming out. 'Hey, Chloë,' he said, 'is Gracie in there?'

'Stop hanging around the girls' toilets, you perv,' said Chloë, unhelpfully.

'She's out in the car park,' said Jane Philips as she passed them.

Kevin and Tim headed back through the hall and across to the car park where a number of English and American students were running around incongruously in their disco gear, playing some kind of volleyball. Some of the girls had taken off their high-heeled shoes or sandals and were running barefoot.

'Has anyone seen Gra—' began Kevin, loudly, and then a hand fell upon his shoulder.

He spun round, ready to apologize, but instead

231

gasped with surprise. 'Dad! What are you doing here?' He had arranged to walk back with Tim this evening; he wasn't expecting to be collected.

The flickering disco lights lit up one side of Dad's face, leaving the other in shadow. His father's visible eye looked hooded and his mouth was a straight, compressed line. 'Son,' he said, and in that one word, a sudden collapse occurred inside Kevin. He knew right away that something awful had happened.

'Who is it?' he whispered.

'Your nan. She was in a car accident,' he said. 'They took her to hospital. Your mum's with her now. Come on. We have to go.'

Chapter 21

Dad's Audi smelt of leather and air freshener. The little green plastic emerald in its card swung from the glove compartment handle, sending out a chemical trail of something meant to be flowery. It made him feel sick. The motion of it, rocking back and forth, back and forth, nearly made him scream.

Nan was dying.

Little green emerald. Swing right. Swing left.

Nan was dying.

CarFresh, it read on the card. *CarFresh*. Patent pending.

Nan was dying.

Swing right. Swing left. For more information on other *CarFresh* products go to www.car-fresh.com

Dying.

Or call the CareLine on 0800 111 778.

Hello! CareLine! My nan is in hospital and she's

dying. Can you freshen my car? Can you freshen my car? Can you—

'*Kevin!*' Dad was staring at him. Kevin realized he'd wrenched the CarFresh emerald off the glove compartment door and cracked it hard against the dashboard.

'Kevin! It's all right, son. She's in the best place. They're taking care of her.'

Kevin looked round at his dad and his dad looked carefully through the windscreen.

The hospital was a blur of polished floors and pale yellow energy-saving light panels overhead, as he and Dad checked in with three different receptions and were pointed deeper and deeper into the warren of corridors. At last they found Mum, curled up in a corner of another waiting area, a plastic cup of cold tea in her hand. She looked lost and small, like a child. She put the tea down and got up to hug Kevin as soon as she saw them. Her cheek was wet. She didn't say anything and a little more of his insides collapsed.

'How is she?' asked Dad.

'The same,' said Mum in a flat, squashed voice. She pulled Kevin across to the brown leather-effect seats and made him sit down. 'She was in a crash on the way home,' she explained. 'A bad one. She's hurt her head and she's in a coma.' She gulped and then took a steadying breath through her nose.

234

'Will she be OK?' asked Kevin, feeling his eyes fill up. Mum's face, blurry in front of him, creased into a half smile as she shrugged.

'We don't know,' she said. 'She . . . she might not, Kevin. You need to know that.' She bit her lip and took another breath.

'Can we do anything?' said Kevin, scrubbing at his eyes.

'No, mate,' said Dad, sitting down on the other seat beside him. 'We just have to wait and hope . . . and pray, I guess.'

> *What Kevin Rutley Wants*
> *1. Nan to live.*
> *None of the other stuff matters now.*
> *Dear Abandinus. Dear god. My god.*
> *The God god. Any god. Any god listening.*
> *Please.*
> *Let Nan live.*

Hours passed. 11 p.m. Midnight. 1 a.m. Mum was allowed in to see Nan but nobody else was. Kevin wasn't sure whether he wanted to or not. He could only imagine Nan being *Nan*. Smiling, laughing, scolding, giving him embarrassing hugs, driving her Peugeot, buying him a toy Labrador, making him drink Coke when he was car sick. He could not imagine her any other way. At least . . . he *could*. A vision of her face all bruised and swollen and cut, with those little plastic tubes running into her nose, flashed through his mind. He just didn't want to know that it was real. If he saw it and it was real, there would be another collapse inside him. And maybe nowhere would be left to offer a perch for his hope.

Worse, much worse, than this thought, was the idea that this was his fault. Because now he knew Arimanius was right. He *did* want something else this night. A new prayer. And if he had not attracted the attention of the underworld god, maybe this would not have happened.

Dear Abandinus, he murmured, over and over again. *Let Nan live. Please. Please hear me. Let Nan live.*

Now his belly crunched up and froze inside him as he remembered something else—Nan swerving her car on the way to the disco. 'Some stupid woman in the road,' she had said. 'Must have dropped something.' So, the woman would have been bent over on the tarmac. He knew now who it was. Saitada, the Goddess of Grief, weeping and wailing the portent of death, right in front of them. And he hadn't even noticed. He had been way too focused on himself.

Even with all the warnings, from Saitada and Cuda and the cucullati, even seeing the way that

Ancasta had reacted to the name 'Arimanius', he had thought he was handling it just fine. He and Tim and Gracie had been smugly celebrating their good fortune just this afternoon. Look at *us*! The Chosen Three!

Now he realized what the Greek myth storytellers had meant when they used the word 'hubris'. It was when a mere mortal thought he could handle the gods and didn't need to watch his step. A kind of pride. And it always led to downfall. Strutting about to impress Emma, revelling in his new sportiness, fighting Mike Mears, even getting smug about his spots disappearing. Oh yes—and shrugging off the attempts of an underworld god to lure him into the dark. This was all hubris. And now he was paying for it.

At 2.15 a.m., when the doctor said there was no change and Mum told Dad to take him home, he didn't protest. He did not want to leave Mum or Nan, but he desperately wanted to get to the shrine and light the candles and get Abandinus to help. He'd committed the offence of hubris and there was nothing he could do now but throw himself on the mercy of the gods.

The problem was that he had to wait for Dad to go to sleep. By the time the snoring began in the bottom bunk it was 3.10 a.m. and just beginning to get light in the eastern sky. Kevin crept out of bed and downstairs, collecting the matches from the drawer in the kitchen. The cool pre-dawn air made him shiver inside his thin pyjamas as he shuffled up the garden in his untied trainers. Abandinus's shrine stood in its usual place, awaiting his attention. He tried to light the candles but there was a breeze in just the wrong direction which kept blowing out the match before the wick could ignite. He began to shake with frustration and fear. Maybe it was too late anyway. Maybe Nan had died and Mum just hadn't been able to bring herself to phone them and tell them. He tried his fifth match and then, when this failed, laid his head on the shrine and wept.

And as he wept he sent up a prayer to Abandinus. It didn't even have words. Abandinus must *know* how he was needed. He must. He would come. He would save Nan. He was a *god*, for god's sake! A *god*. He must be able to save her. And Kevin was his chosen one, wasn't he? He'd been good and done the shrine and the hymn thing, with Tim, and got some more followers with Gracie's help. He'd been good.

But Kevin also realized that he'd been selfish. He hadn't done any of that stuff for any noble reason. He was just excited about what a god could do for him. On the other hand, Abandinus hadn't *asked* him to pray for anything noble. He had only asked for a shrine and a hymn and some worship—that was all about *him*, wasn't it? Maybe he wasn't the kind of god that really cared much about world peace and human suffering and all that. Certainly, nothing he'd seen of any of the gods had led him to believe they cared much about anyone at all. Ancasta was a bit shallow and catty when it came down to it. Semitas was bad-tempered and resentful. Maponus was vague and vain. Abandinus was vainer still. True, he *had* stopped Ancasta from 'damaging' his chosen one, but that was probably just a matter of annoyance because she was playing with Kevin—and Kevin was *Abandinus's* plaything.

But Kevin knew he had to stop thinking this way. He *had* to believe Abandinus was good and godly and would help him. He began to pray out loud, begging for Nan's life. 'Save her, and I will do whatever you want, Abandinus,' he begged. 'I'll be the best worshipper ever. Whatever you want. Just save her.'

By the time the pale yellow glow of dawn began to slide across the sky, Kevin was just slumped against the shrine, moving his lips. Abandinus had not come. *Abandon-us*, more like, thought Kevin. Anger began to surge through him. Where was his god when he *really* needed him? Ever since Arimanius had shown up, Abandinus had been harder and harder to reach.

239

Why? Because Kevin *really* needed him. When he had just wanted stupid stuff like a computer games console and a girl at school to notice him, *no* problem. But the moment he needed his god for something really important—*zip*, as Gracie would say.

Kevin ran back into the house, scrubbing at his eyes and trying to get a grip. He picked up the phone in the hallway and called Mum's mobile. She answered quickly but sounded sleepy and vague. 'Hello? Yes?'

'Mum—it's me. I can't sleep. What's happening?'

Mum sighed. 'It's much the same, love. Nan's still in a coma.'

'Well, that's . . . that's not so bad, is it?' he said. 'I mean . . . no news is good news, isn't it? She hasn't got worse.'

Mum sighed again. 'It doesn't really work like that, Kevin, with comas. The longer someone is in a coma . . . well . . . the less good it looks. We mustn't give up hope, sweetheart, but we need to be ready . . . to . . . ' She tailed off and Kevin found himself nodding miserably at the phone.

'Yeah, OK,' he said.

'It's really early,' said Mum. 'Go back to bed, love. You don't need to go to school if you don't want to.'

'OK,' he said.

'I will call you, the minute I hear anything, OK?' she said.

'OK. Bye.' Kevin put down the phone. Now he knew for sure. Abandinus *had* abandoned him just when he needed him the most. He sat down on the little stripy stool next to the telephone table and his bare ankle brushed against something furry. He reached down and pulled out the stuffed toy Labrador which Nan had bought for him at Houghton. He pressed it to his face, screwing up his eyes, and tried to get control of the feeling inside him. Rage. It was dark, dark rage. His own personal god was no good to him. He had been messed around and duped. And in his mind he could not help but see Arimanius. And he could not help but hear Arimanius saying, 'Take what you want. Not just what is given.'

He *needed* to take. He needed to take Nan's life and keep it safe. And what if Arimanius was an underworld god? What of it? Yes, he was scary. But so was Ancasta and so was Abandinus. They *looked* nice but they did horrible things, like possessing him and making him dance and whirling Gracie about in a tornado. What had Arimanius done to him? Nothing!

Kevin stood up and opened the front door. It was light now, although low cloud in the west lent a pearly grey shadow to the morning, in spite of the sun's rays in the east. Kevin bent to do up his laces and then ran out into the street.

'OK, Arimanius,' he called, pelting down towards the corner of the road, where the underworld god had first spoken to them all in a dream. 'You win. I'm coming.'

He flung himself at the lamp-post on the corner and stared wildly about. 'Come on, then!' he yelled. 'Where are you? Where are you now?!'

Nothing happened, except his rage grew even blacker. After a minute of waiting, he realized that he had only *actually* seen Arimanius at the school. All the other sightings had been in dreams, as far as he knew. Only at the school had he been certain that he was awake—and what had the god said? That this was his 'cradle'. Under a school! He kicked the lamp-post and ran on to Amberton Secondary, a light rain now spattering his cheeks as the cloud from the west crept across the sky, low and damp, blotting out the dawn light. It was growing later, and yet getting darker.

He ran full pelt, tipping himself forward and saving himself from falling with each desperate step towards the school, hurtling along the middle of the road, because it seemed faster than the flagstones of the pavement. The rain was coming harder now, soaking through his pyjamas and making the soles of his trainers squeak and squelch on the oily wet road. A jogger paused on the corner and stared at him. And he must have been a sight because he even heard the jogger call after him, before the sound was swept away by the pounding of his heart, pushing his blood around his body at ever greater speed, resounding in his ears.

He skidded as he turned the corner into the road his school was in, and for three seconds lay sprawled on the tarmac, a brand new graze stinging up his left leg and arm and elbow. He disregarded it as he'd disregarded the pain of fighting Mike Mears last night, and bounded up to the gate. He cursed and bashed his head against the wet metal bars in fury. It was sealed with a chain and a padlock. No matter, he told himself, and grabbed the blunt spikes at the top of the gate, finding a foothold in a cross-bar halfway up the gate. The gate and the fence were at least two metres high, but he swung himself up with an athletic spring that would have amazed and infuriated Rob White, had he seen it. And as he tilted across the top, before the spikes could find a soft spot to impale, he simply launched himself forward and landed on the concrete on the far side where a brutal whack jarred through his ankles, tipping him over onto his hands and knees with a yelp of pain.

He got up and ran to the far side of the staff car

park where the low hedges and undergrowth formed a dark green barrier between the cars and the school garden. Here was where Arimanius had appeared a few hours ago. Here. His eyes raked the undergrowth, seeking the dark light. *Desperate* for the dark light.

'Arimanius!' he yelled as the rain fell even harder, plastering his hair to his scalp and his pyjamas to his skin. 'You win! I'm back! You want me? Come now! Give me what I want! Prove you're not lying.'

And as much as he wanted to see the underworld god, he still could not help the voice in his head whimpering as the dark light began to shine out of the peaty earth. *Oh no not the dark light no not the dark light don't don't don't go to the oh not the dark light no . . .*

The clawed yellow fingernails came first, driving up through the soil at speed, and the bulky arms followed, longer than they should be, like a primate's arms, then the matted dark fur of the god's leonine head breached the surface and his red eyes rose up out of the roots and leaf litter, making Kevin whimper, in spite of his fury and his determination. Just the top of the god's curled black lip was out now, but dark light was streaming out from under it. The cave entrance he'd seen last night rose just above Arimanius like a stone hood, the hedge rising with it and tilting backwards. Rays of dark lights stretched out and moved towards Kevin's fingers, which were splayed on the edge of the tarmac as he bent over on his knees.

'Pray,' said Arimanius, exhaling more dark light and a bitter smell, like dead things.

'Will you save my nan?' croaked Kevin.

'Pray to the dark light,' said Arimanius. 'Take what you want, not what is given.'

'But can you save her?' yelled Kevin. 'Tell me!'

'Faith, Kevin,' said Arimanius. '*Belief.*' The dark light crept towards Kevin's fingers.

He screwed his eyes shut and tried to think. This was the *only* way . . . wasn't it? He felt sick. Horribly sick. Terrified and alone. If he didn't pray to Arimanius, Nan would die. The certainty of it was lapping around him like a cold puddle, seeping into him. He opened his eyes and saw the dark light lapping around him too, but not touching him. It was only three or four centimetres away from his fingers. All he had to do was reach across. He shifted his weight onto one hand and began to slide the other and Arimanius's dreadful smile grew wider and dark light fell from it like an oil slick.

SLAP. Another hand fell over his. The warmth of it took his breath away.

'Go back to the underworld. You're wrong. This one isn't yours.'

Kevin shrieked, 'NOOOO!' He struggled to move

his hand towards the dark light but he was pinned down. An arm went across his shoulders and throat. He flapped wildly with his unpinned hand as he was tilted back, but it was no good. A shaft of golden-white light was flashing around and it cut through the dark light like a laser, leaving the oily flow of Arimanius's awful exhalation cut into ribbons and recoiling like a squid's tentacles.

'You WILL come to me,' roared the god as he sank back into the earth and Kevin screamed. He was terrified the god would still claim him. And terrified that he might not.

Someone slapped him hard across the face. He stopped screaming. For a long time he did not even breathe, his lungs shut tight, just as they had in the dream. He slumped forward, seeing the hand still pinning his own to the ground, hearing a voice and having no clue who it was or where it came from.

Someone punched him on the chest. 'Breathe, Kevin! Breathe!' The impact made him snatch in a ragged breath and at last he looked up. The face that looked back at him was vaguely familiar. The man picked up a mirror and his teeth were chattering. 'Are you back? Did the dark light touch you? Did it? Did it touch you, Kevin?'

'No,' said Kevin, with a sob. 'And now she'll die. Now she'll die.'

Chapter 22

Greg McCrae dragged him to his feet and back across the car park to the school gates. The padlock was cracked in two. It had been old and rusty and had broken easily when hit with a large stone. The professor pushed the gate open and steered Kevin through it, past a dented car with no wing mirror.

'We need to get you home,' he said. 'You're in shock.'

'N-n-not home. No,' said Kevin, remembering that his dad was there and he could not hope to explain all this.

'OK, not home. We'll go back to the community centre. You can get dry there and have some sugary tea and tell me all about it.'

Kevin barely noticed the journey. His mind was in a slow, grey spin. Had he sentenced Nan to death? Had he just failed? Or had he just been saved? As soon as relief washed across him, horror at the outcome swamped him again.

Within minutes he found himself being led across the community centre floor, the main hall dim in the early morning light and smelling still of damp wood-block, and then through to a small, private room with dark wood panelling, shelves and shelves of books, a stone fireplace, and an aged sofa piled with threadbare cushions. Beyond this room was a small kitchen with old oak surfaces and lemon-painted wooden cabinets, and off *this* was a bathroom.

'These are my living quarters while I'm working here,' explained Greg. 'Go through to the bathroom and use the shower to warm yourself up. There's a fresh towel on the back of the door. Chuck your PJs out and I'll sling them in the tumble dryer. They'll be done in ten minutes. I'll make tea. Don't be too long.'

Kevin's mind went blank and he numbly followed Greg's directions. When he emerged from the shower, towelling himself dry, he found his pyjamas resting on a chair by the bathroom door, dry and warm. He got into them and went back out into the kitchen.

'Ah. Good. You look a lot better,' said Greg. Wearing running trousers and a zip–up runner's top, he was sitting at an old wooden table, with two mugs placed on it and a plate of ginger cake, cut into slices.

'Come on. Drink some tea. Eat some cake. It'll do you good.'

Kevin did as he was told. He had no urge to eat or drink, but something of the shock still in him made him obedient. The tea was sweet and seemed to unlock the clamped down feeling in his throat. The cake was shockingly spicy, even though he knew it a was just a standard Lyons bar cake, like his mum bought sometimes. It was as if he'd been away in space and had just landed back on earth—everything was new and intense.

'Better?' said Greg, at length, peering over his own mug of tea.

Kevin nodded.

'Why did you go to him?' asked Greg. 'You knew he was bad news. You were terrified of him. What made you do that?'

'How did you *know*?' asked Kevin, amazement beginning to dissolve his numbness.

'I didn't know. Not for sure,' said Greg, reaching for some cake. 'But it's not often a kid asks you about a lion-headed god, hot on the heels of describing the cucullati. Something about it spooked me. Something about *you* spooked me. Made me do a bit of research—into the small gods, and into you. Turns out you weren't the type to be winding me up. Your mate,

Tim, yes, but not you. And Gracie gave me some clues, too, when I asked about your "project". She was working really hard to *not* tell me something. And Gracie's pretty up front normally. I began to think about the old small gods again, for the first time in . . . years.'

'But you couldn't believe they were *real*,' said Kevin. 'Nobody believes in ancient gods these days. Nobody. People don't believe in anything any more.'

Greg took a bite of cake and looked at him while he munched and swallowed. 'You're assuming a lot about people.'

Kevin dropped his head into his hands. He really wanted to tell the whole story now.

'Go on,' said Greg, as if he could read his mind. 'Tell me.'

'It started,' said Kevin, ' . . . in a watermill.'

Greg had made and drunk another cup of tea by the time Kevin finished his story, ending on his desperate unanswered prayers to Abandinus in the early hours and his race through the rain to find Arimanius again at the school. He left nothing out. Not even the Emma Greening stuff.

When he finished, there was silence. Kevin had not looked at Greg too often during his story, in case he saw an expression of disbelief or amusement. Only once had he heard the man catch his breath and he still hadn't looked. Now he had to.

Greg's face was thoughtful as he ran his fingers through his hair and then knotted them at the back of his head, his elbows wide. 'You think Abandinus deserted you?' he said, eventually.

'Well . . . yeah,' said Kevin.

'Hmmm,' said Greg. 'Gods move in mysterious ways, you know.'

'Yeah, I do,' grunted Kevin. 'Usually mysteriously unhelpful ways.'

'Why do you think I was out running?' said Greg and Kevin blinked with surprise, remembering the jogger who had called out to him as he'd run to the school.

'Oh—that was *you*,' he said.

'Yes—and I do go running, but not normally at half past five in the morning.' Greg brought his hands back to the table and drummed on it lightly with his fingers. 'I couldn't sleep. Kept getting woken up by dreams . . . or maybe not dreams. There was some character in a robe with fish swimming about in it. Kept prodding me in the back and saying I needed to go to school.' He smiled in a rueful, lopsided way.

Kevin dropped his last chunk of cake back on to his plate. 'Abandinus?'

'Well, do you know anyone else who fits that description?'

'That's him.' Kevin felt a wave of emotion rush at him. 'You mean . . . you think he *didn't* abandon me?'

'I think he woke me up and sent me out running for a reason.'

'But why didn't he just show up himself? He could have smitten Arimanius or something.'

Greg shook his head. 'Look . . . I know a fair bit about the old gods. I'll show you some of my books sometime. I've got some really ancient ones, out of print these days, with much more detail in them than anything you could find on the internet. The gods play complicated games with complicated rules. Maybe Abandinus didn't want to inflame the situation. Getting in between warring gods is no picnic for a squash-able life form. The one thing that I have noticed is that whenever humans get caught up in those games, they usually come off quite badly.' He paused and drummed his fingers thoughtfully on the table, looking distant for a few seconds before continuing. 'Just think about the Greek myths! Orpheus getting torn to pieces by bad tempered goddesses because his lute playing was a bit off; Perseus having to kill his own grandfather to satisfy a prophecy; Bellerophon doomed to wander the earth alone and in misery because he dared to try to meet up with Zeus.'

'But those are just made up stories!' protested Kevin.

'Almost certainly,' said Greg. 'After all, who would ever believe such a thing?'

'You think they really happened?' marvelled Kevin.

Greg smiled and shook his head. 'I think all kinds of amazing things have happened over the time we've been on this planet—and, of course, they've been hugely embellished by humans over the centuries. I bet someone called Icarus really *did* have a crack at flying with beeswax wings and plummeted to his death trying. I bet some bloke called Theseus really did battle a bull in an underground maze for the entertainment of a king. But it's how those stories got written up by the local tabloid press which has kept them in our memories and turned them into myths. Much more fun if there's a god or two involved.'

'So what now—you think the "gods" part was just made up?' Kevin shook his head, trying to keep up.

'I don't think that. I think . . . ' Greg sighed and pushed his hands through his hair again. 'Sometimes, yes. But other times . . . I think our planet is full of unexplained things . . . all sorts of entities . . . like the one we met this morning. But I believe we *power* them ourselves. We give them shape and credence and importance, just like you gave to Abandinus. And they *grow* when we do. They become more real—in the way that we all understand *real*. And more powerful.'

Kevin nodded. He remembered Abandinus saying to him, 'The power of belief is greater than you can comprehend, Kevin.' And hadn't they all bought into that—him and Tim and Gracie? They had gone all out to boost Abandinus with a shrine and a hymn and prayers and internet followers.

'So . . . you think we've just, sort of, *created* Arimanius ourselves. Out of nothing?'

Greg shook his head again. 'Not out of nothing. You've all done a little bit of research, yes? Skimmed through lists of ancient Celtic gods on the internet and so on?' Kevin nodded and Greg continued: 'Well, you probably picked up more information than you realized. Arimanius would have been right there in the alphabet of lesser gods, under "A", along with Abandinus. And Ancasta. Or maybe it's just that Abandinus has a history with Arimanius, and your belief in Abandinus just spread beyond the one god, to the other gods in his immediate realm.'

'It does make a *kind* of sense,' said Kevin.

'Well, as much sense as any of this can ever make

to us,' said Greg, getting up and taking the empty mugs to the sink. 'I don't really pretend to understand it all. I just know that there is stuff out there—and in here,' he tapped his head, 'that we simply don't have enough information on. I've always kept an open mind, and maybe that's why I got to see your underworld god. I'd rather *not* have,' he winced. 'But when I saw you running through the rain, looking possessed and horrified, I found that I knew what was happening. Now,' he turned back from the sink, 'I've already done breaking and entering and vehicle vandalism for you today.' He grinned as Kevin furrowed his brow, confused. 'I had to snap a wing mirror off a car so I could shine daylight at Arimanius,' he explained. 'I reckoned an underworld god would find that a bit nasty.'

'But there wasn't any light,' said Kevin. 'It was dark and cloudy and rainy.'

'There was light,' said Greg. 'Just not for you. You'd already started pulling the dark towards you. Anyway, like I said, two crimes is enough for one morning. Let's not have me getting done for kidnapping a minor. I've got to get you home now, and you need to find out how your nan is.'

Kevin nodded and got to his feet. He felt a deep resigned sadness now, about Nan, rather than a raging horror. As if it was already too late.

'Thank you,' he said, as Greg walked him back down the quiet morning streets. 'For stopping me touching the dark light. I wanted to save Nan, but I'm not sure it would have worked even if I had. I think he might have been conning me.'

As they reached the gate, the house silent and communicating no news of anything, Greg said, 'Look—you need to try to find a bit of peace inside yourself for a while. I hope that's the last you see of Arimanius. I really do. But his kind feeds on stress and anger and sadness—and there's no way you can avoid feeling those things, whatever happens to your nan. You're a teenager after all. Try to stay calm and maybe lay off the shrine and hymn and praying stuff for a little while. Keep off all the gods' radar. For your own sake—and everyone else's. The sooner Arimanius gets forgotten, the quicker his power will subside. I shudder to think what he might be capable of if you got *him* a whole load of internet followers.' Greg really did shudder, resting his hand on the wet wooden gate.

'What—what do you think he might do?' asked Kevin. 'If he got a lot of worshippers?'

Greg shrugged but didn't quite pull it off. It was hard to look casual, talking about Arimanius. 'Under-world gods aren't all evil,' he said. 'They have . . .

different values. Some of them have even been known to protect communities of their followers at times, but those communities would usually pay quite dearly for an underworld god's protection. The sacrifices for underworld gods are worse. And many of them glory in violence and catastrophe. Of course, all the gods like to play games, but underworld gods' games tend to have a higher body count . . . When they get annoyed they can smite whole towns. And not getting what he wants is pretty annoying to any god. '

Kevin gulped.

'But it might be fine,' Greg went on, now rubbing his hands together briskly. 'It might be. At the moment you and Tim and Gracie are the only mortals who know about him—and now me, too, of course. We *all* need to start dismissing him from our thoughts as soon as possible. Cut off his energy source. I'm going to talk to Gracie, Kevin, OK? She is kind of in my charge and I need to know she's OK. I'll tell her everything I've told you when I see her after school today. Maybe you should talk to Tim, eh?'

'OK,' said Kevin, feeling tiredness roll over him like a mist. 'I will talk to Tim.'

'Good boy,' said Greg, patting him on the shoulder and sending him up the path. 'Block him out, OK? Happy thoughts, only. If you possibly can . . . Come and see me again as soon as you want to, and let me know how it's going.'

Kevin let himself in and closed the door behind him, breathing deeply and slowly and hearing Dad's faint snores upstairs. Maybe he *could* sleep for a while now. He went into the sitting room and curled up on the sofa and sleep took him in seconds.

Three hours later he was awoken by the telephone.

'Is it Nan?' he burbled into the receiver. 'Is there news?'

'Yes,' said Mum.

Chapter 23

'She's opened her eyes!' Kevin shook Dad awake in the bottom bunk. 'We've got to go back! We can see her!'

Dad grinned and rubbed his son's head. 'Good news!' he mumbled, sitting up.

'She hasn't said anything yet,' said Kevin, with a gulp. 'They don't know if there's been any brain damage.' He shivered. He couldn't bear to think of Nan being brain damaged. She was always so sharp and bright and funny. How could she ever *not* be?

They threw on some clothes and shoes and Dad made Kevin drink some orange juice and eat a biscuit before they left. He also rang the school and told them that Kevin wouldn't be in today (which they'd probably already worked out, an hour into the school day) and briefly explained why. Less than fifteen minutes since the call from Mum, they were in the car heading back to the hospital. The sun was shining and there was no sign of the deluge just a few hours ago when Kevin had run through the streets.

At the hospital, Mum was looking a better colour than last night, and she was actually *drinking* the tea she was holding now. She gave Kevin a hug and Dad hugged them both. 'What's the news?' he asked.

'I've been in to see her and she smiled at me and said hello,' said Mum. 'So that's good. But it's still early days. Until the swelling's gone down on her brain we won't know how bad the damage is.'

'Can we see her?' asked Kevin.

'Yes,' said Mum. 'For a little while.' She led them to a nurses' station and consulted with the sister who smiled at Kevin and said she thought it would do his grandmother good to see him for a few minutes. She led them down the corridor to a small side ward.

'Well, she's out of ITU and on fifteen minute obs now,' the sister said to Mum, who nodded and then looked back and translated to Kevin and Dad: 'She came out of intensive care, which is good—but they have to check on her every fifteen minutes and she's all wired up to monitors and alarms and stuff. OK?'

Kevin knew she was preparing him to not be shocked when he saw Nan. So he kept his smile in place as they walked in and he saw Nan's face, mottled purple and yellow with bruises and surrounded in a kind of brace thing which kept her head and neck still. There weren't any tubes going into her nose or mouth, but two seemed to be going into her left wrist, delivering colourless fluids. He walked over to the bed. Nan's swollen eyelids were closed but she was breathing normally. The room was stiflingly hot and smelt sweetish, like the cheap car freshener he'd wrecked last night. Despite the heat, Nan's fingers were cool when he took her hand.

'Hi there. Are you with us?' said Mum, taking her mother's other hand, and Nan's eyes flickered open. 'Kevin's here. Look!' said Mum and Nan's eyes slid sideways and she smiled sleepily at him.

'Hello, sweetheart,' she burbled. Relief flooded through him. She was the same. She was *his* nan. Whatever had been damaged, she was still his nan. He felt tears come but blinked them back.

'Hello, you,' he said, squeezing her cool fingers.

'How much of my car is left?' sighed Nan, still smiling at him.

'Not much,' said Mum, with a shudder. She dug a picture out of her bag. 'The police came in earlier and left me a spare shot of the accident scene. It's a good job you're fully insured, Mum.' She waved a print which showed the little red Peugeot tipped onto its side with the bonnet and radiator grille crunched up in a snarl of metal. Emergency workers in one corner gave off white flares as their light reflective clothing reacted to the camera flash. 'They got to you really fast, because there was a fire crew just returning from a false alarm around the corner,' said Mum. 'That probably saved your life.'

Nan smiled sadly. 'Loved that little car,' she sighed.

'Well, you can get a brand new one with the insurance money, as soon as you're out. Mum . . . can you remember what happened?'

'Not really,' said Nan. 'It's a bit of a blur. Maybe when I've got all this cobblers off my head I'll be able to think straight.'

The nurse put her head around the door. 'Just a couple more minutes now,' she said. She eyed Kevin's dad and added: 'Should really be just two at a time.'

'Sorry—I'll go,' he said. 'Bye, Gwen. Good to see you're in one piece.'

'Thanks, Jason,' smiled Nan, and she was looking tired.

Mum got up. 'I'll leave you with just Kevin for a couple of minutes,' she said and followed Dad out.

Kevin sat on the chair next to the bed. He noticed that Mum had left the photo on the blanket by Nan's feet and picked it up as he spoke gently to her. 'How are you feeling? Does it hurt?'

'My throat's a bit sore,' said Nan, 'and my head

feels like it's full of hot custard. But I'm OK, Kevin. It's not my time yet, you know!'

Kevin felt a chill go across him. At least one god had thought differently last night. He stared at the photo. It was hard to imagine how anyone had got out of that car alive. He looked closer and saw something which made a series of chills hurry after the first. In the bottom right-hand corner, despite the glare of the emergency lighting, three long fingers of dark light reached across the tarmac.

'Strange though,' murmured Nan.

'What?' said Kevin, gulping and trying to keep his voice normal.

'Maybe I hit a bird,' said Nan.

'A bird?'

'Maybe. Because there were lots of feathers.'

'Time up,' said the nurse, putting her head round the corner.

'Really?' said Kevin. He desperately wanted to ask Nan more.

The nurse stepped into the room and allowed the door to close. She walked to him and put her left hand on his shoulder. Her long hair was in braids and her blue eyes were tearful. She held an egg in her right hand. Coolness pulsed through him and his skin prickled. 'It is not done, Kevin,' she said.

263

'Cuda!' he whispered. He glanced back at Nan but she was asleep again. She didn't even wake as the three stooped little figures ran, giggling, past the window on the narrow sill outside (three storeys above the hospital car park).

'Aye,' said Cuda. 'There is a madness for mortals in our realm this day. How can it end? The underworld claims for balance. Saitada cannot be wrong. Seek the help of the lover. This is all I can tell you.'

'Time up,' said the nurse, putting her head around the corner.

Kevin was gaping into the space where Cuda had been.

'Come on, love,' said the nurse—the real one this time. 'Let her rest.'

At midday, after a lot of sitting around and tea drinking, Mum persuaded Dad to take Kevin home. 'You need to come home, too,' he'd said. 'Get some sleep.'

But Mum wouldn't. 'Not yet,' she said. 'I can't leave yet. You two go. Kevin can make lunch.'

'*I* can make lunch,' sighed Dad. 'Honestly, Kate, do you really think I'm that useless?'

She shook her head and bit her lip. 'I know you're not, Jason. I'm sorry.'

'Kevin *can* get himself some lunch,' said Dad, 'and I am coming back with something hot for you—and a change of clothes, and something to read.'

She smiled. 'Thank you. That would be good.'

In spite of everything his head was trying to wrap around—the state of poor Nan, the dark light in the photo, the remark about feathers and the appearance of Cuda, all spinning around his head like the contents of a surreal washing machine—Kevin's romance detector shot up on to full alert. Mum and Dad were being nice to each other. Could this mean . . . ?

'Come on, Kev,' said Dad, and led him back to the car. Shutting the driver's door he picked up his mobile phone and dialled a number. Kevin couldn't hear who answered but soon realized it was voicemail by the way Dad spoke. 'Hello. It's me. My ex-mum-in-law's been in an accident and I'm looking after Kevin. It's made me think about a lot of things you said. I think we need to talk. Call me, OK?'

'Who was the message for?' asked Kevin as the engine started.

'Lorna,' said Dad.

'What's going on?'

Dad smiled at him, his face tired and creased-looking, and his hand went up to the earring to twist it. 'Stuff,' he said and shrugged.

Kevin was none the wiser, but he didn't push. His brain just slid back to the scary puzzle he'd been grappling with all morning. Cuda was *still* warning him. After Greg had stopped him touching the dark light and dragged him away from the school he had imagined that his dealings with Arimanius were all over. That come what may he would just have to accept whatever happened to Nan. Cuda seemed to think it was all far from over.

So had Abandinus been there? Was he at the crash scene, scattering feathers? Was he *involved*? Did *he* want Nan to die, too? Kevin's heart seemed to crunch up inside him at this thought. Could his own god betray him? But *why*? Why *would* he?

The fact is, he told himself, you don't know a *thing* about *your god*. You want to think he's good because he's done stuff for you—but what do you really *know* about him? All the nice friendly chats and helping out in goal could be a big con. But again . . . argued his other self . . . *why*? Because gods play games, he answered back, smartly. Like Greg said, they play their own games with their own rules and you're just a mortal and you've got no hope of understanding. And everyone knows that when mortals mix with gods, mortals come off the worst. Every time. And anyone they care about. Look at

266

Nan. Would this have happened at all if you hadn't started stirring things up with that stupid shrine and the hymns and the prayers and the emails? Saitada and Arimanius had only shown up *after* all that. Who would be next? Mum? Dad?

'Here we go,' said Dad, pulling up to the house.

In ten minutes Dad headed out again, with a flask of tomato soup and some buttered bread wrapped up in foil and a bag containing Mum's clothes and toiletries and the book she was currently reading.

'Just take it easy. Watch some telly. Have some lunch,' advised Dad before the door shut behind him.

Kevin stood in the dining room and stared through the French windows down the garden. Part of him yearned to run down to the shrine and try to get Abandinus to come. He longed to have the god explain everything to him. Make it all clear and understandable and . . . *safe*. Tell him he was protected and all the fuss was over now. Everything would be all right and no dark light would ever reach for him again.

But no. Greg had said he must keep his head down, and he was right. What had Cuda said, back in the side ward? 'There is a madness for mortals in our realm this day.' Yes—the god realm was all twitchy with him, and probably Tim and Gracie too. He should warn them not to pray or send any more emails or anything. He should warn them that this small gods game was over. Definitely *over*.

Even as he thought this, there was a hammering at the front door which made him yelp with shock.

He ran down the hall, already making out the familiar shapes on the other side of the mottled glass. He pulled the door open and found Tim and Gracie, out of breath and pink in the face, on the front step.

'Kevin! You're here!' gasped Tim.

'Oh thank goodness,' sighed Gracie.

'What? What's happening?' demanded Kevin.

'We were going to ask *you* that,' said Gracie. 'Mike Mears has vanished. And we thought you'd gone too!'

'What happened to you last night?' Tim looked tired and stressed. 'You went off with your dad, looking like death, mate! You didn't tell me why and the school wouldn't tell us either.'

'Why aren't you two *at* school?' asked Kevin, ushering them into the house and shutting the door.

Tim and Gracie looked at each other. 'We bunked off,' said Tim. 'It was nuts there, anyway. Police all over the place, teachers all freaked out. We just took off at lunchtime. We had to find you.'

'My nan was in a car crash,' said Kevin.

Gracie and Tim stared at him. 'Oh god,' murmured Gracie, with panic threading through her voice. 'Saitada . . . she said there would be death. She said you would sorrow! She said . . . '

'Nan's alive!' cut in Kevin. 'But . . . I don't know how. And . . . I think I might be in trouble.'

'Why?' asked Tim. Then he stared at Kevin, clearly not liking his expression. 'What did you do?'

'I . . . I went to Arimanius,' said Kevin.

They both gaped at him, and then Gracie slowly shook her head.

'Yeah . . . seems your dream was right, Gracie,' said Kevin, with a bitter smile. 'He offered me anything I wanted, last night after I had that fight with Mike Mears. I said no then. I said *no* . . . ' Still they stared at him, horrified. 'But then my nan was dying!' he pleaded. 'She was *dying*! Arimanius *said* I would want something else that night. Something I hadn't already asked for, and he was right. And Abandinus didn't come! He didn't help! He just . . . let me down. So I ran back to Arimanius.'

Gracie and Tim seemed frozen. 'You . . . ' muttered Gracie. 'You said yes to him? Don't you know what an underworld god *is*?'

Kevin closed his eyes, revisiting the doom-laden shroud of the early morning rain, the fingers of dark

269

light reaching for him, waiting for him to reach back. 'It's OK,' he said. 'I was . . . saved.'

'What?' said both of them, in unison.

'Look—I need a cup of tea,' said Kevin, sounding like his mum. 'I'll make us all one and I'll tell you what happened.'

Five minutes later, when they were all sitting around the kitchen table, clasping hot mugs and foraging through the biscuit tin, which Mum had filled again, he told them about Greg and what had happened.

'Whoa,' breathed Gracie. 'I always knew he was *intense* about ancient British culture and all that—but he really *does* know his stuff. I never really thought it before, but . . . ' she tilted her head to one side, considering, ' . . . I guess he's kind of cool. That mirror trick against an underworld god. Yep. That was cool.'

'Anyway, he thinks we should keep our heads down now and just stop getting the gods so . . . excited,' said Kevin. 'And I think he's right. Even Cuda said they're all shook up about us in god world today.'

'Cuda?' queried Tim. 'She's been back?'

'Yep. Disguised as a nurse while I was in with Nan,' said Kevin. 'So look . . . I think we have to just cool it all down now. No more shrine visits or prayers. No more hymns. No more chain emails. And most of all Greg said we have to put Arimanius out of our minds now. Thinking about him . . . well, it's like praying to Abandinus. It powers him up.'

They were all silent for a while. Thinking about the thing they shouldn't be thinking about.

'So . . . you think it's really over?' said Gracie, at length. 'You think if we stop worshipping, the gods will just pack up and go home?' She didn't sound convinced.

'I don't know!' Kevin scrubbed at his eyes and sighed. 'I just know that it's all too big. I can't deal with any more of it. I want to be normal.'

'I wish I hadn't done the email thing now,' said Gracie, lifting her mug of tea to her mouth with a shaky hand. 'I did a search on line last night and there are a few people talking about Abandinus . . . on forums and chat sites, you know. Just a few, but it's definitely catching on.'

Kevin sighed. 'It's too late to worry about that now. Just don't ever mention . . . the other one,' he said. 'And let's just try to forget everything. The good stuff too.'

'So, you'd give it all back then?' said Gracie, after a sip of tea. 'All the sporty stuff—the Wii—your mum and dad back together—Emma Greening noticing you.'

'Yes,' said Kevin. 'And anyway, it's not what I thought it would be. I haven't even *looked* at the Wii since I first played it. There hasn't been time. Mum and Dad aren't *really* back together. They're not happy even if they're here in the same house. The sporty stuff . . . ' he sighed again, ' . . . was brilliant while it lasted but it only got me a bloody nose. And Emma . . . ' He shook his head and grinned, remembering the dancing last night and Emma's non-stop alarm clock giggling.

Then he remembered shouting at Gracie. He looked at her across his mug. 'I'm sorry about having a go at you last night. It was over the top.'

Gracie shrugged and fiddled with one of her plaits. 'No, you were right. I shouldn't have called up Ancasta. After what's happened since then, I know that more than ever. Ancasta likes me and I think she's amazing . . . but you can't really trust the gods to be on your side. You did look incredible, though, doing your tango!'

Tim pulled the £165 out of his pocket. It was still bundled up, untouched. 'S'pose I've got to hand this in to an orphanage or something then,' he grunted. And then he smiled at them widely, showing white, even teeth. 'And I guess these'll have to go back!'

Gracie and Kevin stared at his mouth and then at

each other. 'They've always looked like that, you idiot!' laughed Kevin.

'Nah,' said Tim. 'I checked this morning in the mirror. They're definitely better!'

'So. We're agreed. It's all over. We don't do any more gods stuff,' said Kevin. 'We won't bother them and they won't bother us.'

They nodded, solemnly. Kevin put out his hands and took one of theirs in each. 'C'mon,' he said, going a little pink. 'Three-way shake on it.' Gracie and Tim took each other's hands as well and they all gave three heavy shakes around the table.

'So,' said Gracie, after a long pause. 'What else do we do for fun?'

There was a sudden loud knock, which made them all jump. Flashing blue light could be seen through the front door when Kevin peered into the hallway—along with two dark figures on the doorstep. He stared back at Gracie and Tim, behind him. 'It's the police!'

'Don't worry,' said Tim. 'They'll just want to ask you about Mike Mears. You remember? I told you—he's disappeared. They might have found out about the fight you had. They were bound to come and ask you about it.'

The door knocked loudly again. 'Just go and let them in,' said Gracie. 'We'll stay here with you and back you up. Tell them you didn't murder him or anything.' She giggled nervously, but Kevin wasn't laughing. Even as he'd put a foot into the hallway, something made him freeze. Something about the door.

'Kevin, are you in there?' called a policewoman in a motherly voice, through the letter box. 'Open up, please. It's the police. Don't be afraid. We just need to talk to you about last night.'

'Go *on*!' said Tim. 'Or they'll think you're guilty or something. It's the same ones that were at the school today.'

But Kevin could not move and now he was barring their way as they tried to pass him and let the police in themselves. 'STOP!' he whispered. '*Look!*'

Down at the bottom of the front door there was a shadow. It was a glowing red-blue-grey colour and it was moving like the tentacles of a squid, reaching slowly out across the mat.

Oh no no no no not again not the dark light, whimpered his mind.

Kevin knew that if they tried to run across to the dining room and out through the patio doors they would be seen. Five seconds later he was standing on the sink unit and bashing open the kitchen window.

'Are you *nuts*?' hissed Tim, urgently, as the knocking on the door was joined by the metallic clinks of one of the officers trying to break the lock. 'You can't run away from the police!'

'He's not running away from the police,' whispered Gracie, climbing up on the sink behind Kevin and shooting a terrified glance at the kitchen door. 'He's running away from *that*!'

A low curling cloud of dark light was now creeping around it. Tim snatched in a shocked breath and then followed Kevin and Gracie through the kitchen window.

Chapter 24

Thirty seconds later Kevin broke their pledge. He fell at the stone shrine and yelled, 'Abandinus! Help! The dark light is coming! Help us!'

They stood, panicking, around the shrine, *willing* their god to arrive. But he didn't.

'Oh no!' cried Gracie, standing by the greenhouse and staring back down the garden. 'I can see it! It's coming!'

Kevin ran to her side and saw the dark light was curling out of the kitchen window.

'Over here!' yelled Tim, hefting himself up into one of the apple trees. Its low branches reached across the high fence into next door's garden. With one more glance at the shrine, which still showed no sign of Abandinus or any other god, Kevin grabbed Gracie's arm and ran down the garden to the old tree. They leapt up its slanting trunk, snatching handholds in its branches, and followed

Tim to the fence. Tim was already in next door's garden, peering along the side alley of their house. He shook his head at them as they made to run down the alley. 'Too close!' he whispered. 'The police will see you.'

'Maybe they can help,' said Gracie. 'They might save us from the dark light if we go with them.'

'No,' said Kevin. 'The dark light came *with* them. It hitched a ride and they didn't even know.' He pictured the police car parked by the hedges at the school, the dark light snaking up through the earth from Arimanius's cradle, slithering into the shadow beneath the wheels and clinging to the underside of the vehicle. 'They can't keep us safe.'

Tim was already climbing the fence to the next garden along. He nearly fell into a pond on the other side, and guided Kevin and Gracie down so they wouldn't do the same. Adrenaline was pounding through Kevin's body, giving him power to keep vaulting fences and walls and ignore the scrapes, cuts, and grazes he got along the way. It must have been the same for Tim and Gracie, because they kept up with each other across four gardens before running down a side passage and out into the road far enough along to avoid the police car and crew, although they could still see the blue flashing light and a small knot of interested neighbours and passers-by who were wondering what all the fuss was about.

'Can you see it? Can you see it?' Kevin hissed, looking all around him for more dark light as his heartbeat clattered through him.

'No,' said Gracie. She shuddered. 'But I can *feel* it. We need to run. *This* way!'

They ran, keeping low, to the end of the road. Kevin fought back panic and guilt. Arimanius must still think he might give in. He had not been strong enough. It was true. He *might* have given in if Greg hadn't stopped him.

'We—need—Greg!' he puffed as they reached the corner and broke into a full height run. 'We've got to get to the community centre.'

'FASTER!' screamed Gracie, grabbing on to him and Tim and looking back over her shoulder with terror. 'It's coming!'

And it was. Kevin saw the cloud of dark light travelling the shadow beneath the spread of an unkempt hedge just beyond the corner they'd turned. It was bubbling and churning and fingers of blackness probed and stabbed out of the front of it, marking him. Marking them all. Tim had turned round too, and seemed unable to tear his eyes away from the oncoming darkness. He was staggering along backwards and then he pitched over the kerb and fell out into the road.

There was a screech of brakes and a ringing thud

and Kevin spun round to see Tim on the bonnet of a car. 'TIIIIM!' he shrieked. This could NOT be happening! Not another road accident! Not another one!

But Tim was getting up on his hands and knees and staring through the windscreen, gaping, and the driver was getting out of the car. And he wasn't shouting at them or checking for damage. He was just grabbing Tim and bundling him into the back seat. Gracie was following and now Kevin pulled himself out of his freeze and threw himself into the passenger seat, gasping with shock and relief.

'Seat belts on,' said Greg McCrae. 'This might get bumpy.' He did a violent three point turn and then accelerated along the road, flicking anxious glances into his rear-view mirror as Gracie and Tim and Kevin all stared through the back window.

'Is it still following?' said Greg, changing gear.

'Yes!' whimpered Gracie, clipping in her seat belt with shaking hands. 'But I think we're getting away.'

'Any sign of Abandinus?'

'No,' said Kevin and it came out almost as a sob. 'We agreed we were going to stop. No more worshipping or anything. But then—'

'Are you OK, Tim? Are you hurt?' said Greg, still flicking glances at the mirror.

'I'm OK,' grunted Tim.

'We were going to stop!' went on Kevin. 'We said we would! Why is Arimanius still after us? And where's Abandinus?'

'Gods don't give up easily, not when they're trying to prove a point,' muttered Greg. 'And I think I know where Abandinus is.'

'Where?' said Kevin.

'Back in the River Ouse.'

'What? You mean he's just gone home and forgotten us—waaaaaah,' Kevin grabbed a strap above the car door and hung on as Greg turned violently on a roundabout and took the A road to the west.

'How close, Grace?' yelled Greg.

'I can still see it,' she called back. 'But I don't *think* it's closer. I think we might be leaving it behind.'

'He's not forgotten you, Kevin,' said Greg. 'At least I don't believe that. I think he's trying to give the impression he doesn't care about you.'

'Why?' shrieked Kevin as they hit a bump in the road and nearly took off before smacking down again with tooth-rattling velocity. 'OW!' he added.

'No grandkids for *my* mum,' squeaked Tim from the back seat and Gracie winced at him.

'Sorry!' said Greg. 'Really can't slow down. We need to get to the river.'

'What?' yelled Tim. 'The river? Why?'

'To get Abandinus to help out.'

'But you just said he doesn't care!' said Kevin.

'No—I said he's been *trying* to give the *impression* he doesn't care. There's a difference.'

'I don't understand,' wailed Kevin.

'Dark light getting closer!' bawled Tim, from the back seat. Kevin twisted round and saw a smoky line snaking down a hill, probably only a mile behind them. It made his insides go cold with fear as he realized that it could exist outside the shadows.

'Look,' went on Greg, stepping on the accelerator and pushing the needle up to seventy mph on the dial as they shot along the A road, overtaking a caravan with a frightening swerve, 'when Arimanius started paying serious attention to you, Abandinus *stopped* paying attention to you. It was only *after* Abandinus found out, presumably from Ancasta or Maponus, that he stopped showing up. He and Arimanius must have some kind of history—something that means Arimanius wants to hurt anyone Abandinus cares about. So Abandinus is pretending he doesn't care about *you*.'

'But why doesn't he just go and *smite* Arimanius?' demanded Kevin.

'Oh, do pay attention!' snapped Greg, actually taking his hands off the wheel to wave them in the air in frustration. 'He's a bloody *god*! They are *both* gods. Gods are *immortal*!'

'Ah,' acknowledged Kevin.

'That doesn't mean they can't hurt, annoy, and otherwise aggravate each other,' went on Greg, his hands now safely back where they should be. 'They do have feelings ... although that might be hard to believe at times.' He fell silent and stared broodingly through the windscreen.

'It's fallen back a bit,' updated Gracie, from the back seat, still staring at the view behind them. 'But it's still coming!'

'How can it be out in daylight?' asked Tim. 'It's an underworld god, yeah? I mean—shouldn't it shrivel up or something?'

'You're thinking of vampires,' said Gracie.

'No, he's right,' said Greg. 'Gods from the underworld can't walk directly into the light, but they have plenty of minions to create darkness for them. A sort of advance party.' He flicked his eyes back to the mirror and shook his head. 'He's in there all right. Waiting to come out and play. When he's good and ready. That's gods for you.' Once again, an expression stole across his face and was gone again—like a shallow wave on the sand.

Kevin felt a sensation of *knowing* slip across

him. He stared at Greg's profile as the man gripped the wheel and scanned the road ahead. 'You—you haven't learnt all this from *books* . . . have you?' he said, leaning forward in his seat so he could see the man's eyes. 'You *know* this stuff! You *know* it. You . . . something happened to you too, didn't it?'

Greg shot him a look of surprise and seemed to have to catch his breath. 'Look . . . Kevin . . . we're trying to outrun the dark forces of the underworld in a Fiat 1.6. This is not the time!'

'No! This *is* the time! You have to tell us. What happened to you?'

Greg gritted his teeth and overtook a lorry as it lumbered up a gradual incline, making the engine shriek with protest as he jammed down to third gear and jerked the car so hard he nearly gave everyone whiplash. 'I was eighteen!' he yelled, above the racket he was making. 'I was at university in Southampton.'

He pulled past the lorry and back into lane seconds before another lorry roared around the bend in the oncoming lane. Everyone gasped and then Kevin prodded 'Go on!'

'I was in the canoe club with my mate, Tom. We went out one day. Left the boatshed in good weather at Woodmill, but got hit by this squall, just on the edge of Southampton Water. We both went under.'

He fell silent and Kevin could see that what lay before the man's eyes was not just the winding road ahead, but a scene from his past. As fresh now as then, judging by the way his mouth tightened to a thin line. 'I should have drowned,' went on Greg, at length. 'But I didn't. Tom did.'

There was a pause. 'Why should it have been you?' asked Gracie, who had turned back to the front and was paying close attention. 'Why you?'

'Tom was better in every way than I was. A better canoeist, a better swimmer—fitter, sharper. If either one of us was going to get out of that squall alive, it was him. My number was up. I was trapped in the canoe, head down in an undertow, and I couldn't get up. I was weakening and Tom was getting out—kicking his legs in the water. Trying to make it towards me and get me out too. But I knew he was too late. I was breathing in water by then and I knew . . . I knew I was dying.'

'But you didn't die, did you?' said Gracie.

'Dark light still coming,' reported Tim, remaining glued to the back window. 'But not gaining.'

'I *should* have died,' said Greg. 'I *was* dying. My vision was going. My senses were cutting out. But then this . . . beautiful creature . . . swam up to me and pressed her mouth against mine and gave me air. She breathed air into me that came straight from a meadow in summer. Sweet, fresh, cool . . . and she wrapped her arms around me and pulled me out of the water.'

'Ancasta,' breathed Gracie. 'You *know* Ancasta! You were in the River Itchen! That's Ancasta's river!'

Greg said nothing for a while and Kevin felt compelled to look back. The dark light was still following, but, as Tim said, no closer. He looked back at the professor, who was still breaking the speed limit in spite of his revelations. 'What happened to Tom?'

'Ancasta chose me,' said Greg. 'Tom's body was found under the Itchen Bridge. I was found on Netley Shore. I was unconscious but just about alive.'

'So—why blame yourself?' said Gracie.

'Because she *chose* me! And she swapped us over. Tom was not meant to die. It was *my* fate, but she interfered and sacrificed him for me.'

'That's still not your fault,' said Gracie.

'Isn't it? I saw her little inscription at an archaeology display the week before. I was a history student and we visited a lot of these places. I touched the stone and did a quick prayer for her protection and offered my undying love.'

'Really?' asked Gracie.

'Yes. In front of Tom and some other mates. For a laugh. I was *messing around*. And I had no idea what

I was messing around *with*. I got what I asked for. I didn't know at the time that it would cost Tom's life.'

'Don't want to diss your story, prof,' said Tim, 'but the dark light's looking closer again.' They all snapped round to look and now the dark light was streaming along the middle of the road, half a mile behind them, like the soot from a subterranean steam engine, passing right through any vehicles in its way while their occupants drove on obliviously.

'Damn!' growled Greg, pounding at the accelerator. 'Damn! Damn! Why did I have to get such a stupid car?

'It's a professor thing,' said Gracie. 'You couldn't help yourself.'

'Big thirsty four-by-four next time,' promised Greg. 'With a SatNav and climate control and bloody turbo bloody boost. Kevin, get that road map in the door. Tell me how far we are from the River Ouse.'

Kevin scrabbled for the map and found the right pages. 'Where are we now?' he asked.

'We're on the A11—we just passed a roundabout turn off to the A1075,' said Greg, glancing edgily into the rear-view mirror and pressing his right foot down until the engine whined in protest. They crested the top of the long hill and picked up more speed as the dual carriageway descended.

'The Little Ouse is about four miles, I think,' said Kevin, squinting at the map and feeling distinctly car sick. 'It goes through Thetford. But I met Abandinus in Houghton—by the watermill! It's a lot further to there!'

'The river itself should be enough,' said Greg. 'It had better be. I don't think we can outrun Arimanius for much longer.'

'It's falling behind a bit!' whooped Tim. 'Maybe he's giving up!'

'Maybe . . .' said Greg, although he didn't sound convinced.

'So . . . did you see Ancasta again?' asked Gracie.

Greg didn't answer. 'You *did*! Didn't you?' said Gracie. He shook his head impatiently. 'Wait! Wait up! You . . . you didn't just see her once. You . . .' Gracie paused to smile, with wonder and certainty. 'You were *together* with her.'

'All right, Gracie! You win the prize!' snapped Greg. 'That's how I know—gods and mortals do not mix. Ancasta totally messed up my life.'

'Well, at least she *gave* you a life before she messed it up,' observed Tim. 'And, man . . . she is *hot*!'

'You have no idea,' sighed Greg. 'How can any human build any kind of future with a goddess? Or a god? They *love* human spirit. Human emotions. These

287

are the only things they can never truly control. Doesn't stop them trying though. It's almost impossible to get away.'

'Are you telling me you *dumped* a goddess?' gasped Gracie.

Greg winced. 'Like I said—you have *no idea*!'

'OH GOD!' yelled Gracie. 'NO! NO! NO! Not your crazy English CONES. NO!'

The road ahead was narrowing rapidly. A row of bright orange witches' hats suddenly forced the traffic down to one lane and what was a free-flowing road became sluggish and slow.

'Oh, this is not good!' groaned Greg, easing off the accelerator as the gap between them and a BMW ahead got shorter and shorter.

'Go! Go!' yelped Gracie. 'You have to go! It's coming for us!'

In the rear window Kevin could see the thick black snake of dark light speeding down the hill behind them, shooting under and over the cars, close enough that he could make out the wriggling of a thousand tentacles within it. He could *feel* the low ache of despair and helplessness rolling ahead of it in an evil clammy fog and he noticed, for the first time, that birds were flying wildly away from it, fleeing left and right through the air in panicky swirls. Two or three vehicles also swerved in its wake and at least one crashed into the hard shoulder. Arimanius was getting reckless in pursuit.

'Let me out,' said Kevin, suddenly, reaching for the door handle. 'He wants me. There is no reason why he should take any of you.'

Greg smashed his hand down on the central locking switch and bellowed. 'NO! You're not getting out!'

'Go! Go! Go!' squeaked Gracie again. 'Just drive through the cones!'

And Greg did. He floored the accelerator pedal and trucked straight through the line of cones and into the empty lane. The cones cracked and boomed against the car and one rolled up over the bonnet and across the windscreen, making them all yell out with fright as it cracked the glass.

The empty carriageway ran on as normal for more than a mile, which they covered in seconds, at more than eighty mph, careless of the honking horns of aggravated fellow motorists, trapped in a bumper to bumper jam alongside them. But soon a large metal Men At Work sign loomed in front of them, two metres high and weighted by sacks of wet sand. Gracie screamed. Beyond the signs was a steaming lane of tar, newly laid and treacherous as a swamp.

Greg glanced back over his shoulder as they all began to shout with rising panic. The dark light was only a quarter of a mile behind them and gaining. He did not put his foot to the brake but pressed the accelerator pedal even harder down to the floor. The crash through the metal sign shattered the windscreen into an opaque crazed fresco. Greg punched through it, clearing a hole to see through, and little glass diamonds scattered all over them, some speckled with his blood. His left hand was streaming with it. Ahead of them, workmen in fluorescent tabards leapt for their lives, as the car flew past, but it was no good because the hot tar was slowing them down; grabbing and sucking at the tyres and relentlessly pulling back their speed.

'Out! Let me out!' cried Kevin, bashing and struggling against the door handle while Greg held down the LOCK button with his free hand and shook his head grimly. Kevin howled with despair, because he now knew this had all been for nothing. All that he could do was walk back to the dark light and give himself to Arimanius and hope the god would leave the rest of them alone. Knowing it was the only way made spirals of terror run through his every nerve and sinew. But maybe it would be a relief. Maybe it would somehow be bearable. Better to decide and go because the dark light was a thickening column now, its length closing together like a concertina, coiling itself tight, ready to spring. Kevin could hear it. It sounded like the whispers, groans, and wheedling cries of a million resentful souls, topped off with the screech of blades on metal and underpinned with a mind-numbing, bowel-shaking sub-bass rumble.

The car ground to a sticky halt, despite Greg's foot stamping desperately on the accelerator and his frantic grinding of the gears and clutch. The dark light spread out across the carriageway and Kevin saw the red eyes of Arimanius down low in it.

Game over.

'Oi! Can't you read a SIGN?' came an earthy, resentful voice.

A stocky figure in a Day-Glo vest stepped across the ruined sticky tarmac behind them, carrying a large STOP/GO board on a pole and planting the sign squarely in front of the billowing cloud.

'IT SAYS *CONVERGE INTO THE LEFT-HAND LANE!*' bellowed the figure, holding the plastic peaked hard hat on his head against the clammy warm wind that was pulsing ahead of the cloud.

'It's . . . SEMITAS!' squawked Kevin. 'Semitas! God of roads and pathways!'

Semitas turned to look at them through the windscreen.

'You'd better go,' he said, scratching at his grizzled beard with his free hand. 'I can't keep this obstruction up for long. Oi!' He sent three Men At Work signs bowling into the cloud as the tentacles in it squirmed forward. 'SENSIBLE AND COURTEOUS TRAFFIC FLOW IS KEY TO THE TRUNK ROUTE SYSTEM OF BRITAIN! *DON'T MESS* WITH MY TRUNK ROUTE, YOU UGLY LUMP OF FUR!'

'We can't go!' wailed Kevin. 'We're stuck!'

And then Semitas turned round and opened his mouth. He blew a vast, churning ball of icy blue air directly towards them. 'DOWN!' yelled Greg, smacking Kevin's head onto his knees as the godly exhalation swept through the car, smashing through the rear screen and funnelling straight through the broken front screen. Gracie and Tim ducked just in time as ice crystals and broken glass flew all over the ceiling of the car and froze everything above shoulder height. The blast swept on down the road ahead and cooled the hot tar in seconds.

'Go! Go!' yelled Gracie, again. Greg revved the engine once more and there was a squelch as the tyres ripped out of the tar beneath them.

Kevin had just enough time to see a small kid, his face suctioned to the window of a VW campervan in amazement, before they shot down the newly hardened lane.

'I can see the river!' yelled Tim, lifting his voice

above the whistling of the air rushing through the windscreen as the car picked up more and more speed on the empty road. 'Is that our river? Is that the Ouse?'

'Yes,' yelled back Kevin. The river snaked through a wooded valley which sank away from the road in lush green slopes to their right.

Gracie, clinging on to the back headrest and glancing behind, shouted, 'The dark light cloud is getting bigger around Semitas. I think it'll get past him soon. How do we get to the river?'

'This way!' shouted Greg, and veered the car abruptly off the road, ploughed straight through a low hedge, and shot down the hill towards a broad gap between the trees. 'Hold on! I might be about to kill us all . . .'

Chapter 25

There was a lot of screaming. Kevin wasn't sure whether any of it came from him, but some of it was just forced out of them as the Fiat bounced, rolled, hurtled and kangarooed down the steep hillside, before slaloming sideways down the wet grass, shooting across a narrow gravel path and then crashing through low scrub which sent vicious switches of thorny greenery right through the broken windscreen, along with one rusty coil of barbed wire. It was a wonder none of them lost an eye.

'THE RIVEEEEEER!' screamed Gracie. 'STOOOOP!'

The wide blue-green ribbon of the Ouse was suddenly right before them. Greg floored the brakes and the car slid, its tyres shrieking and the undercarriage hammering and groaning, round in a semicircle. There was an almighty crunch as it struck a thick tree stump on the bank, and then the back swung out across the water, and began to tilt down.

'We're going in! We're going in!' yelled Tim, scrabbling out of his seat belt.

'Lean to the front!' bawled Greg. 'Everyone—to the front!' And he sprawled forward, right through the jagged frame of the windscreen, desperately counter-balancing. Kevin joined him, sticking his head through the frame along with one shoulder and arm. Gracie leapt through the gap between the front seats. The back end of the car lifted, agonizingly slowly, and the front settled down onto the bank, which flattened out alongside the river.

'OK—Gracie,' gurgled Greg. 'Carefully get the passenger door open. Climb through and hold onto the door. Anchor it with all your weight.'

'OK,' said Gracie, in a high, scared voice. She clambered over Kevin's back and opened the door, which swung out and forward, making the car go up and down like a seesaw again—but less vigorously. Everyone yelped and then Gracie jumped out, making the car judder alarmingly and begin to tilt once more, but, with a grunt of effort she pulled the door out as far as it could go and hung back on it, using all her weight to keep the car steady.

'Now you, Tim,' gasped Greg. 'Go out my side and

do the same thing with the door.' Kevin could tell he was in pain, but couldn't see why. He could guess, though.

Tim followed Gracie's maneouvre on the driver's side and was soon hanging off the door. With no weight in the back now, the car steadied. But by getting out of the front, Kevin and Greg ran the risk of messing up the balance again and getting caught up as the car flipped back again.

'It should be OK,' Greg said. 'The weight of the engine should hold it down. But you go first, Kevin. I'll stay here until the last moment.'

Kevin pulled his head and arm back through the windscreen, trying not to make any sudden movements. Then he twisted and threw himself sideways out of the car.

'HELP!' squeaked Gracie, as the Fiat began to slide back again. Kevin ran round and pinned down the bumper. Greg lost no time in climbing through the shattered glass frame and slithering head first across the bonnet. He tumbled off the front, leaving a long smear of blood behind him. His chest was covered with puncture wounds and brilliant red flowers were blooming across his white shirt.

'OK—let it go!' he instructed and they did so, jumping clear. With a grinding, groaning sound, the wrecked car upended and slid into the river.

'Abandinus won't like *that* much,' observed Gracie.

'Or *that*,' said Tim. His face was twitching with fear as he stared back up the hillside they'd just travelled so violently. Kevin, Gracie, and Greg followed his gaze. An avalanche of malign blackness was rushing down the hill, filled with the writhing and screeching advance party of Arimanius.

'Now what?' whimpered Gracie, grabbing Kevin's arm.

'Abandinus!' yelled Greg, scanning the river. 'Abandinus! Do not let your followers down! They need you *now*!'

The dark light cloud was just seconds away from enveloping them all. Kevin turned to look at the water. 'Dear Abandinus! Please help us! We pray to you for deliverance!' He glanced back at the cloud. It was not slowing down. 'We pray for . . . for safe passage through fast flowing water.' He grabbed Gracie's shoulders. 'Sorry,' he said. And then he pushed her off the bank. She screamed, but before she'd hit the water he was pushing Tim too, who also yelped with fright. Now Kevin turned to Greg who looked grey with fear as he surveyed the water. He had almost drowned in a river after all. 'You have to trust!' yelled Kevin. 'And it's better than *that*!' As the dark light lapped within feet of them, two red eyes peering out of its depths, Kevin turned and leapt into the water.

The coldness took his breath away, but he struck out into the river, pushing away from the bank. Gracie and Tim were doing the same, swimming towards the roof of the Fiat which was all that could be seen of the submerged vehicle, floating slowly downstream. A splash behind him confirmed that Greg had overcome his fear and followed them.

Kevin reached the floating car roof and grabbed the edge of it, treading water. He had no idea how deep the river was, but his feet couldn't touch the bottom and the current against his body was strong. Very strong. Gracie and Tim were also clinging to the Fiat and Greg was swimming steadily for them. Up on the bank the dark cloud bubbled up high and Arimanius climbed up out of it, as if he'd been on steps leading up from below ground. He stared at Kevin and grinned, the unearthly dark light seeping out from between his teeth.

'Why are you here?' yelled Kevin, his teeth beginning to chatter. 'I turned *back*!'

Arimanius waggled one finger and slowly shook his lion head, the grin never wavering. 'You were stopped,' he argued. 'You did not turn back of your own accord. You belong to me. This you know. This you have known for days.'

'I DON'T!' yelled Kevin. 'You tricked me! You blackmailed me!'

'You chose to take what I offered,' said Arimanius.

'I didn't!' yelled back Kevin.

'And yet your grandmother *lives*!' smiled the god. 'She remains on this earth while her place beyond is empty. Do you think this can be done . . . free of charge?'

The water around them began to churn as a cold breeze funnelled along between the banks. Further downstream two swans flapped low across the water.

'Do you think gifts from the gods are *really* gifts, Kevin?' went on Arimanius. 'Do you think nothing is expected in return? Even Abandinus wants *something*.'

'I'll give it all back!' bawled Kevin. 'It's all stupid anyway! I don't care about computer games or being good at sports or Emma Greening fancying me. None of that matters!'

'Oh, none of your god-given treats matter?' Arimanius knelt down on the bank and leant out across the water, his red eyes burning with amusement. He began to laugh so hard tears ran from those eyes—tears that looked like lava. 'Do you speak for your friends?'

Tim and Gracie, still clinging to the car beside Kevin, gulped and stared at him.

'Now, let's see . . . ' said Arimanius, wiping the lava away and sending it in droplets into the river, where it sent up jets of steam. 'When a law has been broken, what one god giveth, another can take away.'

'They don't care about their gifts either!' Kevin glanced at his friends and Tim nodded, reached into his pocket and threw the roll of banknotes into the river. Gracie nodded too—very slightly—but she looked scared.

Arimanius laughed again and pointed one of his thick yellow curved nails at Tim. 'Smile,' he sang, 'though your heart is breaking . . . '

Tim smiled. His lips suddenly drew back into a ghastly grin, although his eyes widened in horror. His even white teeth began to move. They twisted in his gums like living things, and a bloom of yellow, green, and brown began to spread across them. Then they began to fall out. Tim gurgled with horror and put his hands to his lips, in time to catch the first three or four of them as they dropped out of his gums, now as black as ancient fossils. Gracie screamed and Kevin screwed up his eyes. How could he let this happen? How could he let Tim suffer like this?

'Vanity,' snorted Arimanius with a wave of his hand. 'Oh—you make it so easy for me!'

'Abandinuuus!' bellowed Greg, who was still

swimming around them, as if he was searching for the god among the streaming green water weed.

Tim leant forward, spitting and retching, and when he raised his face his cheeks were shrunken in around his toothless jaws, like an old man. He was gasping and sniffing and trying not to cry.

'And what of little Gracie? Your gift is unimportant too?' said Arimanius. 'Or maybe you could persuade Kevin that it's worth something to you.'

Gracie's gift? What was that? What was it? thought Kevin feverishly. She had never written out a list like he and Tim had. He had no idea what she wanted. What had she asked for? What had she got from Abandinus?

'Oh no,' moaned Gracie, and let out a long whistling breath, like a pierced inflatable toy. Her hand went to her chest and she hunched over as she held on to the car roof. A wheezing groan followed and then her chin lifted with a shudder, her mouth open and her eyes wide with fear. She gasped for breath and he could see that a trickle of air was getting in. Just a tiny trickle. As if she was sucking it in through a straw. The wheezing sound she made was awful. It sounded like children screaming in a choir from hell. In—out. In—out. Tighter and tighter. Thinner and thinner.

'Where's your inhaler?' He grabbed at her arm

but she barely looked at him as she shook her head. And then he remembered. The day of showing off at tennis. She had thrown her inhaler in the bin, convinced that Abandinus had cured her.

'Just—keep breathing!' he pleaded as the water churned up higher around them. Gracie rolled her eyes and gave him a *look* which said, 'Well—OK then! If you *say so*!' But under it she was terrified.

'*I know!*' said Arimanius, in a voice filled with child-like glee. 'A proper *sacrifice*. A life for a life. And without her little blue anti-wheeze box, Gracie will fit the bill just fine. It shouldn't take long. Just smile and wave, Kevin, and then I'll know we have a deal. She can take your grandmother's place and all will be balanced! Can't say fairer than that. You won't even have to come into the dark light to shake my hand.'

'ABANDINUS! PLEEEEASE!' screamed Kevin.

Gracie's eyes rolled up into her head and she let go of the car roof and slid into the water. Before Kevin could dive in after her Greg reached her and grabbed her head, pulling her chin up above the current. But it didn't make much difference to Gracie. Above or below the water, no air could get into her lungs. She was dying.

'OK! Have me! I will be your sacrifice!' sobbed Kevin. 'Stop this! Save her!'

'Aah—but I should tell you—*she* is one option,' said Arimanius. 'Give me Gracie, and you walk away in light. Give me yourself and you must come into the dark light. Come to me now and she lives—turn away and she dies. But know that if you come to me, it will be for ever . . . You have about thirty seconds to decide. After that, little whee-whee-wheezy Gracie will make the decision for you.'

He reached his muscled arm across the water and stretched out his long-clawed fingers, beckoning to Kevin. Kevin moaned with miserable horror. He really had no choice.

But, before he could put his own shaking hand out towards the claws, he realized that a weird pummelling sound was in the air around them. Looking up he saw a vast flock of swans beating the air with their wings just feet above them, sending a pulsing downdraught over his head and shoulders and whipping up the surface of the river. He had never seen or felt anything like it. The whiteness of their feathers was almost glowing, so that their odd orange and black beaks and feet seemed to float in a pearly cloud. Then he heard Greg cry out in triumph as a spinning funnel of river shot up in front of him, sending the cloud of white feathered birds up higher above it, and plunging them all into a localized storm of river droplets and white feathers. Abandinus, his robe shot through with flickering ribbon-like eels, looked furious as he floated up beneath the swans. 'You DARE to seduce my chosen one?' he bellowed and the words clapped off the water like thunder while the swans above them hissed in fury.

'Aboud thime,' whimpered Tim, gummily.

'I *dare*!' said Arimanius, although he retreated from the shore a little way and the cloud behind contracted to just a few metres around him. '*He* reached for *me*! Did you not see?'

'You are nothing but trickery. You cannot claim him on trickery!' roared Abandinus. 'Get OFF my river, you seething pile of gutless worms!' A sheet of river water struck Arimanius, making him steam violently and stagger back slightly. But he stepped back up to the edge of the bank and glowered at the river god.

'You KNOW there is unbalance in the realm!' seethed Arimanius. 'You KNOW there must be sacrifice.'

'And YOU know you cannot claim him through trickery,' argued Abandinus. He waved one arm up at the swans and they moved closer in the air like a winged ballet and the glare of their combined whiteness seemed to push at Arimanius, making him take another step back. But still he returned and leant out, low, to sneer at his foe.

'You cannot deny it, river god. There is a gap in the beyond, unfilled. A sacrifice MUST be made. You know this because the fault is *yours*!'

Abandinus said nothing. He turned and stared at Kevin, and the swan hissing and rough water subsided a little, so that only Gracie's thin, failing wheeze could be heard.

'Return their gifts,' he said to Arimanius. 'Or I will seek out your own new follower and exact my revenge.'

Arimanius shrugged and laughed and fanned his claws out like a magician. At once Tim's teeth were back, white and even and in their place. And Gracie was sucking in great lungfuls of air, coughing and gasping, as she and Greg splashed back through the water towards the car roof.

'And now what happens?' said Arimanius, standing with his arms folded across his leather-clad chest. 'We are in a stalemate, Abandinus. You are a sentimental cretin. You put a wound in the fabric of your world and mine. Tell your boy what must be.'

Abandinus turned back to Kevin again and shook his head slowly. 'I am at fault,' he said. 'I should have warned you. I should have told you the rules. Your grandmother lives when she should not have. I should have hardened my heart to you and let it be.'

'You—you saved her?' said Kevin. 'I thought Arimanius did!'

'No, he just sent you portents and fear so you would beg for my help. And I should have ignored your prayers, but I intervened.'

'You mean . . . he set us up?' Kevin murmured.

'Yes. He did,' said Abandinus in a voice drenched with regret. 'I should not have intervened.'

Kevin remembered now the feathers in the police photo. He pictured Abandinus exploding into the crash like a godly air bag, saving Nan from fatal injury at the last second.

'So . . . what he's saying is true?' he murmured. 'There really *does* have to be a sacrifice?'

Abandinus nodded slowly. 'I have cheated the balance of life and death. Sometimes this goes unnoticed. Sometimes . . . not. I cannot undo this. I cannot return and kill your grandmother. If I could, I would.'

'But I couldn't bear that,' said Kevin and a sad stillness began to sink through him.

'So . . . another life is forfeit,' said Abandinus with a gentleness in his voice that Kevin had never heard before. He understood what it meant.

'And . . . if I choose to die . . . *he* doesn't get me?' he waved at Arimanius, whose grin was fading up on the river bank.

'He does not. He is owed nothing. But going to him is another kind of death and that is an option you still have. Service to Arimanius. It is an extraordinary existence. Some would choose it gladly.'

Kevin stared into the dark light, heard its song, and shuddered. He turned away and looked back at Abandinus. 'Is drowning easy?' he said, dropping his gaze to the water.

'No,' said Abandinus. 'It is not.'

'Well,' said Kevin. 'It'll have to do.' And he pushed himself down under the water and made for the car. As his ears filled with river water the world seemed already gone and this helped him to think rationally, in spite of the emotions tearing through him. He knew that he could bob up again too easily once he lost consciousness, and that might save him. He would need to anchor himself inside the Fiat until he was dead.

It was hard to see it. The river was dark green, overshadowed by the cloud from the underworld, but the beige leather seats eventually bloomed into view and he fumbled for the seat belt, still holding his breath. He knew he would breathe in water soon, but first he needed to buckle up. One last time. He found the belt and used it to pull himself further down. Above him he could just hear distant, warped shouts and screams and around him he could feel the eddies of anguished limbs flailing against the current. He hoped Abandinus would keep his friends up on the surface. It would be too awful if they tried to save him.

Clunk. Click. The clasp was in. He allowed himself a look around and offered up a vague prayer to any decent god listening. *Look after Mum and Dad and Gracie and Tim and Nan . . . and Lorna . . . and even Emma Greening and Mike Mears and . . .* A stream of bubbles blew past his eyes, little balls of light winking farewell to him. He emptied his lungs completely, closed his eyes and readied himself for his first breath of river water and the pain and then the oblivion that would follow.

Chapter 26

At first the force around his body confused him. It could just have been the fierce current. His eyes would not open. His lungs were shut tight like a plastic bag. Soon they would fill with water, but the impulse to breathe had not yet overpowered the instinct not to. Yet he was amazingly calm. Closed. Finished. Over and done with.

But no—he was being rocked and pummelled and pulled. He opened his eyes and saw dark hair wave past them, a forehead, a hand and a bloodied shirt. He was being wrenched away from his sacrificial final act. He began to fight, flailing punches out but not landing any. Seconds later he was dragged to the surface of the water and flung against the far bank.

'Stop it! Stop fighting me! Stop it!' spluttered Greg.

'But I *have* to do this,' wept Kevin, in between

tearing gasps as oxygen shot back into his hungry lungs. Oh god, this was hard enough but he had made his peace with this life. To have to do it *again*? 'I have to!' he bawled. 'Or I have to go with *him*!' He pointed to the other bank of the river, but as the water dripped out of his eyes he saw that Arima-nius was no longer there. A normal light bathed the green water and the grassy bank, where Tim and Gracie now sat, holding on to each other and sob-bing. Scores of swans dotted the river around them, calm and serene.

'You should have let *me* go!' Greg was shouting, waist deep in water. 'I would have done it! I've already had eighteen years of borrowed life. I *owe* much more than you do!'

'But I wouldn't have let you, my love,' came a silken voice and Ancasta rose out of the water and put her arms around Greg's shoulders, her fingertips trac-ing the puncture wounds, instantly healing them. 'You know that.' Greg's face puckered with sadness and yearning and he shook his head.

'Ancasta,' he sighed, putting one hand over hers and closing his eyes. 'When will you let me go?'

'When you let *me* go,' she whispered, pressing her lips to his hair and then sinking back into the water. 'But you never will.' She vanished into the river.

Kevin found himself lying on the bank, the warm sun making his sodden clothes steam. Abandinus sat down next to him, crossing his legs and laying his staff down alongside them. Fine white feathers spiralled down and stuck to Kevin's wet cheek.

'I don't understand,' he mumbled, almost too tired to talk. 'I was supposed to die.'

'You did die,' said Abandinus. 'In every single way but one. You gave yourself up entirely, in thought and deed and spirit. You did that for your friends and your family. I let you go and so did Arimanius.'

'So . . . what happened?'

'There is a moment—a moment between worlds—when it is *just* possible to return. When the connection floats, untethered but still present, between one realm and the next. Some of your kind call it an out-of-body experience but it is more than this. Greg has been in this moment—so he had a sense for it. When Arimanius had gone back to the underworld, the professor knew there was still a moment left when you might be brought back. So I did not prevent him trying.'

'But,' Kevin eased himself up on one elbow, 'what about the deal with Arimanius?'

'It is served. He cannot return to claim you.'

'And Tim and Gracie?'

'They are safe this day,' smiled Abandinus. 'And I am proud. I chose wisely. You are great of heart. You will do great things by my name.'

Kevin sat up. He looked at Abandinus and wondered if he had ever had a choice.

Chapter 27

They walked home in just over an hour. Tim, Gracie, and Kevin followed a cross-country route pointed out to them by Abandinus, while Greg stayed at the riverside to deal with the emergency services.

Several appalled motorists had dialled 999 as the Fiat had shot past them through cones and the metal sign and onto the steaming tar of the newly laid lane. Fortunately, with the traffic jam tailing back more than three miles, the police, fire and rescue, and ambulance took a long time to reach the spot where some swore the car had shot right off the road.

The workmen who had narrowly escaped with their lives all told the police the same story. A man driving a Fiat had hurtled through the metal signs towards them, shouting that his brakes were gone. He was alone in the car. Semitas rested a pitch-stained finger on each of their heads and directed their statements but neither they nor the police noticed they were in the presence of a god.

The ambulance crew found the driver by the banks of the River Ouse, apparently in shock, staring into the water, drenched and bloody (although with no obvious wounds). He was being regarded as something of a hero, as he had steered away from the line of traffic and avoided carnage by allowing his car to crash off the road. All this Tim discovered later when he watched the evening news. The professor's 'miraculous escape from death after a dramatic river plunge' was the second story. The first one was about the teenager who'd gone missing overnight but had been found safe and well, asleep under a hedge in his own school grounds. Mike Mears seemed unharmed and his parents thought maybe someone had spiked his drink at the school disco and left him unconscious until he was found by the school caretaker the following afternoon. Mike didn't seem to remember much, confirming this suspicion. Tests on his blood were being carried out and witnesses appealed for.

Kevin lay on the sofa, listening to Mum clattering about in the kitchen, making spaghetti Bolognese. Nan was doing OK, so she had finally felt able to leave the hospital. Dad was gone. Back to Lorna. His stuff was removed from Kevin's room and the smell of Lorna's house had gone with it. Mum was singing to herself in her slightly tuneless voice. It was the first time she had sung in days, he realized. Dad being back had squashed any singing out of her. Kevin understood, finally, that they really weren't happy together and no amount of asking for godly help was going to change that. They couldn't control human spirit or emotions, Greg had said. He guessed that meant human love too.

'I'm sorry if you got your hopes up, Kev,' Dad had said on the phone, earlier, not long after Kevin had staggered into the empty house, about half an hour before Mum got home. 'I know you've probably hoped me and your mum would get back together again for a long time—but you know, we just can't be happy side by side. I do love her . . . and I think she loves me . . . but I'm *really happy* with Lorna.'

'Even with all the club music,' Kevin had said, with a forlorn laugh.

'Even with that,' Dad laughed back. 'Seeing your nan in hospital—well, it made me think about what was important. Lorna wanted to get married and I thought I didn't—that's really why we fell out. But thinking about how our lives can just snap and end in the blink of an eye . . . seeing the photo of that crunched-up car . . . it made me realize I *did* want to marry her. Do you see? It felt like the gods were giving me a prod, if that doesn't sound too stupid.'

'Stupid? Actually, no,' said Kevin, smiling into the phone. 'It's OK, Dad. I like Lorna and I want you both to be happy.'

'Even if . . . there's a little brother or sister for you one day . . . ?'

'That would be cool,' Kevin had told him. And actually, he thought it would.

Mum came in with two dishes of spaghetti and a spoon and fork for each of them. They cuddled up on the sofa and started to eat. 'I'm glad you got out for a walk with your friends,' said Mum, between mouthfuls. 'Not good to sit around worrying. A nice refreshing country walk was just what you needed. We all drive far too much these days.' She laughed and pointed as the final news round-up showed footage of a Fiat being dragged out of a river by emergency vehicles. 'See! Look where it gets you.' She hadn't noticed the soaked clothes in the laundry basket yet.

The three of them met up in the playground at break on Monday. Until then they had all stayed away from each other. No phone calls, no visits. Kevin guessed that it had all been just too overwhelming. Even on their long cross country walk home, they'd said very little. Tim had lost all his teeth in a truly horrific way, Gracie had nearly choked to death, and Kevin . . . well, he *had* died, according to Abandinus, and his friends had had to watch that. It was no wonder they were quiet.

He had slept for most of the weekend, late in his room, until Mum got him up on both Saturday and Sunday morning, calling him lazy and taking him off to the hospital to see Nan, who was now sitting up without anything attached to her head or wrist, reading spy thrillers and doing crosswords. And then more sleep in the car on the way back from each visit and still more out in the garden, lying in the grass with a book covering his face. He did not go down past the greenhouse to the shrine. He did not even think about it.

'So . . . how are we all?' asked Gracie, taking both their hands in hers. A week ago they would have pulled stupid faces and wrestled their hands back, embarrassed. Not today.

'I'm OK,' shrugged Tim. 'Not sure how much of . . . *that* . . . really happened.'

'How about you, Gracie?' asked Kevin. He still got a nasty clench inside when he remembered the asthma attack in the river.

'I'm cool,' she said. She fished her inhaler out of

her pocket. 'But I'm not throwing this away again in a hurry. And you? Mr Nearly Dead.'

Kevin smiled. All his sleep had been cool, pale green, and dreamless. He felt rested but different. As if all the signposts of his life had been tilted round, just a little bit, never to point quite the same way again. 'I'm all right,' he said.

'So,' Gracie linked arms with them and they walked along towards the school field, choosing the route that did not go near the car park and the hedge, 'are we still the Chosen Three, do you think?'

They didn't say anything for a long time. Then Kevin stopped and looked at them both. 'I think we'll always be. It's just how much we *want* to be that's the question. I think we won't see much of Abandinus or any of the others if we decide we really don't want to. It'll fade. After all, Greg didn't see Ancasta for years, did he? Not once he'd decided to move on.'

'No . . . not until he came back here. You know he moved to the States, don't you? To get away from English rivers, I guess. He came back here with us,' said Gracie. 'Must have thought he was safe after all this time, I guess. Poor professor! I saw him this morning, looking round a used car lot.'

'A four-by-four?' grinned Tim.

She nodded. 'With SatNav.'

'Anyway,' went on Gracie, after a few seconds. 'Once I'm back in the States I'm guessing that's it for me. I don't think English gods are going to get frequent flyer miles on my behalf.'

'Oh. When do you go back?' Kevin felt a stab of disappointment. He'd forgotten Gracie was only here for a student visit. It seemed as if she'd *always* been around.

'In two weeks,' she said, biting her lip. She looked at Kevin, her turquoise eyes wide and sincere. 'I can't believe it. I—don't want to go.'

'Do you have to?' asked Kevin.

'Well, unless there's some divine intervention and my dad miraculously gets offered a top job here . . . yes.' She smiled, sadly. 'You never *know* . . . '

Kevin wanted to hug her but . . . well, this was school. A hug-free zone.

'Yo! Muttley!' They all jumped, the intensity of the moment broken. Mike Mears, fresh from his mystery disappearance, was strutting along the edge of the field with Chad and two other American girl students, Emma Greening and one of her friends. 'How's the disco dancing, twinkle-toes?'

Kevin shrugged. 'I don't dance any more,' he called back.

Emma walked across and sidled up to him. 'You

were the best dancer *ever*,' she said. 'You were amazing!' And she went off into her alarm clock giggle before pouting up at him. 'Was I amazing too?'

'I just can't *tell* you how amazing you were!' said Kevin.

'You can,' she invited, playing with her hair.

'No, really,' beamed Kevin. 'I can't.'

She stared at him, confused. And then went off into another peel of giggles. 'You are *so funny!*' She turned and skipped away, glancing over her shoulder. 'Come and talk to me!'

'Not today!' called back Kevin with a cheery wave.

'Yeah right! You are *so funny. See you in a minute!*'

Gracie put her hands over her face. 'I can't believe you just turned her *down*!'

'I can't believe she doesn't believe it!' sniggered Tim as Emma rejoined Mike and the rest of the group.

Kevin grinned and stuffed his hands in his pockets. He glanced across at the 'in crowd' and saw that Mike Mears was watching him closely, leaning against one of the small trees on the edge of the field.

'So what really happened to Mike, then?' he asked Tim and Gracie. 'I can't believe anyone really spiked his drink.'

'I don't think they can have,' said Gracie. 'The tests must have come back negative for drugs or his mom and dad would already be suing the school, don't you think? It all went very quiet over the weekend.'

'So what was he doing all the time he was missing?' asked Tim. 'Where did he go? D'you reckon he sneaked off somewhere with one of the American girls or something? Sorry, Gracie,' he added. 'But he is always chatting them up. And you're all a sucker for a posh English accent.'

'Two things!' said Gracie, folding her arms and eyeing him haughtily. 'One—we are *not* all a sucker for an English accent, and two, all the girls are living with English families, being chaperoned. How *could* they slip off for a night of thrilling East Anglian snogging, huh?'

'So what *was* he doing?' said Tim, quickly (and wisely) abandoning his first theory. 'Where was he the last time anyone saw him?'

Kevin felt the skin on his arms and neck prickle. He tried to ignore it, but there was no getting away from it. 'I think I was the last one to see him,' he said. 'Near Arimanius's cradle.'

Tim and Gracie stared at him. 'And where was he going, when you saw him there?'

'I thought he was heading back into the school

hall, after I'd told him he'd won the fight,' murmured Kevin, unwillingly casting his mind back to the disco night. 'But I didn't look. I was too busy staring at Arimanius and hoping Mike wouldn't see him.'

'He must have gone back in,' reasoned Tim. 'Because if he had seen, you know . . . thingy that we're not supposed to be thinking or talking about any more . . . well, you'd have heard him screaming and wetting his pants, wouldn't you?'

Kevin nodded slowly. 'Yeah. You're right. He must have gone back in. And then got really drunk on some illegal cider or something and just . . . staggered back outside and fallen into the bushes.' Even as he was saying it, he knew it was ludicrous. He expected Tim and Gracie to look at each other and then back at him and then start gasping in horror and realization. But they didn't. Gracie changed the subject and she and Tim were laughing about something while his brain did memory backflips. He was back in the river and Arimanius and Abandinus were locked into their thunderous godly row and . . . what had Abandinus said? Suddenly it replayed inside his head like a DVD, complete with the downdraught from the swans' wings and the storm of river water. 'Return their gifts,' Abandinus said. 'Or I will seek out your own new follower and exact my revenge.'

New follower. Arimanius had a *new follower*. Someone had entered his cradle beneath the school grounds. Someone who was more attracted by the dark light than repelled by it. Who?

Tim and Gracie were still talking and laughing. Kevin looked past them to the little group further down the sports field. Chad was saying something and all the girls were laughing, but Mike—Mike was still leaning against the tree, gazing right back at Kevin.

Mike was *saying* something. Mouthing something at him that Chad and Emma and the rest were not aware of. Kevin felt his skin prickle again as he read Mike's lips.

'*Chosen one . . . ?*' Mike grinned, tilted his head, and watched closely.

Gracie and Tim were still talking to each other, still laughing. Kevin stared back at Mike and then let his head drop in a slight nod. '*Yes,*' he mouthed back, '*chosen one.*' An acknowledgement. A warning.

Mike ran his hand through his floppy fringe and smiled widely. '*Me too,*' he mouthed. And something glimmered behind his teeth.

Dark light.

Acknowledgements

With thanks to David Rankine and Sorita D'Este for their fabulous A–Z, The Isles of the Many Gods, to Southampton archaeologists for finding Ancasta's shrine, and to all the local British deities we made, who sleep, unremembered.

Ali Sparkes

Ali Sparkes was a journalist and BBC broadcaster until she chucked in the safe job to go dangerously freelance and try her hand at writing comedy scripts. Her first venture was as a comedy columnist on *Woman's Hour* and later on *Home Truths*. Not long after, she discovered her real love was writing children's fiction.

Ali grew up adoring adventure stories about kids who mess about in the woods and still likes to mess about in the woods herself whenever possible. She lives with her husband and two sons in Southampton, England.

Check out **www.alisparkes.com** for the latest news on Ali's forthcoming books.

Read on for an extract of
Car-Jacked, also by Ali Sparkes...

Once Mum's mind was made up it was impossible to change. She had made up her mind, for instance, that Jack would be in college by the time he was fourteen. And as he'd already taken his first ten GCSEs—and passed them all with A*s—he guessed he would be. And then he would take around six A Levels in one year before zooming straight into Oxford or Cambridge by the time he turned fifteen. Mum couldn't wait.

So, while his cousins, Jason and Callum, were hanging around the skate park and worrying about spots and girls and how to get a better score on Halo or Call of Duty or whatever they were into by then, he would be hanging around with eighteen-year-olds who wouldn't want anything to do with him. Not because he was deeply uncool (which, of course, he was) but because his *MOTHER* would be meeting him every day after lectures and making sure he wasn't sloping off for a junk food frenzy.

Jack groaned, lay down on the back seat and pulled the tartan car blanket over him from head to foot.

Ten seconds later the door opened and Dad thumped heavily into the driver seat, keyed the ignition at speed and shot out of the petrol station so fast that Jack was flattened into the upholstery in the rear.

Wow! Dad and Mum had had their rows before but this was obviously a bad one. As far as Jack could recall, Dad had never actually abandoned her before. He must have snapped.

He lay staring at the chinks of light in the blanket, wondering what to say to Dad. He felt a bit guilty. He had deliberately wound Mum up because he'd been fed up with her idea of a 'holiday'. . . but he didn't really mean for it all to go off like this. Dad sometimes lost it with Mum . . . but to leave her all alone at a petrol station in the middle of nowhere?

Jack knew he should say sorry. Tell Dad it was his fault; say he should go back. He would apologize to Mum and make it better.

He began to burrow out of the blanket and then froze. His first peek between the front seats showed a hand grasping the gearstick and wrenching it violently forward as the car veered around a tight bend on the narrow road, at breathtaking speed.

The hand was large and masculine. It had long lean fingers and blood smeared across its knuckles.

It was not his dad's.

Ready for more incredible adventures?
Try these ...

SIMON NICHOLSON

YOUNG HOUDINI

Trickster, Magician, Daredevil: the legend begins.

THE MAGICIAN'S FIRE

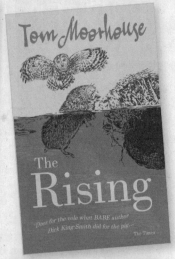

Tom Moorhouse

The Rising

'Does for the vole what BABE author Dick King-Smith did for the pig...'
The Times

CAKES IN SPACE

BY PHILIP REEVE AND SARAH McINTYRE

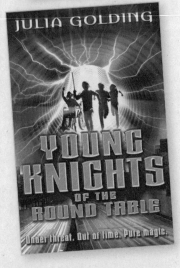

JULIA GOLDING

YOUNG KNIGHTS OF THE ROUND TABLE

Under threat. Out of time. Pure magic.